# A BREED APART

## JAMES S. KELLY

# A Breed Apart

A Novel

James S. Kelly

ISBN: 978-1-961677-80-7

Library of Congress Control Number: 2023913607

Printed in the United States of America

Published by

info@thequippyquill.com
(302) 295-2278

# Other Books

By JAMES S. KELLY


**Westerns**
A Man of Breeding
A Breed Apart
The Downtrodden Breed


**Mysteries**
I Didn't Forget
Not In My BackyardInterned


**Civil War**
Magnolia


**Viet Nam War**
The Long Walk Home

# ACKNOWLEDGEMENTS

**Spouse**
Patricia

**Children**
James Jr.
Mark
Nancy
Michelle

**Friends**
John and Nancy Orchard
Robert and Marilyn Lang
Don and Noreen Pate
Lyndon Beauchene

**Relatives**
Jim and Ethel
Lancaster Thomas Kelly
Maryann Kelly

# CONTENTS

# PROLOGUE

The noontime sun in the southwest part of the United States shows no favoritism. It is equally brutal to animal and human life, alike. He and the woman had been waiting since dawn and the longer they waited, the more intense the sun became. It had taken two full days by horseback to make their way to this remote location. Consequently, they were tired and their horses were exhausted and dehydrated. Jason Brown didn't know how he'd been persuaded to make a journey to this secluded and desolate site; he must have been drunk. At this time of day in the desert, on a spring day, the bugs and sand fleas could eat you alive. The insects seemed to be attracted to his weeklong facial hair and the filthy ragged clothing, he was wearing. He wanted to get up and move around but he didn't want to attract the attention of some cowboy that could be passing on the trail nearby. His companion seemed to be completely relaxed and was sitting on the ground with her legs crossed. She was wearing men's denim pants and a red checkered shirt, accentuated by a blue scarf around her neck. Her hair was cut short and her face scrubbed clean of any of the cosmetics, she normally wore. What bothered him most about her was that she was chewing tobacco. He could see the stain on her teeth even at this distance. Funny it didn't bother him the other night when he was banging her as hard as he could.

They'd arrived early at this dry watering hole in Cane Springs Canyon, about thirty miles from Globe, Arizona. They didn't want to attract any attention, though both knew that what they were waiting for, could be several hours late. Brown looked over at her and she smiled back. It had been a week since they originally met. It wasn't that he liked her; she was just a convenience for the moment. He couldn't speak for the woman, but she seemed to be excited about what they were soon to do.

It was only ten days ago when he was punching cattle and wondering why he was working at the Bar T, outside Mammoth Arizona, a small spread of two thousand acres with a few hundred head of cattle. On Friday afternoon, as was customary, the ranch foreman summoned the five hands and paid them their wages. When it was Brown's turn, the foreman said, "i want you to go up to the line shack on Monday. We're missing about twenty steers. Find as many as you can and bring them back at the end of next week."

The timing was perfect for Brown. If nothing else, the foreman's request was all he needed to make up his mind. "No, I'm going to move on. I've had my fill of cows for the rest of my life."

He picked up a bedroll, saddlebag and mounted his horse and then rode out the main gate. Brown rode for three hours before he came to the town of Mammoth, where he normally spent his pay on the weekends. He didn't know what he was looking for, but it wasn't working as a cowboy, there had to be more to life than that. He tied his horse to the rail out front and walked up the steps and entered the saloon, through the red cafe doors. Two of the men who worked at the Bar T beat him here and were talking to two of the working girls. Brown sat at one of the vacant stools and tried to enter into a conversation with the two cowboys, but they were only interested in the women. After sitting at the bar for an hour, quenching a week long thirst, he got the itch that guys get when they haven't been with a woman for some time. He looked around the bar to see if there might be other women available, but the only two in the bar were with the cowboys. After another beer, he asked the bartender if there was some other place where he could get his knob polished. The bartender smiled. He'd been asked that question before.

"There's a tent across the street; ask for Pearl."

To fortify himself, Brown had another two beers before he walked across the street to the tent, opened the flap and walked in. She had on a clean dress; her hair was combed back and she smelled good. But it was her smile that made it all work. There were two cots in the tent. One was for business, while the other was piled high with women's clothing. He was anxious and threw his clothes on top of the pile, paid two dollars and waited while she took off her clothes. Perhaps to heighten his anticipation, she took her time in removing her clothes. He was rough and quick; he wasn't there to please her. Yet, she asked him to stay when his time was up. So he lay back on the cot and she climbed on top of him. Now this was more like it, Brown said to himself.

It was after another go that she made her pitch about robbing the Globe to Florence Stage- coach. He started to get up but she was on top and prevailed upon him to listen. She told him that this line hadn't been robbed in a long time and probably wouldn't have a guard on board. His ego took a stab; he thought she wanted him to stay for another round, because he was so good in bed. What she needed was a male partner. He must have said yes because he was here in the brush, smelling like horse crap, waiting for the stage. Still, he didn't remember saying yes. He only remembered saying that he never robbed a stagecoach or something to that effect.

"I don't want you to rob a stage; I want you to help me rob the stage," she responded.

She went by the name of Pearl Hart and was born in Canada, twenty eight years ago. Brown had never met anyone from Canada. In fact, he didn't believe she was from Canada because she didn't speak French; but she could swear as well as any man he ever met. This wasn't his thing. He didn't like doing something that he'd never done before and had to rely on a partner for direction, and especially a woman. He stood up and peered over one of large cactus bushes that dominated the landscape, to see if anything was coming.

"Better get down before someone sees you." It was the first thing she'd said in the past hour. He didn't mind sleeping with her but he didn't like her telling him what to do.

He was tempted to walk over and give her his backhand. Instead, he checked his colt 45 one more time. He was a little nervous and besides, he didn't have anything else to do, while they were waiting. Brown wasn't sure he'd need to fire the gun today but it didn't matter, he just wanted to be ready. She had a

38 revolver stuck in her belt, but he wasn't sure he could rely on her. Hell, he didn't really know her, so why was he here? He had a good mind to just leave. Maybe that hardware store job he left in Tucson to be a cowboy, wasn't so bad after all. Then there was the gal who worked in the general store next door. She was good for at least twice a week.

Pearl's plan called for placing a couple of large rocks on the trail forcing the stagecoach to stop. Brown had placed enough good sized rocks on one side of the trail, soon after they reached this site. When the stagecoach stopped, Brown would approach the stage from one side and Pearl from the other. Brown never heard of a stagecoach being robbed by a woman. He wondered if that was the main reason he was here. The truth was he needed some action. It'd been four months since he'd made a score; all he had left from his wages at the Bar T, was five dollars. In spite of her assurances, he wondered if there'd be a strong box on the stage or any cash with the passengers. He could get shot for nothing. Well, he was here, so he might as well go through with it.

Just as he sat back down and leaned against one of the boulders that dotted the desert land- scape, he heard the stagecoach coming. They quickly pushed all the large rocks across the trail, then hid behind one of the large cactus bushes bordering the pathway. Just then a Con- cord Coach came into sight. There was a team of four horses pulling the stagecoach and a lot of dust trailing behind. Brown hoped that whoever was driving, would see the rocks in time and pull to a stop. He could hear the wheels screech and the coachman swear as he pulled on the reins and practically stood on the brake. The stage stopped just as the front wheels touched the rocks. With his hand on a pistol, the driver took his time to look around the area before climbing down; there was no guard with him. Brown and Hart waited until the driver lifted one of the rocks and then made their move. He crossed behind the stage while she snuck up behind the driver and stuck a 38 into his back.

"Don't make a move or cry out, if you want to live," she said.

The driver might have been confused by the high pitched voice of the robber but not by the gun in his back. He raised his hands and turned around. Five foot tall Pearl Hart was standing in front of the six foot two inch tall driver, with her 38 aimed at the his chest; she had a big smile on her face.

"Now look here, don't point that gun at me. I'll do what you want," the driver said to Pearl.

"You bet your life you'll do what I want. "Some of the passengers were looking out the window, but all remained in the coach so Brown yelled. "Get out of the stage and come out with your hands in the air."

When the passengers didn't react fast enough, Brown banged his revolver against the side of the stage twice. Immediately the door nearest Pearl flew open and four passengers stepped down from the cab; two of the four were women. Pearl lined up the four passengers and the driver alongside the stage while Brown climbed up to where the driver sat and grabbed the pouch, nestled in a corner of the boot. There was four hundred and thirty one dollars in the pouch. While Brown was busy with the pouch, Pearl told the men to clean out their pockets and place everything in a hat, lying on the ground. Hart had the women passengers dump the contents of their purses into the same hat. They got another twenty seven dollars from the passengers along with three revolvers, two rings, a silver broach and a small whiskey flask. Pearl then did something that annoyed Brown. She returned a dollar to each of the passengers and thanked them for their generosity. Each of the passengers said thank you, as she meted out the dollars.

Before they released the four passengers, Brown unhitched the horses from the stage and drove them a few hundred yards toward Globe. Hart made the passengers and driver climb back inside the stagecoach, until Brown returned. The passengers were very vocal about being left without horses and their guns.

"It's too hot inside the coach."

"You can get out after we leave, "Brown said. "What if some robbers come by, what are we going to do?"

"Tell them we took all your money," Brown answered

# CHAPTER ONE

**B**rown figured they'd have at least a two hour head start before a posse was sent after them. With a telegraph office in every small town, it was conceivable that the stagecoach driver would collect the horses and ride to the nearest town for help. That would probably be Globe and their sheriff would send out a description of Brown and Hart to all the towns within a hundred mile radius. Robbing stagecoaches in the era of the telegraph was almost a lost art. Brown and Hart mounted their horses that were tethered to a cactus bush about twenty yards from the trail, and rode off. They were headed toward the town of Mammoth, which lay about seventy miles northeast of Tucson. Hart had taken the money pouch from Brown as he was unhitching the horses and tied it to the horn on her saddle. They alternated riding the horses for thirty minutes and then walking them for another thirty minutes. Brown wasn't sure when a posse would come upon them, so he wanted the horses to be as fresh as possible.

They bypassed the small towns of Haydon and Winkleman and rode parallel to the San Pedro River. They didn't encounter anyone directly though they saw a couple of cowboys chasing some stray cattle as they travelled close to the Rising Sun Ranch, outside Haydon. Around five o'clock, he signaled her to stop. 111 think we need to find a place to camp. I'd suggest somewhere along the river bed. That would probably be the safest."

The only coverage they could find was in a curved section of the riverbank, which was carved by the hydraulic action of the river. Brown could see that most of the large boulders were near the far bank of the river. During the rainy season, the dynamics of the onrush of water carved out one side of the river while forcing the large boulders to the other side. It would be dangerous to be here in the rainy sea- son but in May 1899, it was no problem. Though a campfire was out of the question, they had enough blankets to keep them warm. The dry bread, ham and cheese Hart bought two days before was sufficient and the river provided enough water for their needs. Brown tended to the horses and tethered them to some small logs he found along the river bank. Hart unpacked the horses and set up their bedrolls together. He could tell that Hart was tired, but she seemed to be game. It'd be a long tough day for someone like Brown, who was raised on this life. He could imagine how hard it'd been on her, but she didn't complain. She was as lusty as the other night and a lot better company than any cowhand; he really didn't mind having her along. She shared some personal experiences with him as they lay together before falling asleep.

She'd was born Pearl Taylor and lived in a small farming community near Montreal, Canada. She met Frank Hart, who came through town one winter looking for work. He tried bartending in the only saloon in town and boarded with her family until spring of the following year. That's when he and Pearl eloped to Montreal. During a five year marriage, marred by much abuse, several separation and then frequent reconciliations, Pearl had two children. After

Hart broke her jaw during one of his drunken stupors, Pearl left town and moved to Buffalo. Her mother took in the couple's two children with the understanding that once settled, Pearl would send for the mother and the two children. Brown told her about his stint as a cowhand and faro dealer, but that was a far as he'd go. It wasn't his manner to share anything personal. You never knew when it would come back to haunt you, was his philosophy

That night she slept with an arm and a leg crossed over him as he lay on his back. He got up at dawn and lighted a small fire, heated some coffee and gave her a cup as she stirred and sat up. They dressed in silence. As they were breaking camp, he asked for his share of the proceeds from the robbery.

"Why?" She asked.

"We agreed to split the take and I want my half now."

He knew she had a gun in her waist band so he turned to face her in the event she'd draw down on him. Yes, they 'd been intimate, but money had a way of altering people's perspective. "And if I don't want to split it now, what then?" she asked.

As soon as the last word left her mouth, Brown drew his Colt 45 and pointed it directly at Hart. "Put your gun on the ground, "he demanded.

There were tears in her eyes as she fumbled with the gun. As soon as the gun was on the ground, Brown kicked it away. "I want the money now. You really overplayed your hand; we're splitting up."

"I was just kidding. I was going to split with you. You don't have to take it all. I came up with the plan and did my share of the work. You can't leave me with nothing."

She handed him the money and he counted it in front of her. "The four dollars you gave the passengers comes out of your share," Brown said

He dropped two hundred twenty five dollars, one of the rings and the silver broach on the ground in front of her. "I'll keep one of the rings, two guns and the whiskey flask. Buy yourself a new dress with the money. I'll leave one of the guns up the trail about fifty yards. No one will ever know that you were in on the robbery, especially if we're not together. This is best for both of us. They'll be looking for two male robbers, one short and thin; the other tall with a beard."

"I thought you liked me?"

"You're okay. I enjoyed the sex and I didn't steal from you, so that ought to answer your question."

Hart hadn't made any attempt to retrieve her share of the loot before she approached him and put her arms around his waist. She laid her head on his chest. "I don't want to split up. I really like you. Take me with you."

"I ride alone"

# CHAPTER TWO

After Brown left Pearl on the river bank, she lay down and cried. She really liked him and wondered what she could have done differently. She wasn't trying to keep all the money for herself. It just felt so good to be able to say she robbed a stagecoach; she probably gave off the wrong vibes to him; but he overreacted. She didn't know where to go or what to do, so she curled up in the fetal position and fell asleep. She awoke several times that night to relieve herself and try to determine what she should do next. In each case, she pulled the blanket over her head and went back to sleep and cried. That's where she was when Sheriff Truman and his posse found her around noon, the next day. Though she put up a struggle and tried to shoot the sheriff with her 38 revolver, she was easily overpowered. They all got a good look at her before they let her dress, well screw them. She was placed on her horse and her hands were tied in front. She was quiet the entire ride to jail and wouldn't respond to any inquiry. Initially, she was taken to the lockup in Florence, but that was only for a few days. It didn't have facilities for women, so she was moved to the larger prison in Tucson.

When Pearl was captured, the first thing the sheriff asked was, why did she rob the stage? The second was, who was her accomplice? Pearl ignored both questions and although the sheriff repeated the questions several times, she just smiled. Once they arrived at the jail, she was allowed to change into a dress that she carried in her saddlebag. She was placed in a part of the facility where there were no male inmates, though her cell was no different from those of the male prisoners. It was a walled ten foot square enclosure, with no window and it smelled of prisoners from days gone by. Her thin mattress lay on a wooden platform. For security purposes there was no metal in the bed construction. All her possessions had been confiscated along with the loot from the stagecoach robbery; the warden retained these in his office.

While awaiting trial, Pearl became an overnight sensation. The media flocked to the Tucson Jail to photograph and interview her; they nicknamed her, The Bandit Queen. The media was especially fascinated with the token of the one dollar, Pearl remitted to each passenger after she robbed the Globe to Florence route. Reporters continually asked her why she did that. "I felt sorry for the people on the stage. I wanted them to know that Pearl had a heart," she laughed out loud. She always enjoyed that question.

With Pearl as the media darling, the guards and the warden at the Tucson Prison were over- whelmed with attention. They were constantly asked by the press what Pearl was doing, what she had for breakfast and dinner or what Pearl had to say about various subjects. Consequently, the guards' names appeared in the paper and they in turn became celebrities. The warden had clippings of the newspaper articles about Pearl with his name in them, posted on the walls of his office.

He never objected to a newspaper photographer's request for a photo of him and Pearl together. She was allowed freedom of movement throughout the institution and unlimited visits from politicians looking for a photo opportunity. Although she was without funds, two lawyers offered their services in defense of the charges that were brought against her. Four months into her incarceration, Pearl walked out of Tucson Prison, strolled into town, borrowed a horse and escaped. The warden was in a panic but all was forgiven when she was re- captured two weeks later at Beauregard's Boarding House two blocks from the prison.

Joseph Gordon became her attorney and he petitioned the court to drop all charges against Pearl, on the grounds that she was manipulated by her male accomplice. When that wasn't accepted by the judge, Pearl pled not guilty. Her trial was a media circus. After court was adjourned each day, she would hold a press conference that could last as long as two hours. Pearl wasn't adverse to manipulating the press or tell the truth on an as needed basis; her goal was an acquittal. Though she hadn't seen her children or mother in three years, Pearl broke down in tears on the witness stand telling the jury that she only went through with the stagecoach robbery to get enough money to help her ailing mother and feed her children. She didn't name Brown as her accomplice; yet, she implied that she feared for her life, if she didn't help him; she was an unwilling accomplice. The jury believed her and voted for acquittal. Pearl was free.

The authorities in Arizona weren't amused and Pearl's acquittal by the jury was going to be short-lived. She gathered up her belongings, said goodbye to her favorite guards, kissed the warden on the lips and walked out the main gate; she was immediately arrested. The state charged her with mail fraud, though Pearl didn't even know what mail fraud was. This time her notoriety was ignored by the court, and after a brief trial, she was found guilty. She was sent to the Territorial Prison in Yuma for a term of five years. Gordon appealed her conviction on the grounds of double jeopardy, but he was unsuccessful. After several motions that went nowhere, he moved on to other cases.

While in Yuma, her fame spread across the state and she was given even more special treatment, than she had at Tucson. This included a larger cell which opened to a small yard, where she maintained a flower garden. Though an inmate, she had celebrity status and was given unusual privileges. Pearl was able to entertain reporters and any elected official who wanted to be photographed with her. It wasn't unusual to see the Media Darling in the small courtyard, sitting in her rocking chair talking to two re- porters, while one of the guards brought coffee or tea to the group.

Being the only female prisoner in a heretofore all male prison, wasn't lost on Pearl. She used her female allure to improve her situation and attract male guards and trustees, to do her bidding. It wasn't unusual for Pearl to have at least one paying admirer a day, visiting her cell. The guards were her favorite. They had access to the outside world and were willing to bring things into the prison that Pearl needed in return for some pleasure, as she referred to it. Within the first six months of her incarceration, Pearl opened up a savings account in the Yuma Federal Bank. She had over a thousand dollars accumulated by the time she was pardoned, after serving a two year jail sentence. The rumor was that she was causing too many problems among the male guards at the facility; the warden wanted her gone. There may have been some truth to the rumor, because the pardon made clear that she was to leave the state of Arizona and never come back.

After the pardon, she moved to Gallup New Mexico, where she worked as a cook and later as a hostess in the Sonora Saloon. She'd gotten her start as a stagecoach robber because she admired the cowboy way of life. On her only day off each week, she'd don male clothes and go horseback riding. The Buffalo Bill Wild West Show particularly mesmerized Pearl. She fancied that she was part of the show performing a stagecoach robbery. On some nights, Pearl liked to dress up as a cowboy and go into bars, especially the one where she was working, as a hostess. The bartender knew who she was and was amused at her masquerade and allowed her to continue the scam. In her disguise, she'd start conversations with some of the male patrons and then come back later wearing female clothes and talk to the same men, to see if they'd recognized her. Seldom was she found out.

She often thought about Brown and wondered where he was. Although she was employed her entire time in Gallop, she had gone through most of the money earned in Yuma Prison. Now she was doing menial jobs, just to keep food on her table. She needed more or she'd soon find herself in a broken down hotel with no job, no friends and no hope.

One night she came in the saloon dressed as a man, sat at the bar and ordered a beer. A group of cattle buyers were playing billiards in the corner of the room. Pearl was close enough to overhear them talking about a herd of cattle headed to Tucson and how much they were willing to pay per head. There was a least ten of them but Pearl took particular notice of a gentleman, short in stature and some twenty years her senior. Later that evening, Pearl dressed as a woman, singled out the buyer and asked him if he wanted some company. He was more than willing and after a little encouragement, he bought several rounds of drinks for the two of them. From the bits and pieces of their conversation, Pearl learned that he had two thousand dollars to buy a portion of the herd for his ranch. After another round of drinks, Pearl asked the gentleman if he would walk her to her hotel. He was so anxious that he nearly stum- bled over the table trying to help her up from her chair; he expected to get lucky. The saloon was one street away from her hotel, but they had to pass through an alley to reach it. When they were half way through the alley, the cattle buyer stopped. "There's a horse tethered to a ring on the wall here," he said.

As he pointed at the horse, Pearl pulled out a 38 revolver and hit the man over the head. He fell to the ground, but didn't immediately lose consciousness; he started to rise. Pearl hit him in the head again and this time he didn't move. She went through his pockets, taking his watch and billfold, containing a wad of cash. She didn't stop and count the money; she'd take his word that he had two thousand dollars. Quickly taking off her shoes, petticoat and dress, she reached into the saddlebags of the tethered horse and took out pants, boots, a plaid shirt and a cowboy hat, and changed. Using an old crate to stand on, she swung a leg over the horse and left the cattle buyer lying on the ground.

She wondered if he was dead, but it didn't matter, even though this was the first time she'd ever been violent with anyone. But now, she had had enough money to move on with her life.

One thing, Brown taught her was, to leave the scene as quickly as possible so that she'd have a good head start on any posse. Dressed as a young cowboy, she made her way on horseback toward Phoenix; she liked her chances.

# CHAPTER THREE

**B**rown was sitting at a corner table in the Brasoz Saloon outside Tucson having a beer this afternoon. It was a run of the mill place with batwing doors at the entrance, a pot belly stove in the corner next to a billiards table and very little furniture. The dancing girls had just finished their first routine and were looking for a thirty minute client during their intermission. Two tried to tempt him, but he ignored their pitch. There was a newspaper stuck in the rungs of a chair next to him; it was two days old. He pulled the paper out and opened it up. It was a Rocky Mountain Newspaper and on the third page was an account of the robbery he and Hart had orchestrated. Brown had gotten rid of the beard and filthy rags he wore that day and was dressed in a black suit, a white shirt and a black stringed tie. His black boots were polished and he was wearing a black Stetson hat. His appearance alone made him stand out from the average customer. He made a few scores over the past months, but nothing that would tide him over for more than a month at a time. In between scores, he worked as a bartender, a salesman and a clerk in a general store. The jobs didn't last long, but they lasted long enough to keep food on his plate and until he could make another score.

He hadn't given much thought to Pearl Hart, after he left her at the river bend outside Mam- moth. The newspaper article, said she'd been identified by one of the passengers on the stage and was picked up by Sheriff Truman of Pinal County. She was initially incarcerated in Florence Arizona, and then transferred to Tucson. The newspaper stated that Pearl Hart and her accomplice made the last stagecoach robbery in the United States; it was also the first and only one carried out by a woman. The stagecoach passengers had described her accomplice as six feet tall, one hundred ninety pounds, a month long beard and wearing tattered clothing. Brown smiled and thought the law wouldn't have much luck with that description. He doubted that even Pearl Hart would recognize him now, or could she?

His routine over the past month was to get up about ten, have a late breakfast at the Drake Hotel in downtown Tucson and then read the newspaper in the lobby. Once he finished reading, he'd sit on the hotel porch with some of the salesmen or elected city officials and see what kind of action was available. One of the aldermen was talking about a casino being opened on the outskirts of town, but that wasn't something that interested Brown. As he was talking to an anvil salesman, he noticed a woman across the street looking into the dress shops. Brown's heart almost stopped beating. It was Pearl Hart, but how could it be? She was in prison. The woman looked across at him and the other men on the porch, but Brown was quick enough to shield his face with a newspaper and she continued on. He watched as she entered the general store two doors down. He excused himself and told the other men he had to run an errand; he'd see them tomorrow.

But he had something else on his mind. Brown went back into the hotel, through the kitchen and out the back way. Turning left, he entered the alley between the hotel and a ware- house and stood in the shadows watching the general store across the street. Thirty minutes later, Pearl Hart exited the store with a small package and made her way further up the main street. Brown hugged the wall as he made his way out to the sidewalk, while staying close to the buildings, on this side of the street. Pearl seemed oblivious that Brown was following her. She stopped to talk to a woman on the street and Brown stepped into a doorway so he wouldn't be seen. Soon, Pearl walked on and entered Mrs. Beauregard 's Boarding House, which was directly across the street from where Brown was staying. He was astonished that she was staying across the street from him and he wondered if his luck had changed.

After returning to his room at Mrs. Grady's Boarding House, he read the newspaper article again. Pearl could pose a problem for him now that she was in Tucson, and especially across the street. Was this just a coincidence or was she looking for him? And better yet, would she recognize him if she saw him? The more he thought about it, the more he was convinced that she could. Remembering back to the first night they met, he was clean shaven. Taking a chance on a woman he dumped, wasn't some- thing he was comfortable with. Tucson was too hot for him at the moment, especially, if Pearl had a vendetta.

On another page in the same newspaper, there was an advertisement for a dry goods salesman. Western Outerwear, a Denver based company was seeking to expand its business into the southwestern part of the United States. That evening, Brown informed Mrs. Grady that he was moving out tomorrow. He was careful the next morning as he exited the boarding house through the rear and made his way to the railroad station, through one of the alleys, behind his building. He was on the next train to Santa Fe and when he arrived, he sent off an application to Western Wear emphasizing his sale's experience and had the ability to sell any product. The company responded two weeks later to his hotel in Santa Fe and suggested that he come to Denver and meet with the company's president, Walter Rinehart, A Wednesday morning interview was set up, three weeks hence.

Brown could've spared himself the anguish. If he waited two more days before fleeing, he'd read that Pearl had been arrested at the boarding house across from where he was staying. She'd walked out of the Tucson jail two week earlier and hadn't bothered to leave town. Later, the police acknowledged that someone had recognized Pearl from the many newspaper articles about her and had called the police. Pearl was subsequently retried, found guilty and sent to Yuma Prison.

Travel by train at the turn of the century was not glamorous, but it was certainly better than going by stagecoach. Brown arrived in Denver on Tuesday afternoon, the day before his interview. After checking into the Oxford Hotel, two blocks from the railroad station, he unpacked his black suit and black boots. This was the finest hotel he'd ever stayed in. Not only were there electric lights and steam heating in the rooms, but each room had a separate bathroom. He was short of money but decided to stay one night and enjoy this bit of luxury. He tipped the bell boy a dollar to run his suit over to the laundry for cleaning. "I want that suit back tonight, preferably before eight this evening," Brown told the bell boy.

He bathed, shaved, put on a clean shirt and pants and went to dinner at Gahan's Saloon in Larimer square. This was where Denver started, though the town was initially named Larimer, after an army general, turned businessman. After dinner, he moved into the bar area, sat on a stool and ordered a whiskey, straight up. While sipping his drink, he nodded to a couple of men at the bar and entered into their conversations. After another drink, Brown and two of his recent acquaintances went to the back room of Gahan's where a poker game was underway. He'd played his share of Stud, but the guys at the table were sharks and after a few hands, he decided that he was out of his comfort zone. After saying goodnight to his two acquaintances, he went back to his hotel and reviewed his strategy for tomorrow's interview. Yet, he wasn't even sure he wanted the job. The only thing he was sure of was that he'd applied for a position with this company, to get as far away as possible from Pearl Hart.

The next morning at the designated time Brown walked two blocks to the address that Rinehart sent him. He wasn't sure he had the correct location when he looked at the large two story ramshackle building, painted barn red; this building had seen better days. The financial panic of eighteen hundred ninety three had collapsed the silver industry and many of the manufacturing buildings were in disarray; Western Outerwear seemed to fall into that category. He wondered if he wasn't here on a wild goose chase. Well, he came this far, so he might as well go the rest of the way. He entered what he was to learn later, was the warehouse and corporate headquarters for Western Outerwear. No one was in sight, so Brown walked around inside the rambling building, until he saw a woman counting pants on a table in the middle of the warehouse. He checked the tables where dry goods were stored and then asked the woman where Mr. Reinhart's office was located. He was directed to a rickety set of stairs that led up to the corporate offices on the second floor. After presenting himself to the receptionist, he waited for Walter Reinhart. Soon a short, middle aged man, somewhat on the heavy side, approached him and stuck out his hand. "Mr. Brown, I'm Walter Reinhart, please come back to my office."

The contrast between the two men was evident. Brown was on the plus side of sixfeet, weighing about one hundred ninety pounds. Walter Reinhart was closer to five feet seven inches tall and about the same weight. Brown was ruggedly handsome, wearing a pressed black suit with a white shirt and black tie; his black boots were highly polished. Reinhart was an unattractive man wearing a wrinkled shirt, bow tie and baggy pants. His corporate office was modest at best with a desk, conference table, two chairs and a filing cabinet. Brown could see a pile of dust in one of the corners. Reinhart took his place behind an old oak desk and motioned for Brown to sit in one of the chairs facing him. "I've read your resume. What makes you think you can sell dry goods, Mr. Brown?"

"If the product is any good, it can sell itself. Mostly, you need someone who can get their foot in doors and let the product speak for itself. I'm that man. But let's be realistic, growth in the southwest is very strong and men and women laboring in that area need working clothes. So the question is, which company is going to sup- ply dry goods fast enough to satisfy the demand that exists."

Reinhart was stunned and took a few moments to compose himself before he responded. "Well, you certainly can speak your mind. I think you've summed up the problem. For me the question is, are you the one for the job"

"I am. It's been nearly a month since I responded to your advertisement. I assume we wouldn't be having this interview, if you found the man you were looking for."

"Do you have any letters of recommendation with you?"

From a folder on his lap, Brown produced two letters. One was from James Lancaster, the President of the First National Bank of Santa Fe while the second was from Lew Wallace, the Governor of New Mexico. Reinhart took his time and read both letters. He was pretty sure they were forged. How could a lowly salesman know these men? "These are very impressive letters. What about compensation?" Reinhart asked.

From the same folder, Brown produced a commission schedule. The basis of the schedule was that commissions increased as sales per month increased. If Rinehart wasn't shocked before, he was now. "You can't be serious. We give our salesmen a draw toward a reasonable commission schedule. But what you're suggesting is outrageous."

Reinhart reached into his drawer and produced a commission schedule which he handed to Brown, who ignored it

"I took a look at your warehouse before I came upstairs. It seems that you have a very large inventory and if you don't turn that over quickly, your company is looking at a substantial loss. Merchandise, sitting in a warehouse isn't something a business wants. You're in dire need of a professional salesman, whether it's me or someone else. My commission schedule is fair. If I don't produce, I don't get paid."

"You're pretty sure of yourself, aren't you? I don't know whether I like your attitude." Rinehart was red in the face.

"I didn't come here to fight with you Mr. Rinehart. You have a real problem and I think the solution is to have an aggressive sales per- son like me, moving your product. If I can't produce, you owe me nothing. If I can sell your inventory and get repeat orders, then I want to be paid accordingly."

Reinhart was uncomfortable and he didn't like Brown, but he was in a bind. The four men he previously interviewed for the position, lacked the drive it was going to take. He also wasn't sure they had that something else that would be needed for this venture. Without committing himself, he decided to try another tack. "Why don't we go downstairs, I want to show you what my campaign looks like," Reinhart said.

The warehouse was a series of long tables covered with men's shirts, pants, underwear, jackets, socks, and many more items. There were other tables with women's wear piled on them. Brown checked the label on the pants and shirts and saw that the brand was White Elephant. "Mr. Reinhart, you have more tied up in inventory than I first believed. You really need to move this merchandise."

"It's true that we have a lot of stock, but we haven't as much invested in the merchandise as you may think. Follow me; I want to show you something else."

Brown followed Rinehart to the far end of the warehouse. Rinehart opened a door in the wall and entered a large room; he signaled Brown to follow. There were at least twenty Chinese women making shirts, pants and underwear. Brown checked one of the shirts and noticed that the brand was White Elephant. He turned toward Reinhart; both men smiled and shook hands. The deal was made.

# CHAPTER FOUR

**B**rown picked up a shirt and a pair of pants from one of the tables and followed Rinehart up to his office. They started to discuss strategy. "I think we need to start in Tucson to see if this works, "Rinehart said.

"We'll talk about that later. Right now I'd like to see a few samples of the actual White Elephant Wear and compare them to these imitations of yours."

Reinhart opened a large cardboard box and lifted out a couple of shirts and a pair of pants. He tossed them on the desk in front of Brown, who examined the shirts and then the pants. "The material is the same and the cut is close enough but the labels on yours is not in the same place as White Elephants'," Brown said

"Let me see."

Rinehart put on his glasses and took hold of the two samples Brown had brought upstairs and compared them with the actual White Elephant Wear. "You have a good eye for detail, but is it worth the effort to change the labels on our entire inventory?"

"To me, our first order has to be clean to get them to buy into the scam. Subsequently, we can unload what's downstairs. Do you have prices for all of White Elephant's goods and what you intend to sell the imitations for?" Brown asked

Reinhart handed two lists to Brown, who took his time reviewing them.

"I'd suggest that we lower our prices by fifty cents to a dollar." Brown said.

"Why so much?" Reinhart asked.

"These guys aren't dummies. Most will have a White Elephant Catalog. If they're going to go along with us, it has to be worth it to them. So what does it cost to produce our wear?"

Reinhart showed him a file which detailed the cost to his company for each item.

"If I have to give a little more off, how much are you comfortable with?"

"I don't want to give anything."

"We're in this together. If I don't get any orders, neither of us makes anything. I think you need to be more realistic. There's a lot of money to be made but we won't, if you get too greedy and refuse to work with the emporiums." Brown said.

"'We're not partners. You work for me." Reinhart was red in the face and Brown thought he might have a heart attack.

"If you feel that way, you can keep all the money by selling the goods yourself. See how far you get with that."

Brown didn't say anything and neither did Reinhart. Reinhart looked at some papers on his desk, while Brown sorted through the papers in a folder he had on his lap. Neither would look at each other. They just sat there waiting for the other to speak. After five minutes of silence, Brown got up and walked to the door. He had his handle on the door knob when Reinhart gave in.

"Hold on. I'm flexible but I want all prices approved by me. If you need to cut some prices
to make the deal, I want you to wire me and let me make that decision. I'm still the boss."

Brown wasn't the type of person who'd let anyone have the last word. He wasn't going to let Reinhart be the first. "As long as I get paid, I'll run everything through you." Brown returned to his chair.

"How stable are the Chinese workers? What if they decide to leave and work for another firm?" Brown asked.

"That won't happen."

"Humor me."

"I've contracted with Mr. Lee to provide skilled women for a set price. It's up to Lee to make sure they're here and do the work I want. If someone is sick, he'll send someone to take that person's place." Reinhart couldn't help but smile, as he revealed this information to Brown.

"Are they slaves?"

"I don't know and I don't care. Are you comfortable with starting in Tucson?" Reinhart asked.

"No?" Brown replied.

"I think Tucson is best because I want to stay as far away as possible from the White Elephant headquarters in Dubuque."

"Tucson won't work for me. I'm comfortable with Santa Fe where I was over the last three weeks. If your mind is set on Tucson, I'm out of here."

Okay, we'll start in Santa Fe, "Reinhart responded.

"There on other thing. I want a hundred dollar draw, my commission schedule and I'm not going to quibble over it," Brown said.

Reinhart slammed his fist down on his desk and started to rise, but thought better of it. He nodded his agreement by writing a check to Brown, for one hundred dollars. With two suit- cases full of White Elephant correctly labeled goods, Brown took the train to Santa Fe. He planned to call on the owners of the two largest general stores there, to see if one or both would be receptive to his proposition. He knew that his approach had to be just right. But Brown had faith that the emporium owners would immediately see the amount of profit they could make for a quality brand, at a low price. Rein- hart told him that White Elephant was selling only in the Northeast and Midwest and hadn't planned to enter the southwest territory as of this date. Therefore, Brown was reasonably sure that no one in the southwest would accuse him of selling fraudulent wares.

The walk to the Santa Fe Hotel from the railroad station took only five minutes and after checking in, Brown went to his room and slept until dawn the next morning. After having breakfast on the hotel patio, he made his way to the Plaza. This was the center of the town's commercial, social, political and religious life. The Cathedral of Saint Francis of Assisi was at one end of the square; the Palace of the Governors was at the other end. In the center of this quadrangle lay a large fountain surrounded by a grassy lawn. The Plaza marked the end of the Sante Fe Trail which started in St. Louis Missouri. Originally, it was a Presidio or fort and later became the San Miguel

Mission. Night life and annual events such as the annual Fiesta de Santa Fe, flourished in the Plaza. There were many commercial enterprises located there, including two general stores that Brown was to call on this morning.

Even though Brown was selling imitation work clothes, their quality could match that of White Elephant's. The selling point was the discount he offered for the fake clothes. Each of proprietors had catalogs listing the White Elephant prices; yet, both stores agreed to give Brown an initial order. The owners knew something was wrong, but they were eager for the opportunity to make more profit. Brown wouldn't tell them why the price was so much lower than the catalog price, other than this was an introductory price to initiate a good business relationship.

Within a few months, both stores were giving Brown significant orders. In most cases, Brown was able to obtain repeat orders by having them wire their orders directly to the corporate office. Competing salesmen were suspicious of Brown and wondered how he took over the majority of this territory so quickly. It was inevitable that there would be hard feelings. The problem for his fellow competitors was that the two owners wouldn't divulge their agreement with Western Outerwear.

Brown had a lot of time on his hands and took readily to the night life in Santa Fe. He was introduced to many of the prominent citizens by James Lancaster, the President of the First National Bank. He'd given Western Wear a line of credit soon after Brown received his first order in town. He wondered what this banker would think if he knew that his name had been forged on a letter of recommendation to Reinhart.

It was Lancaster who introduced Brown to Lily Williams at one of the charity events, put on by the wives of several prominent businessmen in town. They immediately started a friendship which soon became an affair. Though both enjoyed the many restaurants that frequented the Plaza, they were discrete about their involvement and generally had their liaisons on picnics or at the homes of some of Lily's lady friends. She talked of marriage but Brown was non-committal. He knew that his stay in Santa Fe would end soon and he wanted to move on without any entanglements. In fact, he was starting to limit his liaisons with Lily to once a week and started looking for other companionship.

Late one evening Brown stopped to have a drink at his favorite saloon intown, but it was a slow evening. There were only a handful of customers in the bar and no one was playing pool. He decided to have only one drink and then walk back to his hotel. As he left the saloon, Brown sensed that he was being followed. He stopped twice to see if he could determine who it was, or if he was just imaging it. Brown wasn't carrying his gun but he did have a small piece of pipe in his coat pocket. He took it out of his pocket. It fit nicely in his right fist which he extended at his side.

As he started to cross the dirt road to his hotel, two men came out of the shadows, bumped into him and Brown stumbled. Each man grabbed one of Brown's arms and dragged him into a nearby alley.

They threw him up against one of the walls. But Brown had anticipated their maneuver and cushioned the collision with his shoulder. He then pivoted and struck the nearest man with his fist that held the pipe and the assailant fell to the ground. The other assailant brandished a knife. He went into a semi crouch and stalked Brown, waving the knife in front of him. He seemed overconfident and was grinning as he crowded Brown, forcing him deeper into the alley. But Brown wasn't as helpless as they thought. When the man parried at Brown with his knife, he sidestepped and swung his clenched fist with the pipe as hard as he could and connected with the man's head. The attacker fell to the ground. When the other man started to get up, Brown kicked him in the head and left both men to their own devises, dusted himself off and made his way the hotel. The word soon spread among a certain element in Santa Fe that Brown wasn't someone to trifle with.

With the Santa Fe market safely within their control, Reinhart wanted to expand their efforts to Tucson, his original choice. "Tucson is not acceptable," Brown said.

"You wanted for a crime there?" Reinhart asked.

Brown knew that he couldn't dodge the issue too much longer, so he gave Reinhart an answer, even if it was a lie. "Look, there's an irate husband who threatened to kill me, if I ever returned to Tucson. His wife was very beautiful and we had a thing. You know how it is," Rein- hart smiled.

Tombstone was experiencing a mass influx of workers, seeking their fortune, primarily due to the major silver strikes in the area. Reinhart agreed that Tombstone would be their next target. It was none too soon. Lily was starting to talk about having children and Brown didn't want to be surprised one day by an unplanned pregnancy. In order to put Lily down softly, he bought a dozen roses, called for her in a two horse carriage and drove to a restaurant in the Plaza. At the end of the evening, he made love to her and told her he'd only be gone a short time. Brown promised to come back for her and they would be married.

He was slowly accumulating some money. The commissions were modest at first and then as more settlers came into the area, he started accumulating quite a savings account. But there wasn't any challenge here. The merchants were wiring their orders directly to Denver. All he had to do was check in with them periodically and correct any problems with the shipments. He wanted to go to Tombstone, but realized that what he really wanted was some action.

Tombstone presented a logistics problem. The rail line hadn't been extended from Tucson and any vendor had to be supplied by freight haulers for an additional cost. But anyone supplying the Tombstone area faced the same problem. He didn't think that was significant. With the major population expansion in the Tombstone area, caused by the number of workers flocking to the silver strike, just outside of town, no one paid any attention to the added cost. Money was plentiful and the workers needed the clothing.

Major building projects were either in the planning or the construction phase; yet, half of the retail buildings had at least one wall covered with canvas. Building materials had to be trans- ported in and were a precious commodity. Many times, the lumber dealer held back delivery and sold it to someone else at a higher price. Such was the price of doing business in a growing city. Money was plentiful and consequently corruption had found its way into every fabric of the commercial community. If you wanted to be a mover and shaker, you had to grease some palms.

Those with money, wanted to enjoy their new found wealth. Chinese, Italian and French restaurants were started and flourished. To augment recreation for the general population, an ice cream parlor, a bowling alley, a Wine House selling imported European Wines and a pub selling Coors Beer were opened. People wanted culture, so a theater was built and well known actors and actresses found their way to Tomb- stone. But the miners needed an outlet as well. In nineteen hundred Tombstone, there were one hundred and ten saloons, several brothels and fourteen gambling halls. The most famous of these was the Birdcage.

Billed as the wickedest theater between New Orleans and San Francisco, the Birdcage pro- vided a variety of shows on a fifteen foot long stage standing five feet above the floor. There was a long bar across one end of the main floor and on the wall behind the bar was a seminude painting of Fatima, a belly dancer, in Oriental dress. Poker was played in the basement while the second floor acted as a brothel. High above the first floor seating area were fourteen cages or boxes with curtains that shielded the occupants, from those on the main floor.

Sally Ferguson an entertainer at the Birdcage Saloon was a frequent companion of Brown's while he was in Tombstone. He'd spend most nights in one of the cages watching her accompany some of the featured singers, that management brought into the Birdcage. She was a few years older, had been married twice and wasn't interested in a commitment. They were intimate but she and Brown had separate rooms, even though the rooms were next to each other on the second floor. Years later, Brown would wonder if he should've stayed in Tombstone.

Like the Santa Fe market, Brown was soon the major supplier of dry goods for the two general stores in Tombstone. After two months, he was able to have repeat sales handled by telegraph between the owners of the general stores and Western Outerwear in Denver. Consequently, he had even more time on his hands and there were other liaisons besides Sally.

While in Santa Fe, a problem with Reinhart surfaced. Brown's initial commissions were mailed to his address at the hotel in Santa Fe. But by the fourth week, he was shorted and then there was a week delay between checks. Brown wired Reinhart and soon the shorted commissions were mailed to him but a pattern was established. Six months later a similar situation occurred in Tombstone. He hadn't received his commissions for the past month and he was angry. Brown decided to confront Rinehart; he took the train to Denver. To make the trip more palatable, Sally Ferguson accompanied him. Before they left Tombstone, Brown notified all four store owner in

Tombstone and Santa Fe that he'd be out of town for a week. If they needed more goods, they could wire West- ern Outerwear directly.

It was three days later when Brown walked into Rinehart's office unannounced.

Reinhart's face turned red as Brown sat down facing him. The owner was not amused by the unannounced arrival. "Why didn't you tell me [45]you were coming? I have a busy day."

"If I told you I was coming, you'd say the same thing."

"Well since you're here, what's on your mind?"

"You know all too well what I'm here for. I moved your imitation products and I want to be paid in a timely manner and I want to be paid what we agreed to."

"The vendors are not paying as fast as you think and I've had to borrow money from my bank to pay you."

"That's a bunch of crap. I check with my retailers on a daily basis and I know they're paying you immediately upon receipt of the goods. If you continue trying to short change me, I'll find another dry goods company and see if they'd like to have me selling their product."

"You can't do that. We have a contract and besides no one else could furnish a product as fast as I do."

"Don't kid yourself. I could put together your setup within a month. The vendors don't know you; they know me. Guess who they'll buy from. If you can find some Chinese scam artist, so can I. Maybe, I can make a deal with Mr. Lee; I could probably make him a partner. If you're trying to cheat me, I assume you're trying to cheat him. Maybe it wouldn't take me more than a week to replace you."

"You can't come in here and threaten me.I know the right people. It'd only take a word from me and you'd be no more." Reinhart had regained some of his composure. He was sitting back smiling at Brown.

Brown sat up straight and opened had suit coat. Sticking out of his wait band was a Colt forty five. Reinhart turned pale and when he spoke his voice was wavering.

"Okay, okay, it won't happen again." "Here's the amount I'm owed to this date. I want a bank draft for that amount plus the cost of my trip here. I'll take the draft to your bank now for payment. If the bank won't honor your draft, I'll come back here and you won't like what I'll do. If you're not here, I know where you live."

Reinhart wrote a draft for the amount owed and handed to Brown.

"From now on, I'll collect the funds from the vendors as soon as delivery is made. I'll deduct my commission so there'd be no more problem with being shorted or not being paid. I'll deposit the balance and have the bank wire your share to you. If they don't have wiring capability, I'll have them mail you the balance. This way, there's less paperwork and both of us get paid faster."

"You can't do that; I'll have you arrested."

Reinhart was standing now and shaking his fist at Brown, who couldn't control his smile at the ridiculous figure in front of him.

"Sure you will. This is a good deal for both of us and yet, you tried to screw it up. I know you're a greedy bastard, but I didn't think you were that dumb. If you don't want to work this way, then I'm out of here and hello Mr. Lee."

"I'll try it for month. You better not try to cheat me."

"You mean like you did to me."

Brown took the draft to the bank in Denver and cashed it. He knew that Reinhart wouldn't stand still for the new procedure very long. He wondered if setting up his own dry goods sup- ply company was realistic. It'd be a lot of work and then there was that other thing. If someone blew the whistle on their scam, Reinhart would take the fall, not Brown. He wondered if he didn't want a score that was a lot bigger. His brief exposure to the culture in Santa Fe and the enormous sums of money available in Tombstone made him question his present occupation. Yet, this was such a good deal for both he and Reinhart that he didn't want to lose it. The cash flow was excellent, but his appetite was greater; he had the itch for something else. Being a dry goods salesman, was not his idea of being a mover and shaker.

He and Sally remained in Denver two more days. They spent most of their nights in the Larimer Square Section of town, eating at the best restaurants and finishing the evening in one of the many saloons that dotted the Old Town area. "You know what I like best about you Sally?" Brown asked.

"Tell me."

"You're fun to be with and I don't have to worry about a commitment."

"I'll drink to that."

With introductions from the two general store owners and the bank president, Brown easily entered the social life of Tombstone and got a taste of the finer things in life and some very interesting people. It was at the Birdcage where he was introduced to William Yates, of Liverpool England. William had inherited a silver mine from his brother, who was shot during a quarrel over cards in the basement of the Birdcage. Whoever shot the brother didn't stay around for a trial. The killer brandished his gun and made his way out to an alley through the basement door. Yates" brother died two days later. William was looking for someone to finance his mining operation. His main problem was that he was a gambler and not a very good one. Each time he put aside sufficient funds to start mining his brother's claim, he ended up in a stud poker game in the basement of the Birdcage and was fleeced of his stake soon thereafter. He could hold his own for the first hour, but the professionals that frequented the poker room soon took advantage of him. Consequently, none of the locals wanted to lend him money or invest in his enterprise.

Investing in someone's business enterprise had never been Brown's objective, but he was intrigued. He considered that he had lived his life primarily on the opposite side of the law. He liked the respectability a professional businessman enjoyed. Even his job as a salesman for Reinhart was really a scam. He wondered what it would be like to be a respected member of society. While Sally was working, Brown and William Yates would have dinner and a few drinks in the Birdcage.

One night Brown asked William how much money he needed to bring up some ore samples.

"One of the mine owners told me that it would take about three thousand dollars to get enough ore out of the mine to see if it contained sufficient silver to bring in sufficient investment capital and expand the operation."

"If I come up with the three thousand dollars, what percentage of the ownership are you willing to give me?" Brown asked.

"I'd be willing to give you a five percent share in the mine."

"You can't be serious. Go find someone who'll take that risk. You can't even borrow enough to pay for your hotel room. One hundred percent of a non-producing mine has the value of zero. On the other hand, a seventy five percent ownership in a producing mine, does have some value. "Brown responded.

When Yates didn't answer, Brown got up to leave. "Hold on. What happens if we need more money before the mine can produce?" Yates asked.

"I'll borrow the money or maybe I'll steal it."

Yates laughed and both men shook hands on the deal. It was subsequently put inwriting, after Brown assured himself that the claim had been registered. The last condition of the agreement was for Brown to visit the mine and assess its value. The next day, he and Yates rode twenty miles southwest of Tombstone to where the mine was located. There were six ore buckets, ten candle spikes and five helmets with oil wick attachments just inside the entrance to the mine and a rock crusher just outside.

Each donned miner's hats they found on the earthen floor and then attached oil wick lamps to the hats. Yates told Brown that the shaft had been dug down about sixty feet. There was a manually operated lift with pulleys and ropes, sitting on top. They got on the lift and descended twenty feet below the surface of the mine and walked the length of a six foot high tunnel extending about fifty feet. Yates could walk erect while Brown had to stoop to keep from hitting his head on the ceiling. The walls of the tunnel were marked with black coloring indicating that Yates' brother had blasted the walls to retrieve some ore. The two went back to the shaft and descended another twenty feet and found a duplicate tunnel, about ninety degrees from the one above, with the same coloring on the walls. The tunnels were honeycombed with wooden supports, which told Brown that some thought went into the excavation. They checked the cribbing in both tunnels and were comfortable that it could support the overhead beams.

When they finished with the second tunnel they went back to the shaft and descend to the bottom which was another twenty feet down. Here is where Yates' brother had stopped. After they surfaced, Brown asked Yates. "What was the value of the silver ore taken out of the mine by your brother?"

From what I remember, my brother told me he'd taken ten loads of crushed ore to the smelter. I don't know what the value was."

"I think we need to visit the smelter and get the answer to that question. Now I've never worked in a mine, but I know we need a good dynamiter and some labor to shovel the rock into the ore buckets, someone to haul it up the shaft and someone to feed the rock into the rock crusher," Brown said.

"I agree we need a dynamiter but I was figuring that you and I would do most of the labor," Yates replied.

"I didn't anticipate doing any of the labor. Being below ground all day in a stooped over position is not something I intend to do. I don't think we know what we have yet. If your brother did a lot of blasting with very little return then we'll have to dig another tunnel. This is looking like a lot more work than I anticipated."

"You're the one who approached me, not the other way around. You're in this with me now."

"I was just talking out loud. Let's go to the smelter and see what results your brother had. Once we agree that this operation can be profitable, then we'll get the necessary equipment and supplies and hire some workers. There're always some Indians hanging outside the OK Corral looking for work. They can break the rocks down and shovel the gravel into the ore buckets. From what I can see, we'll need five men working full time, with you and me taking the ore to the smelter."

They stopped at the smelter on their way back to town, showed the manager a copy of their claim and asked how much ore was processed for Yates' brother's mine. The manager took them back to his office and showed them the percentage of copper, silver and iron that had been extracted from the ore, over a six month period. The claim yielded about eighteen hundred ounces of silver or roughly eighteen hundred dollars. "That's slave wages, Brown said.

"But my brother didn't know what he was doing and he made nearly two thousand dollars, "Yates replied.

"Who the hell do you think we are? We don't know shit about silver mining. We probably won't do as well as your brother. No wonder he was gambling. He had a loser on his hands. I'm going to pass on this. You can have your mine back. I'm out."

"You signed an agreement and the claim was refiled with both our names on it."

"I'll be in town for another two days. We'll refile again and leave my name off. I'm going back to town."

"I'll sue," Yates said.

"Good luck with that."

Saying goodbye to Sally Ferguson was difficult. Brown really wanted to take her with him but she was reluctant. "I have a good job here at the Birdcage and let's face it Brownie, you're not the type to make a commitment. Besides, you like to play around. I knew what you were up to when you pulled the curtain on the cages above the stage. I wasn't mad. I don't see us as permanent. I'll just stay here. If you want to come back, you're more than welcome."

"You know I might just come back and surprise the hell out of you."

Sally smiled, as he walked out of the Birdcage. Usually, it was Brown who was dumping a woman.

# CHAPTER FIVE

**B**isbee Arizona was the largest city between St. Louis and San Francisco. Its growth could be attributed to the major deposits of copper and the more than one hundred copper mines that were spread across the valley, surrounding Bisbee. While Brown was in Denver, Reinhart and he decided that Bisbee was their next market. Similar to his departure from Santa Fe, Brown vacated his room in the Bird Cage, kept his account open at the Tombstone Bank and travelled by stagecoach to Bisbee. The vendors' checks were coming to the banks in Santa Fe and Tombstone. They were taking out Brown's share and forwarding the balance to Reinhart. The two banks agreed to hold onto Brown's share until he set up an ac- count with a bank in Bisbee.

His normal dress was a black suit, white shirt and a black string tie as was the custom for travelling salesmen. His short hair was topped with a black Stetson and his black boots were highly polished. He looked like a successful businessman, though he could easily be mistaken for an undertaker. Rufus Smith, the owner of the only general store in Bisbee was taken with Brown's dry goods sample and especially the price and terms that Brown pro- posed. He had a copy of White Elephant's prices and was surprised that those quoted by Brown were substantially less than stated in the catalog. Bisbee was growing rapidly and dry goods didn't remain on the shelf very long. Smith decided to take a chance with the successful looking man, standing in front of him. After a quick examination of Brown's samples, Smith gave him a significant order.

"If you can deliver within a week or two, Mr. Brown, I'll double the order next time."

"I'll do my best Mr. Smith. I like the idea of a bigger order; my company will be very pleased."

The two men parted and Brown walked to The Paradise Saloon, sat the bar and ordered a whiskey. This was an Irish saloon with the main fare being whiskey. One thing that set this place apart from the other saloons, was that females could be serviced at a side window. One of the women working the bar came over and offered companionship but Brown, although moderately amused, curtly told her that he wasn't interested. He finished two whiskeys and went back to the Bisbee Inn, had dinner and went up to his room. No one paid attention to him at dinner, thinking he was one of the many peddlers and salesmen that had come to Bisbee, once a rich vein of copper was found in the hills. The next morning, as was his pattern in Santa Fe and Tombstone, he walked into the local bank. Armed with the order from Rufus Smith, he asked to speak to the manager. While waiting for him, he took a quick inventory of the number of guards on duty, the tellers and the access to the bank. Franklin Herbert came out of his office, received Brown cordially and asked him to have a seat.

"Mr. Hebert, I received my first order from Mr. Smith at the general store and was assured that if I could deliver in a reasonable time, there would be substantially larger orders in the future." Brown showed Herbert the order.

"I'd like to open a commercial account and have your bank clear any drafts from Mr. Smith and mail a majority of the funds to my employer. When it's time, I'll tell you what percentage of the funds to send. Do you think you can handle the transactions?"

Herbert shifted in his chair and his posture became more erect before he responded, especially since the order from Smith was significant. "We'd be delighted to function in that capacity and I personally will insure that your account is quickly expedited."

"May I ask what safeguards you have in place to prevent fraud and robbery?" Brown asked

"This past month, we've installed a state of the art vault. It's a Diebold and I assure you that it's burglar proof. In addition, we have an armed guard on duty during the day, when the safe is open. As a further precaution, I have the only combination to the vault in this town."

"Do you have sufficient funds on hand to give me the flexibility, should I require more funds to purchase other goods?"

"That's a reasonable question. Though I don't make public the exact amount of funds we have on hand at any one time, I can assure you that we can handle anything between thirty and one hundred thousand dollars. And if necessary, I can supplement that amount within a few days." Herbert couldn't control a smug smile as he leaned over his desk to share this information with Brown, as though he were telling him a secret.

"You seem to have taken enough precautions to warrant my company's trust. I look forward to a long and profitable relationship."

After the initial order, Smith made three additional purchases from Brown in the next month; each was larger than the previous. Smith's draft was cleared immediately and similar to the transactions in the other two towns, Brown subtracted his commission earned. He had the balance wired to a separate account Reinhart had set up in Denver. He didn't want the funds from the White Elephant Scam to show up on Western Outerwear's books. Brown assumed that payment for the Chinese labor, the material purchased for the fake White Elephant Brand and all the logistics associated with this operation was managed under a different company. Reinhart didn't divulge this information to anyone, including Brown.

Franklin Herbert and his wife Kathy welcomed Brown into their home for a dinner party on three occasions over a five month period. At these events, Brown was able to rub elbows with the movers and shakers of Bisbee and gain the confidence of most.

Kathy Herbert was a reasonably attractive woman and a perfect hostess. It was obvious to all at these events, that Franklin Herbert was enamored with his young attractive wife. Al- though not a beauty, Kathy was the handsomest woman within her circle of friends; all the men deferred to her. Brown guessed that Kathy was at least twenty years junior to her husband. After dinner on each occasion, Kathy would escort the women to the living room and Franklin and the male guests would retire to his study.

The men would drink brandy and smoke cigars until late at night, while the women talked about shopping. Much of the conversation between the male guests was centered on the copper mining industry and other commercial enterprises that were coming to Bisbee, because of the copper boom. Brown learned at these par- ties about the plans for an opera house and an extension of the railroad from Tucson. Franklin Herbert took Brown under his wing and made sure he was invited to a luncheon, twice a month where all the prominent businessmen from Bisbee attended. It was during these gatherings that Brown learned a great deal about Herbert, who was from the upper mid-west but attended schools in Boston. He'd been married before and had a grown daughter, who was married and living in Georgia. Herbert wanted to leave his present employer in five years and open up his own bank. He asked Brown to keep that information confidential.

As the guests were leaving after one of their dinners, Kathy grabbed Brown's hand and smiled at him. Brown knew the move and decided to distance himself from the banker 's wife, by leaving without giving his respects. The next day, Kathy Herbert arrived at Brown's hotel around noon and asked the clerk at the reception desk to tell Mr. Brown, she was in the lobby. When he came down the stairs, she invited him to go on a picnic. He graciously accepted, helped her into a one horse carriage and drove with her to Mineral Springs, about a mile outside of Bisbee.
 "This is indeed a pleasure Mrs. Herbert. How did you know I'd be interested?" Brown asked.

"I came to find out why you left so early last night. If my husband or I did anything to offend you, we apologize. We value your friendship. I also sensed that over these past months, you might be bored in our frontier town. I took the liberty to come by your hotel to show you that we in Bisbee can really welcome newcomers. I wasn't sure you'd be free. I just took a chance."

"I feel fortunate that you did."

On the way, Kathy shared with Brown that she was from Tucson, had completed high school and had been working as a bookkeeper in her father's hardware store. Her father, an attorney, had made many investments in the Tucson area and the hardware store was but one of these. Kathy had two proposals of marriage that she didn't take seriously before she was introduced to Franklin Herbert, six years ago by her father. Herbert had been in Tucson on business for his bank when they met. She could tell immediately he was smitten with her, but because of the age difference, she was reticent to encourage him. Herbert postponed his departure for a few days, called upon her father and with his blessing, proposed to her. But, Kathy wasn't sure she wanted to marry someone that much older than she. It was Kathy's mother, who persuaded her daughter to accept Herbert's proposal. She pointed out that although her suitor wasn't young and handsome, his position with the Bisbee National Bank insured Kathy of a good life. It would also open up an interesting social life for the wife of a respected citizen. Her mother was correct on that account but Kathy was correct on the other. Franklin was a little old for her.

Kathy Herbert brought sandwiches, chicken, potato salad and a bottle of light red local wine. They sat down under a large Desert Willow Tree and spread out a blanket, ate some of the chicken and savored the wine. Kathy was wearing a light blue riding outfit with a red Stetson. She blushed slightly when Brown undid the string holding her hat in place and removed her hat. After another glass of wine, he undid the pins holding her hair which was piled high on her head. When her hair fell to her shoulders, she flushed. Brown was enjoying himself. She resisted somewhat as he undid her blouse. When he slid her blouse back over her shoulders, pinning her arms to her sides, exposing her breasts, she moaned. Brown caressed, massaged, kissed and sucked her breasts before he would allow her to lie down. He wanted Kathy Herbert to know he could take her anytime he wanted.

Brown removed the remainder of her clothes and slowly kissed her thighs, moving slowly up her legs until she screamed with anticipation, "Do it, please."

He no sooner entered her when she climaxed. He took his time and soon her passion returned. She climaxed once more before he reached that stage. "Oh my god," she kept saying, over and over.

Kathy lay exhausted cuddled in the crook of Brown's arm for some time and suggested to him that it was time to head back to Bisbee, but Brown hadn't completed the seduction. He stood up and pulled Kathy to her feet. He kissed her hard, cupped her breast and then instructed her to kneel down in front of him. When she realized what he wanted her to do, she resisted. He grabbed her hair in his left hand and guided her face with his right hand to the intended area. "I can't do that," she pleaded.

"Yes you can and you will." Brown twisted her hair in his hand and she cried out in pain, but did as she was told.

When Brown was satisfied, he allowed her to rise but wouldn't let go of her hair. "Whose woman are you?" Brown asked.

"Yours," she cried.

"Okay. When I want you, you'll come. Do you understand?"

"Yes."

"Yes, what?"

"Yes, I'll come to you when you call."

Before Brown would allow her to dress, he fondled her breasts ran his fingers into her moist lips while kissing her. She started to moan and soon Kathy asked if they could do it again. "I have an appointment back in Bisbee. I can't spare the time," he said.

Brown was reserved when it came to sharing his thoughts and what his life was like, before he came to Bisbee. He was an attractive man and had his share of liaisons in Bisbee but Kathy Herbert was the only married woman he was seeing. Their affair started that afternoon at the springs and became more passionate as time passed. Most of their rendezvous were at the mineral springs. On two occasions, when her husband was out of town, Brown spent the night at the Herbert's home. Each time, he made her walk around naked the entire time. He de- lighted in getting her to do what he wanted. One night he made her dance nude in front of him. "I want to see your breasts bounce up and down."

On the two occasions he spent the night with Kathy in the Herbert home, he made her perform oral sex on him in her back yard. "What if someone comes by and sees us?" she cried.

"They'll say that Franklin Herbert is one lucky man."

To Brown, she was nothing more than an attraction and something to do when he was bored. But Kathy was desperately in love and asked Brown if she could leave with him, when he moved on. Although he was non-committal, he didn't discourage her. Brown had other women friends in Bisbee. When confronted by Kathy, he said he had to keep up appearances and besides, she was having sex with her husband. Why shouldn't he have the same fun?

"It's not the same and you know it. I thought you loved me." Kathy said.

"You mean I have to be celibate, but not you. I don't think so."

In the space of eight months Brown had successfully created a monopoly for dry goods in the three towns of Santa Fe, Tombstone and Bisbee. Once he established the monopoly and Reinhart was able to supply the goods In a timely manner, Brown didn't need to go back to the other two towns. All future transactions were handled by telegraph from the store owners, directly to Western Outerwear. Buoyed with the instant success from their scam, Reinhart came to Bisbee to meet with Brown to tell him they should consider expanding their operation, into the Phoenix area. Brown told Reinhart that he was tired and wanted to take a month off.

"We've got a lot of sheep we're selling to; why not shear them as long as we can?" Reinhart responded.

"There are plenty of repeat orders to keep the cash flow coming in. I need some time off. "

"You're going with another company," Reinhart was hysterical.

"Relax; I only need a month off. Besides I'm going to be right here."

# CHAPTER SIX

**W**ith business peaking in all three towns, Brown called upon Franklin Herbert and invited him to lunch at the new Bistro De Francais. He had dined there at least once a week and liked what the chef could do with sauces. The banker was delighted to spend time with his successful client. Over a period of three weeks, they had lunch four times. Brown confessed to Herbert that he always wanted to be a banker and Herbert was more than eager to enlighten the younger man on the nuances of the banking profession. He particularly instructed him on how funds were moved from bank to bank, balances that had to be maintained and contingencies that a good banker had to plan for.

"Next year, we're opening a branch in Tombstone. I know you've been doing business there. I couldn't promise anything but if you're interested, I could suggest to the board of di- rectors that you'd be a good person to head that bank. Everything you'd need to know could be learned in three or four months," Herbert said and Brown smiled.

"I want to thank you for your faith in me. I'll let you know within a few weeks if I'm interested in your generous offer. Tomorrow, I leave for Tucson. I promised my employer that I'd see if we could enter that market. When I come back, I'd like to take you and your wife out to dinner, to repay you for your hospitality and friendship." Brown didn't mention to

Herbert that he'd been intimate with Kathy Herbert on a bi-weekly basis for the past eight months. The night before he left for Tucson, Brown was going to dinner at the French restaurant. When he stepped out on the porch of his hotel, he saw Kathy Herbert arrive in her carriage and tie the reins to the rail out front. He waited as she came up the stairs. "You were going to leave without saying goodbye," Kathy demanded.

"I don't like to discuss my affairs in public. Let's go into the alley on the side. I'll only be gone for two weeks to open up a new territory and then I'd be back. I don't understand your problem."

"I want to go with you."

"I'm sorry, but I'll be busy and won't have time for you. You're better off waiting for me here. I'm coming back and that's when you can decide whether you want to leave with me or stay here with your husband."

She was leaning up against the hotel brick wall in the alley when Brown pushed against her and kissed her passionately. He moved his right hand inside her clothing and held her left breast in his hand. He could feel her heart beating very fast.

Kathy tried to pull away but Brown was too strong for her and she gave into it. He lifted her dress, pulled down her undergarments, put both hands under her buttocks, lifted her up and entered her. He pushed her hard against the wall. She moaned and cried and he told her to be quiet. She climaxed twice and then slumped against the wall as though she was drained. "You're coming back to me, aren't you?"

"I'll be back in two weeks. You can count on that."

It wasn't the addition of new territory for his company, as he told Herbert or a vacation, as he told Reinhart. He was after the money sitting in the Bisbee National Bank. He'd been working on a plan to take as much money as he could carry from the bank, ever since he met Kathy and Franklin Herbert. He couldn't help the self satisfying smile he had on his lips as he thought about it.

True to his word, he made his way by stage to the Tucson area, but not to Tucson proper. He was still concerned about Pearl Hart. The first thing on his agenda was the purchase of two good horses. Brown was a good judge of horse flesh and after a spirited negotiation with the owner of a livery stable in the southern part of Tucson, he bought two horses. He was confident that the two horses would be able to handle the task that he had in mind. Remaining in Tucson only long enough to complete the transaction, he then rode south toward the Mexican border town of Nogales. Brown wrapped his black suit and shirt in plain paper and stuffed them in his saddlebag. He hung his boots over the other horse and then donned a long sleeve plaid shirt, an old hat and cowboy boots.

The road to Nogales was laced with many small towns; Brown bought enough provisions in Tucson to avoid any contact in those towns. To him, those traveling north were looking for work; those traveling south were getting away from something. The fact that no one paid any attention to him, as he passed through the small towns was a tribute to his disguise. He took his time conserving the horses' energy and reached the border town of Nogales in two days. His plan was to stay there for a week, before heading deeper into Mexico. He wanted to give his disguise enough time, so he rented a stall for his horses, a room in the Widow Tulare's boarding house for himself and he paid a week in advance for both.

During that week, Brown bought provisions for three weeks and some mining and camping gear. At night, he was bored and wanted some female companionship but what was available was not to his liking. He fought the urge and hung out in his room. Only a few times, did he slip into the local cantina for some Mexican beer. At the end of the week, he gathered up his provisions, the horses and continued south for another ten miles, before turning due east. The terrain was flat, the mountains were to the south and travel with the two horses wasn't that difficult. He'd travel in daylight and sleep at night. He purposely didn't wash himself or change his clothes. He wanted to look like a miner down on his luck. After traveling for ten days, he turned north and entered the small town of Naco, Mexico, found a livery stable and rented a stall for the larger of his two horses. He stored his extra gear and supplies in a shed outside. There was a sorrel mare for sale at the livery. It appeared sound, so he purchased it for a few dollars and he and the two horses headed to Bisbee.

When Brown was within two miles of Bis-bee, he camped along a dry stream bed with the sorrel and the horse he purchased in Tucson. He went over his plans, made sure the horses were fed and had plenty of water. About midnight, he made his way to Bisbee with both horses. Franklin Herbert and his wife

Kathy lived in a single story home at the end of the main street. He was familiar with the house since he'd eaten dinner there on several occasions and had bedded Kathy Herbert, when Franklin was away. He tied both horses to the fence out back and carefully made his way to the back door. He took his time, making sure that nobody was out and about. Kathy Herbert probably had no idea how helpful she'd been. It was she who told him that there no dogs in the immediate area. But that paled in comparison to what else she did. She was the one who gave him a key to the Herbert 's house.

Brown entered the kitchen and quietly made his way to the front of house, where the master bedroom was located. Herbert and his wife were sound asleep, side by side in bed. Brown leaned all the way over Kathy Herbert and put a knife to the throat of Franklin Herbert, with his left hand. As Kathy became alert, Brown grabbed her small neck in his right hand and told her in a gravel voice to be quiet. Herbert was awake and staring at Brown, but he didn't move or make any noise. Brown's knife was pressing on his neck. " What do you want?' Herbert asked."

"You two are coming with me to the bank and you're going to open the vault. If you don't, and if you cause me any problem, I'll break your wife's neck and slit your throat." To emphasize his point, Brown squeezed Kathy 's neck and she began to choke.

Brown made every effort to disguise his voice, but Herbert understood him and got out of bed. He said, "I can't open the vault, it's on a timer."

Brown grabbed Kathy Herbert by the hair and dragged her out of bed. She stood about five feet tall and weighed one hundred pounds. Brown moved his knife into his left hand. With his right, he grabbed the front of Kathy's nightgown and ripped it down exposing her breasts.

"Dam you Franklin, do something," she screamed while trying to cover up.

Franklin came around the end of the bed and sprang at Brown, who was alert to the move, even though Herbert was coming to his back. Brown pivoted and struck Herbert with his fist knocking him down. Kathy Herbert screamed and tried to go to her husband, but Brown held her back.

Herbert was slow to get up, so Brown grabbed one of Kathy's breasts and squeezed it hard enough to make her yell. Herbert looked up at Brown as though he was pleading. "Alright, I'll open it up. Just don't touch her again."

Brown released Kathy's breast but still held onto her hair. She pulled her nightgown around her and folded her arms over her chest.

"Grab your keys and go out through the kitchen. My horses are tied up out back, your wife and I will follow you. I advise you not to yell out, or call to anyone. I'll cut her throat first and then yours," Brown said.

They walked about a hundred yards trailing the horses behind, before they stopped behind the bank. Brown followed Herbert to the back door while holding Kathy Herbert by the hair. Just before they reached the door, they heard voices coming from one of the houses nearby; all three stopped. Brown pulled the banker's wife in front of him and ran his arm around her neck as though to choke her. When there was quiet, Brown grabbed Kathy's hair again and signaled the banker to continue and open the rear door; all three entered the bank. The moon was out and its rays illuminated a portion of the interior. Brown looked around and said, "open it up."

"I don't know if I can see well enough in this light. We need a candle so I can see the dial," Herbert responded.

Brown pulled Kathy in front of him again, pulled her arms down and pulled the remnants of her nightgown all the way down to her knees, exposing her breasts and thighs. Herbert just stared at his wife's nakedness, so Brown ran his hand down and started massaging her private area.

"Alright, alright, I can do it, just don't touch her anymore and let her cover up," Herbert begged.

Brown allowed Kathy Herbert to cover up but he held onto her hair; it was only a short time before Herbert had the vault open. Brown released a rope tied to two bags around his shoulder and dropped the bags on the floor in front of Herbert. He still held onto Kathy Herbert's 'hair. "Put the currency in these bags. I don't want any coin or gold."

It took Herbert about four minutes to fill the two bags.

Brown pointed to Herbert. "Take a look outside and make sure it's clear; remember I have your wife," he said.

When Brown was comfortable, he instructed Herbert to tie the money bags to the saddle of the sorrel. Brown pushed Kathy Herbert toward the other horse and ordered Herbert to put her in the saddle.

"What are you doing? I got you the money, now let her go."

Herbert was starting to raise his voice, so Brown took out his gun and pointed it at him, while still holding onto Kathy's hair. "If you don't quiet down, I'll shoot you right here. She's going with me so you won't send a posse after me. I'll let her ride back on the horse she's on, as soon as we're clear. Now help her onto the horse and you better not raise an alarm."

Brown grabbed the reins of Kathy Herbert's horse and slowly moved out of town. He wanted to reach Naco, Mexico before daybreak.

When they were within a mile of Naco, Brown turned the horse over to Kathy Herbert and gave her a revolver, which wasn't loaded. If the horse was traced, it would end here in Naco.

"Here's some ammunition for the gun but don't load it until I'm out of sight. I hate to shoot you after all we've been through. Of course, you may want to come with me. That's what you want, isn't it? If you go back, you may have to answer a lot of embarrassing questions."

"I hope you rot in hell, you son-of-bitch. You think I didn't recognize you; you're a pig. I'd rather be poor with Franklin than rich with you," she snarled back at him, as she spurred the horse and rode back toward Bisbee.

# CHAPTER SEVEN

**B**rown picked up his other horse and the supplies he stored at the Naco Livery and rode a mile south before he stopped to change horses. He readjusted the bags of money on the horse he rode, switched his Remington to that horse and continued south for another ten miles before turning west toward Nogales He wasn't worried about a posse because Kathy Herbert wouldn't reach Bisbee before he was at least ten miles south of Naco. It was improbable that she tell the sheriff or her husband that it was Brown, who robbed the bank. He was also fairly certain that the posse wouldn't follow him into Mexico and create a situation, between the two countries. But he knew that news of the robbery would spread soon and his main worry would be Mexican Bandits. They roamed south of the border preying on businessmen and solitary travelers. The bandits rode in small bands of three to six, but there were some groups as large as twenty.

Luckily, the terrain was flat and allowed him to travel at night without too much concern of running into something. It was in the daytime that he was most vulnerable to the bandits. He'd ride for thirty minutes and then walk the horses for thirty minutes. Near dawn, Brown found an area covered by heavy brush, near the foothills to the south. He tethered the horses, gave them some grain and water and quickly fell asleep. He liked to think that he slept with one eye open and would be alert if someone approached his location. It was near four in the afternoon when he heard some movement north of his position. He raised his head and peered through the brush with his binoculars. There were six riders about a mile away traveling east toward Naco. One rider was riding an Appaloosa and another had shiny spurs. Brown waited until he was sure they were out of sight, and then went back to sleep.

To keep the horses fresh he alternated riding between the larger and smaller horse. It was the same with the supplies and bags of money. He felt that it'd take a week of travelling at night to cover the distance to Nogales and he wanted the horses fresh, if and when he needed their stamina. He traveled the next three nights with- out incident and at each dawn, found an area covered by heavy brush and made camp.

Everything was peaceful for the first four days. It was on the fifth afternoon that he heard, what he thought were riders. He took out his binoculars and peered through the brush. There were six of them and they were about a mile north of his position traveling west, the same way he was headed. He noticed one rider with an Appaloosa and another with shiny spurs; they probably were the same group he saw traveling toward Naco, several days ago. Well if they hadn't heard about the robbery before, he was sure they knew about it now. He'd have to be careful if he was to reach Nogales with his life and money. He counted the money yesterday; it totaled Fifty One Thousand Dollars.

At dusk, two days later, Brown decided to lighten the load. He buried the miner tools he brought along as a subterfuge, as well as some extra food. He was only one day away from Nogales and felt that he and the horses could survive with less food if necessary; water was the important subsidy. As long as he and the horses had enough water, they could go longer than anticipated. He stuffed some hardtack for himself and grain for the horses in his saddle bag and rode toward Nogales. Just as dawn broke, he came over a small rise and could see the outline of Nogales. He also could see some riders camped between him and Nogales. He figured it was the riders he'd seen twice before. He knew what they were after; he just wasn't going to give it to them. At least he didn't think he would.

He slowly backed the horses up behind the small rise and fixed his binoculars on the group. They were the same group. It didn't appear that they had seen him, so surprise was still on his side. He stayed awake the next day and continually checked the group to determine if they intended to move on. It appeared that they were staying put, as though they were waiting for someone. Unfortunately, he knew who that was. There wasn't much he could do until night- fall, unless they left; but they didn't. Well, his plan had worked so far. He wasn't going to let a few bandits come between him and his money.

As nightfall came, he could see the embers from the rider's camp fire. Brown knew they 'd have a sentry out somewhere, but the question was, where. Brown scanned the area away from the fire, hoping the sentry would give away his position. He was hoping to catch some light from an occasional cigarette. He thought some more about his situation and came up with a plan. If he wasn't successful, they wouldn't find the money. He picked a spot a hundred yards from the horses and buried the money bags. He was sure he could find the spot when he returned, even if the horses got spooked and ran off.

The most logical choice for the bandits was to change sentries at midnight, or shortly thereafter. About eleven that evening Brown made his way on foot toward their camp site. He planned to be there about midnight. In the event they waited another hour or two to change sentries, he'd still be in position to see where the sentry was located. It took him forty five minutes to cover the ground between him- self and their camp. He stopped only for sixty seconds every ten minutes, to be sure he wasn't discovered. On one occasion, he heard voices and that time he waited five minutes, before continuing on. Brown was surprised the bandits hadn't turned in yet and assumed they were drinking and having a good time thinking about all that money that was going to be theirs. He'd taken off his spurs, before he left his camp and when he reached the bandit's camp, he took off his boots.

It was midnight when he heard some movement to his left and then some muffled voices, followed by someone returning to the camp. Brown was carrying only his knife and a forty five caliber colt. He'd have to be quick and quiet if he was to survive. He had always been able to defend himself, but this was the first time he was to be the attacker and there wasn't just one foe, there were six.

The sentry was sitting down leaning against a burned out log with his rifle resting against his leg. Brown crawled up within fifteen feet of him, then stood straight up and hurled his knife at the sentry striking him just below the heart. The sentry moaned and grabbed at his chest and then leaned over onto his side. Brown rushed forward, pulled the knife from his chest, slit his throat and then looked around to be sure no one heard the moan; one down, five to go. He took a deep breath before crawling closer to the camp fire. That's when he heard movement to his right and he lay flat on the ground. When he heard the flow of water, he knew that one of the bandits was relieving himself. Brown scanned the area and saw the man standing with his back to him, twenty feet away. Moving on his hands and knees ever so slowly, he got close enough to the man, before standing up. He put one hand over the man's mouth and slit his throat with the other. The man was heavy; it took Brown time to move the body further away from the camp fire.

The glow of the fire outlined four men sit- ting in a wide circle. Two were on the opposite side of burning logs, while the remaining two were near each other, between Brown and the fire. These two would be easier to neutralize. The trick was to kill the nearest two without being vulnerable to the two, opposite the fire.

He took a couple of deep breaths to calm himself and rushed the two nearest him, brandishing his knife. He slashed the first man's throat, but missed the second. The bandit rolled over but Brown pounced on him like a cat and struck three times with his knife, feeling bone on a least one occasion.

The bandit was bleeding from his wounds and was lying on his stomach, so Brown turned his attention to the two on the other side of the fire. They were awake and rising to their feet and at the same time grabbing at their weapons. Brown threw his knife and hit one man in the chest but the man had already grabbed his gun and hurriedly fired at Brown, striking him in the left side. Brown felt the impact of the bullet, while the other man, realizing he couldn't reach his gun in time, ran into the night. Brown had no choice. He pulled his knife from the fallen man's chest, slit his throat and ran after the one who'd bolted. It was dark, but the fleeing man was making enough noise for Brown to follow. He slowly narrowed the distance and when he was within a couple of feet, he launched himself at the man and drove him into the dirt, with himself on top. He raised his knife and struck the lethal blow.

Brown rested for a few seconds, checked his side which was still bleeding and then dragged the body back to the camp site. He counted the bodies again; one was missing, so he counted again. There was the sentry, the man who was taking a leak and the one he just ran down. There should be three at the camp site; one was missing. He went over the order of attack again and realized it was the one who he left lying on his stomach; he must have been playing possum. Brown stopped and looked around. Even though he struck the man three times, the blows weren't enough. But where did the he go? Time wasn't on Brown's side. He found six horses tethered to a line between two trees and took off their saddles, then released the lines. He took a whip and struck the horses on their rears. All six horses ran into the night

He cut off the stirrups on all six saddles insuring that they couldn't be used again even if the one who'd escaped, was able to find one of the horses. Brown's side hurt but the bodies needed to be buried. There was a small shovel on one of the saddles and he started digging. Luckily, the dirt was soft and he excavated only deep enough to cover the bodies, their guns and saddles. It took him two hours to bury the five bodies and then he cleaned up the camp, put on his boots and walked back to where he left his horses.

Since the missing bandit could be watching his every move and perhaps lying in ambush, he needed to move on as quickly as possible. He made his way back to camp and retrieved the two horses. The two bags of money were still where he buried them. After digging up the money, he tied the money bags to the smaller horse. Brown was a very controlled individual. He planned for every contingency and didn't like it when something unforeseen happened; he worried that things were unraveling. He removed his shirt and assessed the wound. The bleeding had stopped, but there were separate entry and exit wounds indicating the bullet had passed through his body. His side hurt and he suspected some of his ribs could be broken. He covered the wounds with some liniment, wrapped a bandage around his waist a couple of time and trusted that it would hold.

He was now faced with two new problems. The first was whether someone in the vicinity would come across the bandit 's camp site, poke around and find the five dead bodies. The second was the problem the escaping bandit could create. He remembered striking the bandit three times with his knife; he thought they were lethal enough, but now he wasn't so sure. If he was out there watching, would he be able to strike when he saw an advantage. Brown chastised himself for his failure to kill the bandit; he'd have to be alert every minute from now on.

Distancing himself from this area was his first priority. He didn't know how long it would take someone to discover the site. But once the bodies were found, other problems would be created, such as more bandits to evade and even a posse looking for him. This could be the most expensive fifty one thousand dollars that was ever stolen. As he mounted, he had the feeling that someone was watching him.

# CHAPTER EIGHT

Tommy and Sarah Sanchez were on the way home from their east coast trip, where they settled Sarah's brother's debts. James had pledged all his assets for a scheme his in-laws had undertaken. He subsequently found out that he was the only one in jeopardy. Tommy and Sarah saw through the scheme, paid off her brother's debts and threatened his wife's family with exposure. After a physical confrontation with James' in- laws, Tommy forced them to accept his terms. They looked forward to returning to their ranch in the Santa Ynez Valley. One week on the train was difficult at best for Sarah and Tommy, but with two young children, it was an adventure each day. At night, they couldn't wait to go to sleep.

"Do you feel good about what we did for my brother?" Sarah asked Tommy.

"I do. He helped you when you were down on your luck. It was the least we could do for him. Whether he can stand up and take control of his life, is my real concern. That scheming wife and family of hers has their hooks into him and won't let go easily. I'd be more comfortable if he came with us. His debts are paid and all his investment are completely unencumbered. I know you used at least thirty percent of your resources to pay off all his debts; that was nice of you. James should soon be back to where he was before he married that woman. I'm just not sure whether he'll go through with the divorce."

"I suggested he come for a visit, but he wanted to have some time to think about the future. We'll just have to see how it plays out. I can't live his life. He has to own it," Sarah said.

The twins, Thomas and Helga, were in the sleeper car; Naomi was watching them, leaving Tommy and Sarah with a few moments to themselves. "Going back east has made me realize that a family is the most important thing in life for me. I not only want to spend the remainder of my life with you, Juan, Thomas and Helga, but I'd like to see if my daughter Naiwa can be part of our life. I feel that I've let her down. She's part of me and I feel guilty that I haven't reached out and provided for her and her family. I've never seen her children and our two children have never met her or her children. When we reach Nebraska, I wonder if we can take a detour and visit my daughter at the Pine Ridge Reservation," Sarah asked.

"It's not going to be an easy ride to the reservation; I've been there many times. It's a very depressing place and has some bad memories for me. If we got off at North Platte, Nebraska, it'd take us four days to reach the reservation. I don't know if Thomas and Helga can handle it and I don't know whether I want to expose them to the potential dangers. Wouldn't it be better if we came back without the children?"

"They're our children Tommy. I think they'd view it as an adventure. We could rent a good sized rig and maybe one or two drivers. I know much of the area hasn't been settled yet, but with you along and maybe one or two drivers, I'm comfortable enough to make the trip. Can we at least have the conductor telegraph ahead and see what's available, before we make a decision? Part of the twenty years I spent with the Sioux was at a reservation like Pine Ridge, so I'm well aware of what their life is like."

Tommy could tell that this was important to Sarah. He put his hand on Sarah's thigh and moved it slowly toward her heart shaped area; she smiled. "Give me an answer before you reduce me to a panting female. I just want all my family together and I don't want us to ever be apart. I just hope you understand what I'm going through?"

"I do understand." I'll talk to the conductor and ask him to wire ahead to see if we can rent a carriage and hire two good men to accompany us," Tommy responded.

They were one day out of North Platte before they made a decision. The conductor had an acquaintance in North Platte who he telegraphed when they stopped along the way. They picked up a response two days later when they stopped to take on water. Over the next three days they were able to come up with an acceptable plan. Tommy, Sarah and Naomi discussed it overnight and, in the morning, the decision was unanimous. The entire family would travel to Pine Ridge Reservation and see Naiwa and her family.

When they arrived at the North Platte Station, a six person carriage was waiting and so were three men. The conductor got off the train and introduced Tommy and Sarah to his friend Charlie Johnson, who grew up in the area. "Charlie is a retired engineer for our line and a good friend. He knows everyone in this area and I see he brought along a couple of men; he hopes you can use."

Johnson introduced Tommy and Sarah to Bill Drummond and Saul Peters, the other two men waiting at the depot. I know you don't know me or these two men but Drummond is the former sheriff of North Platte, while Peters is a retired army scout. Both know the area and both have been to the Pine Ridge Reservation. They are the two best men available at this time to guide you on your trip. Why don't you talk to them? If they're not acceptable, I'll look for others, but it'll take some time."

Drummond was an impressive figure weighing over two hundred pounds and exceeding sixfeet in height. Peters was closer to Tommy size and age. He spoke to the two men for a half hour, told them what he had in mind and discussed compensation for the two men. The three shook hands and the two men agreed to drive the family to the reservation. "Can I ask the purpose of this trip Mr. Sanchez?" Drummond asked.

"My wife's daughter lives there."

Tommy could tell that Drummond was surprised. Both Drummond and Peters looked at Sarah and then at each other. "My wife was a Sioux captive and was forced to marry into the Sioux Nation. Now if that's a problem for you two men, we may as well know it now. Before you answer, you should know that I have Indian ancestors. So what's it going to be?"

Peters and Drummond looked at each other, but it was Peters who responded. "This is really none of our business Mr. Sanchez. We just saw a pretty white woman and were surprised that she could have an Indian child. We meant no disrespect Mrs. Sanchez and we'd like to make the trip with you and your family. The fee you proposed is generous, payable one half now and the balance upon completion. We could start as soon as we have enough supplies."

If Sarah had taken offense at Drummond's inquiry, she didn't let on. "I have two small children travelling with us. There will be no drinking on the trip and no smoking around my children. Is that understood?" Both men said yes.

The conductor had reserved two rooms at the hotel for Tommy, Sarah, Naomi and the two children. "I'll check into our rooms," Sarah said and left with Naomi and the two children.

"I'm going to the bank and arrange for financing. You two go to the general store and pick up our supplies. The rule is, if you think we need it, we'll take it. I don't want to be caught short when an emergency arises. I don't think the carriage you brought will carry my family, you two and the supplies. Let's rent a second wagon and a couple of horses, we can return them on the way back. My wife and I can help with the driving."

After Sarah told the two children where they were going and who they were going to see, they wouldn't go to sleep. When they finally dozed off, Tommy, Naomi and Sarah weren't far behind.

Prior to leaving, Tommy telegraphed the Indian Agent at Pine Ridge to let him know the family intended to visit the reservation. Early the next morning, they dressed in riding attire, got in the carriage with Drummond driving. Peters brought up the rear in a two horse wagon with all of their supplies.

Peters and Drummond trailed their horses behind the wagon that Peters was driving. The two men weren't particularly surprised when Tommy purchased two Remingtons, but the surprise was yet to come. Tommy purchased a holster and two colts forty fives. When he asked the proprietor where he could try out the colts, he was told there was a barn in the rear of the general store, with a target pinned to a hay bale. Tommy fired one colt and then the other hitting the center of the target each time. When he fired each from his holster with lightning speed and hit the center of the target each time, Drummond said, "holy shit."

Tommy wanted to keep to the more travelled roads and pass through small towns as much as possible. He knew they'd have to camp out most nights, but he was hoping that there might be lodging in at least one of the towns along the way. The first two days passed without incident. The next afternoon, they came to the town of Valentine, just below the South Dakota border. Two days on the trail for Sarah and Naomi wasn't that difficult, but both women wanted a bath. Though there was no lodging in the town, the barber had a bath tub. Sarah, Naomi and the two children took turns having a bath while Tommy kept close watch so none of locals walked in on the two women. As soon as the baths were over, Tommy gathered up everyone and told them it was time to leave. He was concerned that the size of their entourage might tempt someone.

As they were leaving the town, Tommy noticed four men sitting outside one of saloons in town. They seemed to be taking an interest in the family and watched them as they rode out of town.

Tommy suggested to Drummond and Peters that they find a camp while it was still light outside. When they made camp for the night and after the women and children were lying down, Tommy shared his concern with Drummond and Peters. "I want a guard out all night. We'll do it in shifts of four hours each and I'll take the first shift."

"You think there'll be trouble?" Drummond asked.

"Let's just say, I err on the cautious side."

At ten that evening Tommy was relieved by Peters. Nothing happened during his four hour shift but he sensed something was making the horses restless. Tommy strolled over to the carriage under which, Sarah, Naomi and the two children were asleep. Tommy laid his hand over Sarah's mouth and whispered into her ear. "It's me Sarah. Please don't wake anyone."

Sarah struggled at first but when she realized it was Tommy, she sat up. Tommy said. "I have a feeling we may have visitors tonight and I don't know if I can count on Peters or Drummond. I want you to have your rifle next to you. Drummond is asleep by the fire and Peters is standing watch over near the big rock. I'm going to take a look around. Don't worry, I'll be watching everyone."

"Please don't take any chances, please." Sarah kissed Tommy hard and held onto him. He pulled himself away and slipped into the night.

Tommy had learned from his older brother how to move without much sound. Though he wasn't as gifted as his brother, he could move on prey whether it was man or animal, without being seen or sensed. He heard the four before he saw them. They were crawling toward the camp in twos. One set was coming up behind Peters and the other two were going directly at Drummond. Tommy positioned himself so that he could cover the two crawling toward Drummond. Peters would have to fend for himself. The two in front of Tommy were taking their time. He could hear them whispering, but he couldn't make out what they were saying. At that moment, the pair in front of him changed direction and moved slowly toward the wagon where Sarah, Naomi and the children lie.

Tommy waited as the intruders neared Sarah and then stood up. When they were almost on top of Sarah, a rifle shot rang out and Tommy could see one man stagger and fall down. The other looked at his fallen partner; Tommy shot him through the heart and yelled out to Peters, "watch out behind you."

Peters turned, but it was Drummond who turned on his stomach and shot both men in the chest. Peters quickly recovered, but the two that were shot appeared to be dead. Tommy ran to Sarah who had her rifle pointed at one of the fallen men near her carriage. "Are you okay?" Tommy asked.

"I'm okay but the children are frightened and Naomi is crying. "They checked the two Sarah and Tommy shot. Both were dead.

They walked back to the fire to see if any of the intruders were still alive; they weren't. "I saw you slip into the darkness and I figured you sensed something. I was wide awake when you yelled," Drummond said.

"A good thing for me that you were," Peters said.

"Mrs. Sanchez, where did you learn to shoot like that?" Peters asked.

"My husband is a good teacher. I think I'll tend to the children." Sarah left the three men standing there.

Tommy walked back with Sarah and checked on the children. They'd gone back to sleep. When he came back to the fire he spoke to Drummond and Peters. "All four were in Valentine this afternoon. I wonder if they knew that we were travelling to the reservation. I can't get over the fact that they seemed to know, where the women and children were, "Neither Drummond nor Peters responded.

"Let's bury them now and get some rest. I'll make one more look around to make sure that none of their friends followed them here. I think we'll take their four horses with us. Drummond, you're a former lawman. Who do we tell about these four?" Tommy asked.

"As far as I'm concerned, I'll let the sheriff in Valentine know where to find them, when we get back there. That's if he wants to. I'll check their pockets before Peters and I bury them, to see if they have any identification and I'll give that to the sheriff.

Tommy walked back to where Sarah was waiting. "It's good thing that Drummond was awake. We may have lost Peters." Sarah said.

"Yes, wasn't it," Tommy replied.

# CHAPTER NINE

**O**n the morning of the fourth day, three male members of the Pine Ridge Reservation rode into their camp. They said that they were sent by Chief Red Cloud to welcome them and lead them to the main part of the complex. None of the three spoke English, but conversed in Lakota with Tommy and Sarah. After the family broke camp, they followed behind them

As they came over a ridge, they looked down at a village of tents, many of which were torn, with remnants blowing in the breeze. They had arrived at Pine Ridge Reservation. As they approached the main entrance, they could see a gathering of the village and a banner in Lakota welcoming the son of Sitting Bull. Young Thomas was the first to ask, who's the son of Sit- ting Bull? "Your father is," Sarah responded.

They were warmly received by many of the inhabitants including Chief Red Cloud, a true statesman among the Lakota and a great warrior. Even the Indian Agent was there to welcome Sarah and Tommy. He was probably shocked to see an elegant gentleman get down from his carriage, instead of a Sioux Brave. The villagers chanted Sitting Bull's name in Lakota and many of the young braves pushed to get near to see his son, Tommy Sanchez, as well as the widow of the great warrior, Crazy Horse.

Red Cloud was as much of an attraction for Tommy and Sarah as they were for the villagers. He'd had defeated the American Army in many battles and led the transition from plains life to reservation life for the Sioux. Tommy had met Red Cloud when he came to the Standing Rock Agency to say his farewells to Sitting Bull and his older brother. This was also Crazy Horse Country and Sarah felt joy and sorrow at her homecoming. She looked around, but couldn't pick out her daughter. It was Red Cloud who brought Naiwa and her two children, Chatan and Wachiwi forward.

Tommy helped Sarah down from the carriage and held onto Helga and young Thomas. He could see the look of sheer wonder on their young faces. When Sarah put her arms around her daughter, she noticed how thin Naiwa was and how listless her two children were. "Where's your husband?" Sarah asked.

Naiwa lowered her head and whispered that he was dead. Sarah would learn from Chief Red Cloud that several of the young men on the reservation, including Naiwa's husband, were hung for cattle rustling. The men tried to get jobs in the surrounding towns, but there was still too much apprehension on the part of the white settlers to trust anyone, that looked like an Indian. The rations provided by the Indian Agent weren't enough. They were always hungry. One day six braves decided to do something about their plight. They raided a neighboring ranch and ran off with four steers. The rancher and his cowboys hunted them down, hung the braves and returned the steers to their ranch.

"We were always so hungry. I told him not to go, but he said he had to do it for his family. I knew he felt like he'd been letting us down by not providing us with enough food. He wouldn't look me in the eye the morning he left. When he wasn't back by sundown, I knew something bad had happened. That was six months ago," Naiwa said.

"Why didn't you write? You have my address."

"I didn't want to bother you and your new family. You had it so hard."Naiwa said.

Sarah cried and hugged her daughter. "Well, I'm here now and I intend to look out for you and my two grandchildren."

That night, Tommy and Sarah shared their food with Naiwa and her two children along with Red Cloud and members of the tribal council. It took some time for Red Cloud and the others to tell Tommy and Sarah what life was like on the reservation.

"There is very little food, no jobs and a high mortality rate, especially among the children. There is nothing to look forward to, except death. It's fortunate that Chatan and Wachiwi are still living. Many of their friends are not," Red Cloud said.

The next morning, Tommy met with Drummond and Peters and told them that the family would stay at the reservation for the next three days. "If you want to go off the reservation and hunt somewhere, it's alright with me. I want you back by dinner, the night before we leave and I might add, sober enough to travel. "Tommy smiled, as he said the last words".

"Thanks. We'll get our gear and head out. I hear there's some elk about twenty miles from here and maybe the villagers could use some fresh meat."

Later that morning, Tommy met with Red Cloud and two of the tribal elders. They rode to the site of the Wounded Knee Massacre and counted the wooden crosses that marked the landscape. "How could something like this have happened?" Tommy asked Red Cloud.

"It was the time of the Ghost Dance revival. The army was directed to put a stop to anything that could incite the Sioux. Soldiers were sent to Standing Rock Reservation to arrest Sitting Bull. They feared that he would rally the Indians to mount an attack on the settlers in the area. By this time, all the tribes had been disbanded and the army didn't want a repeat of the Battle of the Little Big Horn. Sitting Bull wasn't part of the Ghost Dance, but he was a symbol that the nations could rally around. That made him the Army's target. When the soldiers attempted to arrest Sitting Bull, he said he was through with war and wanted to live in peace. But that didn't appease the soldiers. They became aggressive, he resisted and they shot him. He died the next day from his wounds.

"Was that what brought on the massacre?"

"After your father was killed, Spotted Elk and many of the Lakotas feared for their lives. Around two hundred fifty men, women and children made their way to Pine Ridge. They were overtaken by the Seventh Cavalry and told to make camp right here." Red Cloud pointed to the spot of their encampment.

"When the army commanding officer arrived, he demanded that Spotted Elk's band be disarmed immediately, which the Lakotas were reluctant to do because they needed their weapons to hunt for food. A confrontation occurred and after much shouting between the two sides, the shooting started. Many of Spotted Elk's people ran; they were rundown and killed by the soldiers. Nearly one hundred and fifty people were slaughtered right here." Red Cloud put his hand over his eyes but Tommy could see a tear on his cheek.

Tommy walked over to the grave markers along the ravine. "Was this the last conflict between the Lakotas and the white soldiers?"

"No. The next day some of our people, who escaped from the massacre set up camp at White Clay Creek, about fifteen miles north of here. Soldiers were sent to bring them back to Pine Ridge. A battle ensued and this time our people beat back the soldiers, who had to be res- cued by the Black, Buffalo Soldiers. There were some small skirmishes for a few months after that, but the battle was essentially over. Our dream of freedom in our own land was gone for- ever. We became prisoners of war. To pour salt on our wounds, all the treaties were disavowed by the white settlers and their government. To make matters worse, gold was discovered; our land was too valuable to leave in our hands. The Dakotas were ours by treaty, yet we were stripped of everything."

Tommy was overcome with emotion when speaking about his father. "Thank you for sharing with me what my people did and how brave they were. My father would not have survived on a reservation. He was a free soul and didn't want to be confined. I remember what it was like moving the entire village to go where the fishing and hunting were better. I loved that life, but when I was sixteen, my father took me up to a place in the hills, where he went to think. It was just the two of us camping out for two days. That's when he told me that I would have to make my way in the white man's world, if I were to survive. He realized the life we knew would end someday. Our land would be taken and the buffalo we needed for food and clothing, would be killed to near extinction. I left the next month. My mother was dead and though I had a half brother, he was much older and already had a squaw and two children."

"Then you know what you must do. Take Naiwa and the two children with you when you leave. She'll not want to go because she's afraid of everything beyond the reservation. She's had very little contact with the white man. I will help convince her. If you don't take her, she and the two children will be dead in a few years. There's no future here. Our way of life is gone. What you see is what it's like here every day."

"Is there anything else that I can do to help you?" Tommy asked.

"You were very generous with the four horses and saddles. Our young men will be happy. There's really not much that can be done. We are forced to live here and rely on the government to take care of us. We have no way to earn money, no education and no skills other than hunting and fishing and that's been taken away from us. Our men die around forty eight years of age and our women live to fifty two. You could leave some food, but it will be gone immediately and then what do we do. The best you can do is to save some of us. Naiwa is a good woman; she'll work hard for you. But it's the children that concern me the most. They know nothing of the way it was and when my age group dies, our culture will probably be destroyed. We must save some of our young."

Tommy left the old chief smoking his pipe and went to find his wife. The children and Naomi were asleep in a tent provided by Red Cloud. Sarah was tending to Naiwa and her two grandchildren. Helga and Thomas had taken to living on the trail and here at the reservation, they were simply in awe of everything. This was a life they never heard about. They were finding out about their mother and father and who Sitting Bull was. They were slowly accepting Chatan and Wachiwi into their family, but didn't quite comprehend that they were uncle and aunt to the two Indian children. Tommy was proud of his family and wondered what it would be like, if they took the other three back with them.

Red Cloud had set up two teepees for Tommy's family, furnishing them with blankets for sleeping. The years had been good to Sarah, but being in the teepee brought back memories of her captivity. She didn't suffer from malnutrition as Naiwa and her children had. But her captors expected her to work long hours, furnish enough wood to keep the camp fire burning all night and in her spare time, skin buffalo. Initially, she competed with the stray dogs for food and slept around the fire at night. The women in the village were especially hard on her, probably because she was pretty and many of the braves looked upon her as a future wife. Soon, the elders noticed that she was blossoming into womanhood. Their council had one of the families take her in and treat her as their daughter, until her marriage to Crazy Horse.

After marriage, Sarah's life stabilized, but she was still expected to work long hours, even while carrying her two children. After Crazy Horse was killed, Sarah stayed at Fort Robinson. with Naiwa and Juan. She was barely surviving and without the sponsorship of General Miles, she would have starved. The soldier's wives treated her as a piranha and a second class citizen because of her Indian children. To make matters worse, Juan was a malcontent and was constantly being apprehended by the soldiers for some infraction, until he ran off with several young braves. He was headed nowhere until Tommy went after him and brought him back to Sarah.

Naiwa was so frail and her two children, with sunken eyes looked dejected. That had to change. She had to help them. Naiwa's two children were older than Thomas and Helga but because of the malnutrition on the reservation, all four children were about the same size. Sarah insisted that Naiwa and her two children bathe while Sarah and Naomi cut the children's hair and then applied a salt and oil solution to clear away the lice common to the reservation. Sarah took Naiwa's and her children's clothes and burned them. She gave two of her dresses to Naiwa and an outfit each to Chatan and Wachiwi. Thomas and Helga wouldn't miss them

Sarah stopped what she was doing and walked toward Tommy. "We can't leave them here. They have no life and no future. We need to take them home with us. I want my daughter and my two grandchildren with me."

"What does Naiwa say?"

"I haven't mentioned it to her yet. I was waiting to talk to you first."

"I'll do whatever you ask. You know that. We have so much and can easily take three more into the family. We can build them a home on the ranch."

"Tommy, there are many memories here for me. Some are good, but most are bad. I don't want to stay here long. I know I'm being foolish, but this was a life I want to forget and I know you above all, can understand that."

The next morning Tommy met with Chief Red Cloud and the tribal elders. Although reluctant, Naiwa agreed to leave with Tommy and Sarah, but Tommy wanted the tribal council to approve her leaving. In addition, he wanted the Indian Agent to sign off. It took the better part of the day, but in the end all parties agreed. Drummond and Peters had returned that evening and were making preparations for the ten to return to the train in North Platte.

That afternoon, Red Cloud took Tommy, Helga, Thomas and some of the reservation children on a tour of Pine Ridge. Helga was in awe of the teepees and the blankets the Indian women wove. Young Thomas played with the young boys who showed him how to use the bow and arrow and throw the lance. But the biggest thrill Thomas got was when his father showed his skill with the bow. Red cloud nailed a cloth to a tree fifty yards away and drew circles around a large cross. Tommy placed arrow after arrow in the center of the target. He then took his time and showed Thomas and Helga the art of the bow and arrow. Thomas wanted to know if Tommy used it to hunt.

Before Tommy could answer, Thomas asked if Tommy had gone on Indian raids against other villages.

"Where did you learn about Indian raids?" "Naomi told me about them and how you snuck up on an entire village without being heard. Are we Indians?' Thomas asked his father.

"I am half Indian. My mother was white. You are one fourth Indian. My father was Sitting Bull and my mother was Elizabeth Kelly. When you go to school, you will hear of Sitting Bull. His Indian name was "Tatonka Yatanka". I could've taken his name when he died. I chose not to. My father was a great man and a great warrior; he was a hero to his people. There will be some books that will portray him as a vicious killer. He wasn't like that. He fought for the rights of his people."

"Do you have any brothers and sister?" Young Thomas asked."I have a half brother named Crow Foot. He's at the Standing Rock Reservation, where my father died."

Red Cloud smiled at the exchange between father and son. "Tommy, I have a surprise for you. I was a good friend of your father's and I was there when he was shot by the tribal police- men, who came to arrest him. Before he died, he asked if I would give you something, if I ever saw you again." Red Cloud handed him Sitting Bull's Headdress. It was a magnificent headdress with bright red and yellow feathers flowing to the ground. Thomas, Helga and the other Indian children took turns trying on the headdress, which was too large for any of them.

Tommy put on the headdress. He was five feet nine inches tall, the same height as his father. He had to turn away from his children because the emotion he felt with the headdress was overwhelming. Red Cloud also gave Tommy a picture of Sitting Bull with the headdress on, standing with Wild Bill Cody at his Wild West Show. "Did you know your father was in Buffalo Bill's Wild West show for a year?"

"I was living in San Diego when I heard the show was in Los Angeles, so I took the stage up to see him. He introduced me to Bill Cody and his new friend Annie Oakley, who he named "Little Sure Shot. He was a little embarrassed at being in the show. He didn't like to lose any battle, even I fit was just pretending."

"I feel that I have honored my friend by being able to satisfy his wish. Here are some other things that Sitting Bull used as a young brave. I want you to take them with you. I hope that you will keep them safe and they'll be a remembrance of what our life was like, but could never be again." Red Cloud presented Tommy with a silver breastplate that Sitting Bull wore over his chest when he went into battle, plus a vest made of buffalo bones. Tommy was stunned with emotion and a tear came to his eye. He knew what Red Cloud was asking. He would protect and treasure them for the remainder of his life.

The children ran ahead and Red Cloud and Tommy followed them at a distance. When they reached Red Cloud's teepee, he said. "I knew your mother. The council said I could have her as my wife. I went to her and told her. She smiled. But Sitting Bull came to our village the next day and when he saw her, he asked the council for her. Sitting Bull was a famous warrior chief at that time and I was but a young brave. The council wanted to befriend the great chief, so they told him that he could have her. She was small with red hair and blue eyes. Her Indian name was "Scarlet Woman", I cried when she died. Sitting Bull wouldn't say it, but I think her death had a marked impact on him for the rest of his life; he never took another wife. I kept a lock of her hair and I want you to have it." Red Cloud took a small pouch from around his neck and handed it to Tommy.

It wasn't only Tommy that was having an epiphany at Pine Ridge. While walking with Naiwa, Sarah was startled when someone whispered her name. She looked around, but couldn't determine who it was. When she heard it again, she looked at an old woman who had a blanket wrapped around her shoulders and was squatting next to a teepee. Sarah was apprehensive. She remembered how badly she was treated for her first five years of captivity, barely staying alive, fighting the dogs for leftovers and dressed in rags. At night she slept on the ground wrapped in smelly blankets. She recalled the beatings the Indian women gave her when she didn't react quickly enough or when they thought she hadn't completed her chores. She feared the men but the women made her life a living hell.

The old woman tried to rise but fell back into a sitting position. Sarah asked her in Lakota if it was she who called out to her. The woman acknowledged that it was she. "I was your foster mother. My husband and I took you in while you were being courted and eventually married Crazy Horse. Do you remember me?"

Sarah knelt down beside the old woman and put her arms around her. Sarah cried but the older woman was stoic. "You are still a pretty woman. I've always wondered what happened to you, after Crazy Horse was killed," the woman said.

There were very few in the tribe that treated Sarah with any common courtesy during her captivity. This woman was the exception. "My two children and I went to live at Fort Robinson. I taught the children at the fort until my brother found me and helped me leave Fort Robinson. Since then I have a new husband and two beautiful children. We live in California." Sarah responded.

Over the next hour, Sarah and her foster mother talked of the old days and how hard things were now. Her husband died five years earlier and she was being taken care of by her son, but it was hard for him. He had a wife and two children and there was only so much food. It was obvious the woman was suffering from malnutrition. Sarah sent Naiwa to the wagons for some food. The old woman was grateful but would only eat a few morsels. "I will share this with my family, "she told Sarah.

Before she left pine Ridge, Sarah arranged to have a supplement of food from the trading post delivered each week to her foster mother. Theirs was a tearful parting. When Sarah suggested the woman could come back to California with her, the woman said she preferred to stay with her son and his family. "This is the only life I know. I'm grateful to you but I want to spend the remainder of my life with my son and his family."

The night before they left, Red Cloud hosted them at his lodge. When dinner was finished, Red Cloud walked beside Tommy while the others went ahead to their teepee. "How well do you know the two men who came with you?"

"Not well at all. The conductor on the train arranged to have them meet us in North Platte. Why?"

"I've watched the way they look at your wife, especially the big one. She's a handsome woman, but their looks are not of admiration, but of lust. I know I'm an old man, but I still see things and I'm not comfortable with those two. I have a suggestion if you don't mind?"

Red Cloud quickly laid out his plan. Tommy didn't make any comment until he was finished. They shook hands and Tommy caught up with Sarah and the rest of his family. That night he told Sarah that Red Cloud suggested they go back home via Chadron and take the train to Sidney Nebraska. "Red Cloud doesn't trust Drummond and Peters. He wants to send some of his braves as escort, especially the ones I gave the horses and rifles to."

Sarah didn't respond, so Tommy asked her what the problem was.

"Tommy, I was present when Crazy Horse was bayoneted by the soldiers and I was part of the group that took his body to his final resting place. I don't know how many of that group is still alive, but none have divulged Crazy Horse's resting place. It's within thirty miles of Chadron and I'd like to go there and pay my respects. I don't know how you feel about my wanting to see my late husband's resting place. If you think it's a bad idea, I will abide by that. Coming back to Pine Ridge has made me look at that part of my life, that I've ignored for many years. You left this life voluntarily; I did not. I could have left Crazy Horse many times, but I did not. I realize you are the love of my life, but I did love my first husband."

"I have no objection at all. There are many things I admire about you, but the one I admire the most, is your loyalty. You don't have to tell me where he's buried until we reach Chadron; I won't divulge it to anyone."

"His resting place is in Hay Springs about thirty miles southeast of Chadron. The day after we reach the town, I'd like only you to escort me to the site. The braves can watch Naomi, Naiwa and the children"

# CHAPTER TEN

**D**rummond and Peters had completed their preparations when Tommy approached them just after dawn. "I appreciate your help during our trip but we're going to change plans and return by train from Chadron. Four of Chief Red Cloud's Braves are going to escort us to Chadron, so we won't need your services any longer. You can go back the way we came and return the wagons and horses. I paid for two weeks rental, so there shouldn't be any other charges. Red Cloud will lend us a buckboard. His braves will bring it back to the reservation. The four braves are offloading our supplies as we speak, though I've left four days supplies for you. I'll pay you the balance we agreed to."

Drummond was the first to raise the issue. "Don't you think you should've consulted with us before you made the change. I don't know Red Cloud. How can you be sure that he's giving you good advice?"

"I know I didn't consult with you, but we made the decision last night. The children are tired and with the addition of three more to our party, Sarah and I felt it was best to take the nearest train home. I was assured by Red Cloud who knows this area probably better than any man alive, that the way to Chadron is well traveled and fairly safe. He was a friend of my father and I trust his judgment."

"I just don't like the way you changed every-thing without letting us in on the planning. It's as though you don't trust us." Drummond said.

"Well, I really don't trust you. That incident on the way to the reservation when you shot the two men is troubling. It was as though you were expecting them. And how did two of the intruders know where the women and children were? Yes I have some concerns."

"You're telling us that we set you up. I don't take that from any man and neither does Peters. I want an apology now and three extra days pay for our work."

"The compensation we agreed upon is what I'll pay and nothing more. Now if you don't want the balance, I'll keep it."

"We'll take it. But a guy out in the plains with three women and four children seems awfully vulnerable to me. You'll need all your luck to make it to Chadron." Tommy didn't like the sneer on Drummond face as he and Peters rode off with the two wagons and their horses.

Parting with the past is traumatic. Tommy wanted to leave but he was sad. Sarah cried and held on to Naiwa as she turned to look back at a past that she wanted to forget. Naiwa was nearly hysterical and it took all of Sarah's understanding to convince her daughter, that it was best for her children that she leave this life behind. Sarah and Tommy held on to Chatan and Wachiwi until they were miles away. The children were apprehensive of the unknown world they were entering. But it was really Helga and young Tommy that helped them with the transition.

Tommy wasn't sure he'd heard the last of Drummond and Peters. He wondered if they had another surprise for him and Sarah. He'd have to be wary. Chadron at the turn of the twentieth century could be described as a metropolis in the plains. It acquired notoriety in eighteen hundred ninety when the Chadron to Chicago Cowboy Horse Race started here. The winning time was thirteen days and sixteen hours and the winner was paid one thousand Dollars.

Chadron's population had grown to seven- teen hundred people and a railroad depot had been added. There were three hotels and two restaurants, in addition to the small businesses found in a western town. The Chadron Grand Hotel had modernized its room by adding bath- room facilities. The rooms were large enough so that all eight were comfortable. The four Indian braves travelling with them, camped outside of town. They were aware that Tommy and Sarah were going to be gone the entire next day and they would be responsible to protect the children and the women left behind.

Needless to say, Sarah and the women were very happy. Pine Ridge Reservation was friendly, but it was hard on the women and children. That night the family ate in a Chinese restaurant; it was a first for the children. They were surprised to see some soldiers in the bar and restaurant. Since Ft Robinson was some- what active, Tommy assumed that the soldiers from the fort were the principal customers of the town. "Did you want to visit Fort Robinson?" Tommy asked Sarah.

"No, it has too many bad memories of before and after Crazy Horse's death. Thanks to General Miles, I and the two children survived, until my brother James found me. I was treated like damaged goods by the women at the fort for having two half breed Indian children. Juan resented our treatment and did the only thing he knew at the time. He rebelled and left the fort. You know the rest.

Before they left for Hay Springs, Tommy met with the four Indian braves who were sheparding them to Chadron. None of four spoke English, only Lakota. Tommy hadn't spoken the language much in the past twenty five years, but he soon was in the flow and was able to get his message across. "The two men, who'd been with us since we left North Platte, have been fired. They don't appear to be happy with that, perhaps they may wish us some harm. I want three of you to watch the children and women while we're gone for the day and I want one of you to trail us at a distance but be ready, in case there's trouble."

The four talked among themselves and indicated which one would follow Tommy and Sarah. One of the braves smiled and pointed to the shortest of the four. "No one can see Walking Silent when he tracks someone. One time he couldn't even find himself." The four laughed and punched at each other. Tommy couldn't help but join in.

When he was satisfied that everyone knew what was expected, Tommy rented a rig and he and Sarah drove to Hay Springs. The four hour trip was hot and dusty and they had to stop several times, to rest the horse and relieve them- selves. But the journey was without incident. Hay Springs was a small town of five hundred people with a long main street and at least ten saloons along the dusty road. They didn't attract any attention as they drove through town and ten minutes later Sarah pointed to a grove of trees. She asked Tommy to stop. He helped her down and she walked to a clump of trees, sat down and leaned back against one of the sturdy trees. To give Sarah some privacy, Tommy walked a hundred yards down the trail, found a shady spot and waited until she was ready to leave.

He had grieved for a loved one, many years ago. Maria Conchita, the daughter of Don Francisco Lopez, of Mexico was the only other woman he ever loved. He was smitten with the young woman as soon as they met. It wasn't long before he asked for her hand in marriage. Tommy and Don Francisco were in business together and the father was delighted that Tommy would become his son-in-law. Once the bridal announcement was made by the father, the two lovers, exhausted from a day long festivities, took a carriage ride to Sierra Springs, set down a blanket and had a couple of glasses of wine. They soon fell asleep in each others arms on the hot, still, summer day. When Tommy woke, there were four men leering down at him and Maria. Before he could get to his feet, Tommy was shot twice. Subsequently, Maria was beaten, raped and strangled.

When the two lovers hadn't returned to the hacienda by nine that evening, Don Francisco and four of his men went searching for them. They found his beautiful daughter lying dead on the ground and her intended on death's doorstep. Tommy hovered between life and death for a week and then slowly recovered. Within three weeks, he was able to go after the four men. Don Francisco wanted to go with him, but Tommy said this was a job for a person with his skills. He didn't kill any of the four when he captured them in their lair. He returned them to Don Francisco and let him determine their fate. The night was pierced with screams that Tommy would always remember. No one mentioned the four men again. No one asked about their fate. It was a though they never existed.

An hour later, Sarah walked back to the carriage and called for Tommy. He could tell she'd been crying. He decided to give her space. It was up to her to tell him how she felt, if she wanted to. They sat in the carriage for over thirty minutes before Sarah composed herself and told Tommy they could go back to Chadron. Sarah hadn't uttered a word since they left Crazy Horse's resting place. Half way back to Chadron, they were stopped by Drummond and Peters, who'd been hiding behind some trees just off the Hay Springs to Chadron Road. Both had their guns drawn.

"We think we deserve more for our services. I know you carry a wad of cash with you, so hand it over and we'll let you pass. If not, it'll get nasty and you won't like what we can do to you and especially your wife."

Drummond and Peters were side by side astride their horses pointing their guns at them. Sarah started to get down from the rig and her movement distracted the two gunmen. "Sit right there missy. I don't want to shoot you, but I will."

For the instant that Drummond and Peters were focused on Sarah, Tommy had eased down to the ground on the other side of the rig. He was wearing a holster and gun and his coat hung back. He was poised for action. "I'm going to give you two a chance to ride off. If not, I'm going to take away your guns and deliver you to the sheriff."

Drummond laughed out loud and turned to Peters. "Can you believe this guy?"

Tommy drew with lightning speed and shot Drummond in the right shoulder. His horse reared and Drummond fell to the ground; his gun dropped from his hand. Just as quickly, Tommy shot Peters in the right arm and his gun fell to the ground. Peters turned his horse and started to leave but the Indian brave that was trailing Tommy and Sarah came up and knocked Peters to the ground. During the confrontation, Sarah had dropped from the rig and had the gun she carried in her purse, trained on Peters and Drummond.

When they were sure the two men were disarmed, Tommy and Sarah bandaged their wounds, as the two lay on the ground, cursing at them. After the wounds were cleaned and bandaged, Tommy and the Indian brave tied Peters and Drummond to their horses and made their way to Hay Springs. The sheriff was an old friend of Drummond and was surprised that he had turned outlaw. Peters was unknown to him, but after taking a deposition from Sarah and Tommy, he arrested Drummond and Peters; he assured Tommy that they would be convicted and sent to prison.

"I appreciate it sheriff. I hope your friendship for Drummond doesn't cloud your thinking. I don't want to keep looking over my shoulder to see if they've escaped. I hope we understand each other."

"Don't worry Mr. Sanchez. Friendship is one thing, but the law is what I serve."

Tommy found the two wagons that Drummond promised to return on his way back; they were behind the livery on Main Street. He paid the owner to deliver the two wagons and four horses back to North Platte.

# CHAPTER ELEVEN

When their train arrived at the San Luis Obispo Station, Tommy telegraphed ahead to the Los Olivos Depot, requesting they contact Sarah's son, Juan. They wanted him to meet them with the six passenger carriage and two horses. Santa Ynez was a young town founded in 1881 by Bishop Francis Mora. He'd been given permission by the US Congress to split the College Ranch, given to the Catholic Church by the Mexican Government, into lots. It was originally named Sagunto and lots sold for six to fifteen dollars an acre. Shortly thereafter, a combined grammar and high school were built to handle the increasing population. A post office was established in eighteen eighty three. But the big impetus to growth was the Southern Pacific Railroad and the feeling that they would extend their line from Santa Barbara to Santa Ynez via the Gaviota Pass. The Santa Ynez Land and Development Company was formed and the boom was on. Unfortunately, Southern Pacific decided not to extend to Santa Ynez and the town suffered through a depression.

When Sarah came to the valley, many of the businesses were still suffering through a recession. There were many vacant buildings in the town and some farms had been abandoned. But, there were still eleven saloons, a livery stable, feed store, pharmacy, blacksmith shop, millinery store and barber shop on Sagunto Street. Doctor Cunnane and his brother who'd come with the first group of settlers, were the practicing physicians in town

Juan had grown into a handsome young man and though his Indian heritage was prominent in his looks and demeanor, Sarah could see some of her traits as well. What a change the last two years had made in the young man. He had been transformed from a malcontent to a responsible citizen. He'd completed his studies in the law and earned a position with a law firm with offices near the depot in Santa Ynez. Sarah was a pragmatist; she knew that it was Tommy's firm, but flexible hand that had made that all possible. Juan still had Crazy Horse's independent streak, but he'd been able to control it well enough to become a respected citizen.

As the train came to a stop across from Mattie's Tavern, they looked out the window and saw Juan sitting in a carriage, with a bouquet of roses on his lap

He recognized his sister Naiwa immediately and tears flowed as they embraced. He spoke Sioux to Chatan and Wachiwi and told them he was their uncle Juan. After a long welcome, he helped Tommy load the children in the back of the carriage and tie the baggage to the rear of the rig. On the ride home Juan couldn't stop talking about the cases assigned to him by his law firm. "I forgot to tell you. There was a bank robbery in Santa Barbara last month. My firm represents the bank and the partners assigned them to me, as a client. It seemed natural, since I'd been working with them on the many loan defaults they suffered during the recent depression from land speculation.

"When did the bank robbery take place?" Tommy asked.

"Three weeks ago. It happened in broad daylight. Two men wearing masks walked into the Santa Barbara National Bank at noon and robbed them of fifteen thousand dollars in currency. Another man was outside holding their horses. The two inside walked casually outside, got on their horses and the three rode north into the hills. The sheriff formed a posse and initially picked up their trail, but lost it near the Painted Cave Area. After a week the posse came back empty handed. Tommy, you know these mountains between Santa Ynez and Santa Barbara, as well as anyone. Can they hole up somewhere where the posse wouldn't be able to find them?"

"Much of that area is known only to the Chumash. Since there isn't much game up there, nobody's hunting or trapping. So yes, they can hide out indefinitely if they have food or if someone is helping them. Water isn't a problem. What does the sheriff say?"

"He doesn't like the idea of a robbery in his town and the bandits escaping. He thinks the only way they could have eluded the posse, was for someone in this area to help them. He also wondered how they went in and out of bank so smoothly without a shot being fired or without any resistance on the part of the guards."

"Where were the guards? Why didn't they try to put up resistance?"

"One was reading a newspaper in the front of the bank. He was quickly overwhelmed, while the other was in the back room relieving himself."

"Pretty convenient to me, what does the sheriff think?"

"He doesn't know, he's just wondering out loud. He questioned both guards and they said it wasn't unusual that one would go to the bathroom during the day. The one guard at the entrance said he saw the two men come into the bank. There was nothing unusual in their manner, until one of them came up behind him, put a gun in his back and took his gun. The guard said there was nothing he could do. Lucky for the bandits they picked the time when one of the guards wasn't available. "Juan winked at Tommy.

The entranceway to the ranch was marked by a large sign, welcome to "Altura Prado". As they rode down their long gravel road, bordered with roses on one side and Bougainvillea climbing up the white fencing on the other side, they let out a sight of relief; they were home It was Sarah who oversaw the planting of the roses and Bougainvillea when she owned part of the current parcel, where their house is situated. The other house, originally used by Don Ortega when he owned the other portion, had been torn down by Tommy, after he and Sarah purchased the land. Sarah took great pride in their ranch and realized how much she missed it while she was away. Thomas and Helga leaped out of the carriage with Chatan and Wachiwi close behind and Naomi bringing up the rear, yelling at them to stop. Tommy lifted Sarah in his arms and carried her to the door of their four bedrooms, single story ranch style home. Sarah kissed him hard and held on as he opened the door, before putting her down inside the house.

Tommy Sanchez was the person Juan admired most and who he tried to emulate. Although he was a teenager when Crazy Horse was killed, Juan remembered how Crazy Horse carried himself. Tommy and Crazy Horse came from the same mold. Both were leaders, both were loyal and both were married to Juan's mother. He remembered how hard his mother worked when she was Crazy Horse's wife and later as his widow. He was ashamed for all the grief he caused her. She was entitled to a good life and a good man. Tommy Sanchez was that man.

Juan's reverie was interrupted by Tommy. "You look fit Juan. Have you been doing any riding?"

"I spent a couple of days as a volunteer with the posse. Actually, it was my employer who suggested I go along. It felt good to be in the saddle for a change instead of being cooped up in a small office, reading law books. I like the law, but every once in a while, I get the urge to go into the mountains. You know what I mean," Tommy smiled.

After dinner, Juan went back to his boarding house in Santa Ynez. The family rested the next day and Tommy took the twins and his two grandchildren fishing the following day. Chatan and Wachiwi had never seen a fishing pole but they caught on quickly. The twins had been cooped up too long on the round trip to Philadelphia. He wanted them to be able to act like children again; none of the four disappointed him. He'd created a small pond on the southeast portion of their ranch and stocked it with bass and some trout; he planned to spend the entire day with the children. Sarah fixed a picnic basket and the kids played games and fished. Young Tommy was upset that he didn't catch a fish, but Helga did.

"It's not right. I'm the man and I should be the one to catch a fish." Young Thomas cried out.

"Sometimes it'sjust luck. You'll catch one next time and so will Chatan and Wachiwi." Tommy said.

Of course, throughout dinner that night, young Thomas had to hear how his sister was the only one to catch a fish. Tommy sat back and smiled. It was good to be home. Two days later, Tommy and Sarah decided to ride out to the south range, have a picnic and look at their cattle pasturing in one of the valleys on the ranch. Naomi prepared a picnic basket for them and Sarah brought along a bottle of wine from their small vineyard on the ranch. They found a place overlooking the valley where a small herd of their cattle was grazing. Sarah laid a blanket, set out the lunch and poured two glasses of wine.

"We haven't been alone for a month Tommy; have you been avoiding me?"

He reached over and pulled her to him and kissed her long. He then undressed her on the blanket.

"What happens if one of the Vaqueros comes up here and sees me lying here naked as a jay bird?' Sarah asked.

"Well, he can't have any of this. I might let him look, but then I'll ask him nicely to leave." He laughed. Sarah swung as hard as she could but Tommy anticipated her. He smothered her swing and drew her to him. Afterward they lay naked in each other arms and talked the talk of married people, who love and enjoy each other. What about Naiwa and the two children?" Tommy asked.

"You can tell she's uncomfortable. This whole experience is a lot for her and especially the children to assimilate. I'm going to give her time. I think she'll come around. Look at Juan. We've done a pretty good job with him, or at least you have. We've got to work on their English if Chatan and Wachiwi are going to school in the fall. I'll wait until that time before I make a decision. Perhaps they could be privately tutored for the first year."

There were twenty Vaqueros to do the various chores associated with raising cattle on their sprawling ranch. The head wrangler Raul Mendoza, and about five of his wranglers met them as they rode into a glen, where about a hundred head of cattle were grazing. Mendoza asked if they could ride a short distances from his men because he wanted to talk to them privately. Raul spoke very little English, so he, Tommy and Sarah, who had an affinity for languages, conversed in Spanish. Their conversation was calm at first and then became intense as Sarah and Tommy asked questions. Raul said they were missing about twenty head of cattle and they'd been missing for about a week. He'd ridden over the entire ranch to find them, but to no avail.

"Most of my riders have been with me for a few years but some are new. I think some of the new men might know what happened to the cattle. I can't be absolutely sure, but I've narrowed it down to three of the new men. I'd been waiting for you to return before I did anything."

"What do you think we should do?" Sarah asked Raul

"I think we should lay a trap and find out who's involved."

"Where do you think the cattle went?" Tommy asked.

"Initially to some other ranch in the area is my best guess, after that I'm not sure"

"Why did you come to that conclusion? Tommy asked."

"Two of the three worked at Star Ranch before they hired on here. That ranch borders our property to the far south."

"Who owns the Star Ranch?" Tommy asked Raul

"I believe it's a man named Singleton. I think he's new to the area, but his foreman isn't. His name is Ed Meade, who used to work for Don Ortega."

Sarah was standing close to Tommy and he could feel her shiver at the mention of the man's name. Raul noticed the look on Sarah's face. "Are you alright Mrs. Sanchez?"

"I'm fine, "Sarah said and got on her horse. Raul, Tommy and Sarah rode back in silence until they reached the ranch house. Tommy asked Raul to come into the house. Sarah went to tend to the children and to tell the cook there'd be a guest for dinner. Tommy and Raul went into Tommy's office, where Tommy offered him a glass of Brandy and a cigar; Raul took the cigar but declined the drink.

"How often do you make a count?" Tommy asked Raul in Spanish.

"We have about seven hundred head of cattle dispersed throughout the ranch. I try to divide the cattle into herds of one hundred each. That way it's easier to track and maintain a count, which I do once a week. Now I don't count every head; I look at the herd and estimate. I can be off by one or two but not twenty. I rotate my men on a weekly basis so that there are about three to four Vaqueros for each one hundred head of cattle. I had the same three watching the herd that's missing twenty head."

"What was their response when you asked where the cattle were?"

"They didn't know. They said the cattle must have wandered off at night. I asked if they searched for them. They said they did but couldn't find them. "Raul responded

"How long have they worked for us?"

"Six months."

Sarah had joined the conversation and Tommy could tell she was agitated. "Raul, this is serious. Ed Meade harassed me when I was here by myself. He hates my husband because Tommy had him fired and then gave him a beating on Sagunto Street in front of Meade's friends. Then Tommy gave him twenty four hours to leave town. That was five years ago. If he's involved, it's because he wants to get back at us."

"Where are the three you suspect?" Tommy asked.

"They're in the bunkhouse. I took them off night duty and haven't paid them this week. I think they expect to be fired. I know I've let you down and I'm sorry. If you want to let me go, I'll understand. Raul said.

"We're going to have dinner first and then we'll take some action." Tommy said

Naomi had the cook prepare ribs, beans and salad tonight, with a good bottle of red wine from the vineyard on their ranch. The children wanted to know why Raul was having dinner with them. Sarah told the children that Raul was a guest and it wasn't polite to ask why he was here. After apple pie and coffee, Tommy and Raul excused themselves and went into Tommy's office at the rear of the house.

"Bring the three into the main barn and make sure they're unarmed. I'll be right there. Don't worry, we'll find out what happened to the twenty head of cattle and we're not going to fire you. I have a great deal of trust in you."

Sarah stopped Tommy as he was leaving his office. "What are you going to do?" She asked.

"I'm going to give them a scare and find out what they know. I want to know if Ed Meade's involved."

"Be careful. Meade scares me. I know you can handle yourself but Meade doesn't play by the same rules as you and I."

"I'll be careful."

Tommy went into his storage barn and picked up three strong ropes. He took his time before he entered the main barn. He wanted the three men, who were standing in the center of the barn, to anticipate what was going to happen. Tommy walked into the barn and stopped in front of the three men. He just stared at them while they kept looking at the ropes in his hand. The significance wasn't lost on the three. Tommy walked away from the three and climbed up into the hay loft. He threw the three ropes over the main beam traversing the width of the barn. After he climbed down, he took his time fashioning a noose in each of the three ropes and then tied the other ends separately to a vertical beam. The nooses hung about five feet above the barn floor and were swinging in the night breeze.

Raul didn't say anything but the three suspected of rustling Tommy 's cattle, attempted to run. Two vaqueros, who came with Raul, leveled their rifles and forced the three back into a small circle. Tommy continued to work on the nooses and then pulled on each to make sure they were tight. By this time, one of the men got on his knees and begged for his life. Still, Tommy didn't say anything or look at the three men. It wasn't but two minutes later that the same man yelled out that it was Ed Meade who approached them with an offer of money, if they 'd looked the other way. Subsequently, all three confessed and begged for their lives. They said the cattle were moved south onto the Star Ranch.

"Tie them up and lock them in one of the storage rooms. Tell them we're not going to hang them now but if we don't find the missing cattle, well just make them guess what we'll do. If they try to escape, we'll hunt them down and hang them." Tommy was addressing Raul in Spanish; he knew the three heard him.

After one of vaqueros moved the three to the storage room, Tommy told Raul to pick two trusted vaqueros and meet him here at mid- night. Tommy planned to make a call on Meade and any of his men that were involved.

"Take the ropes down and bring them with us."

When he returned to the house, Sarah asked Tommy what happened.

"I scared them a little and they confessed to helping Meade steal the cattle."

"What are you going to do now?"

"We're going to pay Ed Meade a visit tonight. The three Raul suspected of rustling our cattle, gave up Meade. He offered them money to look the other way when he and several of his cowhands took our cattle to the Star Ranch."

"Meade bears a grudge against us. He may be waiting to spring a trap on you. I know you can handle Meade but I still want you to be careful. I don't know what the children and I would do if anything happened to you." Sarah started to cry.

He put his arm around her waist and kissed her gently on the lips. "I'll be careful, but I can't let them get away with this. If I turn the other cheek, they'll continue to harass us and that's not acceptable."

"I know. I know."

Meade had been the foreman for Don Ortega before Tommy's marriage to Sarah.

Meade tried to intimidate Sarah and made suggestive comments to her knowing that there wasn't a man around to protect her. She'd complained to Don Ortega, but he either wouldn't or couldn't do anything. When Tommy found out about the harassment he visited Don Ortega late one night and cut off part of his ear and made him promise to fire Meade.

A week after Don Ortega fired Meade, Tommy was in town with Sarah and Naomi. Meade and two of his friends called Tommy out on Sagunto Street in front of about thirty people. Tommy wasn't wearing his guns; they were in the carriage. He tried to reason with the three and when that failed, he walked back to the carriage, put on his guns and approached the three in the middle of the street. Without saying a word, Tommy drew and successively shot the hats off all three, gave Meade a serious beating and told all three to leave town. Subsequently, Don Ortega sold the remainder of his large spread to Tommy and Sarah. That was almost sixyears ago and now Meade has returned.

As far as Tommy knew, Meade's employer at the Star Ranch, a small five hundred acre spread bordering Tommy's and Sarah's large ranch at the southernmost portion, was an absentee owner; they'd never met him. Tommy, Raul and two of his trusted vaqueros made their way south, found the gate that Meade had fashioned, crossed over the creek dividing the two ranches and came up behind the Star bunkhouse. It was two AM. There wasn't a sentry visible anywhere on the ranch so Tommy sent one of the vaqueros up close to the bunkhouse to see if Meade and his men were there. The vaquero reported back that there were six men in the bunkhouse. Four were in bunks and two were asleep around a fire. Tommy instructed one of the vaqueros to remain concealed while he, Raul and the other vaquero approached the bunkhouse.

Raul and the other vaquero grabbed a wooden log and on Tommy's signal they slammed the log into the bunkhouse, splintering the door. Tommy burst in with his gun in front of him. Raul and the other Vaquero were right behind with their rifles pointed at the four in the bunks. Meade and one of his men fell out of their beds; two others sat straight up, but didn't attempt to get up. The two on the floor just lay there. No one went for a gun but Meade was yelling that they were trespassing and for Tommy and his men to get off their property. Tommy directed Raul and the other vaquero to make sure the sixwere unarmed and to march them to the main barn. One of Meade's men tried to run away, but Raul hit him alongside the head with his rifle and knocked him down. That must have discouraged the others because they walked without incident to the main barn. Raul helped the one he hit. When everyone was in the middle of the barn, Raul and his vaquero tied their hands behind their backs. Tommy repeated the procedure he used before and slung the ropes over the main beam, crawled down and set the nooses five feet from the floor. This exercise wasn't lost on Meade and his men.

"You can't do this, we haven't done anything," Meade yelled.

Tommy didn't say anything. He took his time checking and pulling on the nooses before tying the other end to a vertical beam. He then walked up to each of the six and looked into their eyes. When he was certain who he wanted, he selected three of Meade's men. Raul marched the three to the center of the barn and put nooses around their necks. The three didn't speak English but were crying out in Spanish. Two of the three wet their pants. Raul asked each about the twenty head of cattle. Each screamed out that it was Meade's idea and they just went along because it was a job. Meade yelled at them to shut up. When asked who was involved, all three said that all of them rustled the cattle. "Where are they?" Raul asked.

"They were sold in Santa Barbara," was the response. of each except Meade.

Meade kept yelling at the others to shut up. "They're not going to hang us. They're just trying to scare us, so shut up." His analysis was lost on the other five. They were scared and wanted to cooperate.

Tommy walked up to Meade, who wouldn't make eye contact. "I told you to get out of town five years ago and not to come back. I'm going to let the sheriff hang you, but if he doesn't, I'll kill you on sight."

Tommy turned to one of Meade's men. "Who did you sell our cattle to?" Tommy asked in Spanish.

"Some guy at the stockyards," the man said.

"Get their horses. We'll take them to Santa Barbara and turn them over to the sheriff. If they give us any problem on the way, we'll hang them." Tommy said.

Before they left, they found the housekeeper in a small unit near the main house and told her about the six. "Let your employer know that he hired cattle rustlers."

With the six tied to their horses, they rode back the same way they came. It was morning by now and Sarah was up. Juan, who was living in a boarding house behind his law office, had arrived early and caught up on the details of Tommy's raid on the Star Ranch. Sarah and Naomi served breakfast to Raul and his vaqueros on the porch and to Tommy and Juan in the kitchen." What are you going to do with them?' Juan asked Tommy at breakfast.

"We're going to take them to the Sheriff in Santa Barbara."

"You know you don't have the legal right to raid the Star Ranch and threaten Meade and his men with hanging," Juan said.

"They stole twenty head of cattle from our range. I'm not going to let anyone get away with that."

"Tommy you can't threaten men with hanging and expect their confession to be legal," Juan said.

"What's got into you Juan? You've been reading too many law books. There's no law here in the valley. The ranchers have to protect their stock. Meade and the eight aren't innocent men. They're rustlers. Ask Raul. He heard all of them confess. We'll all of them did, except Ed Meade, who was the ring leader. "

"Be careful is all I'm saying, Tommy." Juan reached out his hand.

After breakfast, they picked up the three that were locked in a storage unit and put all nine in a buckboard. They arrived in Santa Barbara about three in the afternoon and gave a statement to the sheriff. Each of Meade's men and the three that worked for Tommy, confessed to their part in the rustling; Meade wouldn't confess to anything.

"My men and I were threatened with hanging, if we didn't confess," Meade said.

"You can tell all of that to the judge. You'll get a fair trial," the sheriff said.

"Sheriff, if I see any of them again, I'm going to hang them. So they better not get off with a light sentence. I don't know if you can find who they sold my cattle to, but he should be tried as well. Those cattle have our registered brand on them," Tommy said.

"Before you go back to your ranch, I wonder if we can talk about the bank robbery, that happened here last month," the sheriff said.

"What do you have in mind?"

"You're the best tracker I know. I wonder if you'd accompany me into the hills to see if you can find anything that the posse missed."

"I've been gone for a few months, so this week is taken. Could we do it at the end of next week?'

"Why don't we plan on Thursday next week?

We can meet here and follow the trail we took trying to find the robbers."

"Do you mind if I bring Juan? I understand he spent a few days with you and the posse."

"See both of you on Thursday."

# CHAPTER TWELVE

**B**ack at his law office, located next to the post office in Santa Ynez, Juan knocked on the door of the senior partner 's office. Hiram T. Jones practiced law in Santa Ynez Valley for five years. "Come on in Juan. I was just finishing up a brief on the Com- stock Suit."

Juan walked in and sat at a chair in front of Jones. "I know that First National Bank is a good client and I don't want to create any problem where one doesn't exist. But I have some concerns that I'd like to share with you."

"Tell me what's on your mind."

"To put it bluntly, it bothers me that the robbery at First National was so clean and fast. They went in, got the money, left and escaped in the hills."

"Well those things happen. Is there something that leads you to believe that there's something else that hasn't been discovered?"

"I not only was with the posse for two days after the robbery, but I went back to the bank and interviewed the employees and management, who were in the bank during the robbery. I'll be the first to tell you that I've never been in a robbery and I never investigated something like this. But, something just doesn't ring true to me."

"And what would that be."

"Nothing happened. It was as though they were following a blueprint. How realistic is that? Two men enter the bank, pass a note and money is given over. There were two guards on duty that day, though one was in the back. The one guard at the entrance was caught by surprise, so he said. It's too clean."

"They're our client. What do you suggest?"

I'd like to do a little investigation on my own. My first thought was that one or both of the guards were involved in some aspect of the robbery. On further reflection, it's possible that someone on the bank staff was in on it, as well. How could the robbers know that one of the guards, stationed at the front wasn't alert while the other would be in the bathroom? It doesn't seem realistic. I have a friend who works at the bank. Would you object if I met him for lunch and asked him what he hears within the bank?"

"I don't have a problem if you want to satisfy your curiosity, but I don't want you to do anything beyond that, without running it by me first. You may want to ask the sheriff if he knows anything about the guards, before you talk to your friend."

"I'd like to go to Santa Barbara in the morning and see what I can uncover, if that's okay with you?"

"I'll give you a day for your investigation, but no more than that. I expect to have an oral re- port the day after tomorrow."

Juan left at three in the morning, rode over the San Marcos Pass and arrived in Santa Barbara by noon. Luckily, his friend was still inside the bank; his lunch hour started in an hour. They agreed to meet at Manny's on lower State Street; the fish stew was the specialty. Joe Morgan met Juan a year ago when

Hiram Jones introduced Juan to the management of the bank. The two men were about the same age and hit it off instantly. They socialized frequently and Morgan introduced Juan to his sister Penelope, who was attracted to Juan. The parents had second thoughts about their daughter socializing with a half breed.

"Did you come all the way to Santa Barbara just to have lunch with me?" Morgan asked.

"I'm here on bank business but what I have to say is confidential. I'm asking you not to re- peat it to anyone."

"This sounds serious. I'll try to keep it confidential, but I owe my allegiance to the bank manager, who I personally like. If you can accept those guidelines, then I'm all for confidentiality."

Juan laid out his concerns and asked if Morgan could get him some background on the two guards.

"Their names are Hennessey and Overton. They've been with the bank for a year and seem to be competent. It's true that Hennessey was in the back and Overton in front, when the robbery occurred. I don't know what Overton could've done differently. I saw the two men enter the bank and one of them immediately moved behind Overton and took his gun from him. The only observation that I would have is, that it was fortuitous that Overton was so near the entrance and neutralized so quickly."

"The bank must have applications on file for Hennessey and Overton. I wonder if I could get copies. You never can tell what may turn up. What about the other employees who were present. Are there any short termers?"

"No. Most have been with the bank for over three years, which is when I was hired. It may take a few days, but I believe I can get you copies of the guards' applications. I'll send them to you in the mail pouch to our branch in Santa Ynez."

"My sister wants to know when you're going to call on her again." Morgan asked.

"I was planning on calling on her this afternoon, if you don't take up too much of my time. Did she really want to see me?"

"Yes, but I don't know why. I introduced you to my sister, but you haven't done anything for me."

"What did you have in mind?"

"I really was hoping that you'd introduce me to the famous Tommy Sanchez. Is he as fast as they say he is?"

"Faster. I'll see what I can do."

Juan had an early dinner with Cynthia Morgan in a restaurant specializing in fish on Stearns Wharf. Later, Juan rented a carriage and they drove on the beach. Their relationship hadn't reached the intimacy stage but, they certainly used the art of petting to the maximum. When Juan drove her home, she took a few minutes to make sure her clothes were properly adjusted. "You know my mother is concerned that you're going to take advantage of me and ruin my reputation. But I wonder why you haven't taken advantage of me. Am I ugly?"

"You are like a beautiful flower. I thought I would introduce you to my mother before I deflowered you." They both laughed and she kissed him and bit his ear before she said good- night and hopped out of the carriage.

Juan returned to Santa Ynez early the next morning. He was more pragmatic than Morgan's sister. He knew that a young half breed attorney in a small law firm would not be warmly embraced by the mothers of young debutantes. He knew that his partial acceptance into the good homes was due to the influence of his mother and Tommy Sanchez. Although his mother was white, he had many features of an Indian. Perhaps the young women in the area were intrigued by his background, but he knew most of the parents were apprehensive of him dating their daughters. We'll he have to get by as best he could and right now he was having a good time.

# CHAPTER THIRTEEN

**B**rown was exhausted. He felt that he needed to be some place where he could relax. He decided to take his chances and go directly to Nogales. Once there, he'd take the train to Tucson, even if Pearl Hart was in the area. He knew the wounded bandit was out there somewhere, but where? Brown recapped the episode at the bandit's camp several times. He was sure he hit flesh each time that he stabbed the man. It's even possible that he hit bone, yet the bandit got away. He couldn't believe that man could survive, but he did.

Just as he was mounting his horse, Brown was struck from behind with a tree branch; he fell to the ground. He was coherent enough to realize that he was in trouble, so he rolled to a sitting position. The rope to the horse carrying the money slipped from his grasp and the horse bolted, but Brown couldn't worry about that at this time. A young Mexican was circling him with a club in one hand and a knife in the other, looking for an opportunity to strike a lethal blow. The man's shirt was covered with blood and he appeared to be limping. This had to be the missing bandit. Brown was on his butt with his right leg and arm extended to parry any blow. He withdrew the knife he carried in his boot and was lashing out with his boot and knife, as the Mexican struck. But the Mexican, who was about five feet six inches tall and one hundred forty pounds, was too quick. He easily dodged Brown's thrusts. Each time Brown made a move to get up or strike out with the knife, he'd receive a blow on his shoulders or arms. On two occasions, his leg was slashed by the man's knife. Brown's holster had twisted when he fell; he was sitting on his gun. Brown struck out with his foot and tried to slide his holster around so he could get to his gun, but he was hit with a blow to his head. He thought he was done but he willed himself to be conscious. He didn't want to die here so he gathered all his strength and lashed out with his knife, but only touched air. He had to get up. Sooner or later one of those blows from the club or the knife would render him helpless. Brown knew he was tiring but he wondered how long the bandit could continue to be this aggressive, since he'd been stabbed three times.

The answer came sooner than Brown expected. The bandit leaped at him while swinging his knife in a downward arc, aiming for Brown's chest. Brown had been waiting for such an opening. He was too big and strong for the bandit, who was weak from the knife wounds and the duel was over quick. As the bandit made the lunge, Brown grabbed the arm holding the knife and reached out with his knife and caught the bandit in the stomach. He heard the man gasp as Brown lifted his arm and cut the man to the heart. The bandit died on top of Brown. When he was sure the man was finished, Brown threw the him off his body and lay on his back for several minutes; he was exhausted. Brown's hands and legs were cut, his head was throbbing and his knee was sore from the number of blows, the bandit rained down on him.

There was blood oozing from the gashes on his right calf. As he checked other parts of his body, he noticed blood coming from a wound on his left shoulder.

Well he was alive, but he was also penniless, unless he found the smaller horse that had bolted. He mounted the larger horse, which remained nearby, during the entire attack and followed the tracks the bolted horse made, as it ran away. Thirty minutes later he came upon the horse. Its reins had caught on a stump and the horse, which was lathered and breathing heavily, couldn't move. It was highly agitated. Brown gave the horse some water and rubbed him with his hands, talking soothingly to it. Eventually, the horse calmed down. He transferred the money bags, which had remained attached to the saddle, to the larger horse and then cut the reins tying the smaller horse to the stump. This time the horse didn't run away, so Brown tethered its reins to his saddle. He rode back to retrieve the gun and supplies lying where he was attacked by the Mexican.

Brown tended to his wounds and ran some cold water over his face. He hurt all over and didn't know if he had the strength to bury the last bandit. He decided not to. He tied a rope around the man's feet and the other end to the horn on his saddle and dragged the corpse to- ward some brush and left him for the coyotes. Brown remounted his horse, grabbed the reins to the smaller horse and rode north.

Nogales, in the eighteen nineties was a sleepy border town of about three hundred people, but it had a train depot; that's what Brown needed. The schedule for the next train to Tuscon was at noon tomorrow. While leading his horses down the main street, he spotted a barber shop. He had almost a month's growth of beard and many cuts and lacerations on his body. He knew that he smelled like a dead horse, but he wanted to get rid of one of the horses, be- fore he did anything else. He walked the horses down the street to the livery stable and sold the smaller horse and saddle to the livery owner. He also made arrangements to stable the larger horse overnight

Carrying the two saddle bags, his black suit, boots and shirt rolled up in newspaper, he walked back to the barber shop. He didn't recognize himself when he looked in the mirror, but he could smell himself. The bath was a welcomed relief. He discarded the clothes he wore for the past thirty days in the barrel next to the tub. He asked the barber for some bandages and lineament. When asked about his wounds, he told the barber he'd been dragged through some brush by his horse. That seemed to satisfy the man. The barber polished Brown's boots and brushed his black suit while he bathed. When Brown left the shop in clean clothes, he looked at his reflection in the window and then walked to the railroad station. He bought a train ticket to Tucson for tomorrow and paid to have his horse stored in a rail car.Brown walked three buildings back down the street and into the boarding house, recommended by the ticket agent. After registering, he carried his saddle- bags up to his room.

Dinner was served at five PM sharp. He was one of seven boarders sitting at the oblong table, listening to the local gossip. No one mentioned the bank robbery in Bisbee. He wasn't concerned about the two elderly women and one older man at the far end of the table, but the others gave him pause. One was a large man who could pass as a law man; he sat at his end of the table, to Brown's right. The other was a younger man who sat directly across from him. This man had a habit of keeping his head lowered, but every once in a while would glance up to see what Brown was doing. Sitting to the young man's right was a young woman, who he learned was on her way to Tucson to visit her family. When asked by one of the elderly women at the table why he stopped at this boarding house, the large man wouldn't give a reason. The younger man volunteered that he was a permanent boarder.

Brown placed his saddlebag containing the money in the boarding house safe before coming to dinner. As soon as he finished eating, he retrieved them and went to his room on the second floor. He hardly slept that night, keeping his clothes on and his gun ready. The two men at the dinner table had him spooked. At breakfast the next morning, only six of those who were at the table the previous evening, were there. The young man, who was the permanent border, was missing. Brown asked the landlady where he was. She said he got up early, checked out and rode north toward Rio Rico. A thought crossed Brown's mind. Would the younger man catch the train and join them before or after he left the Nogales Station. Brown tried on several occasions to enter into a conversation with the large man at the end of the table, but the man wasn't interested.

As Brown waited at the railroad station for the noon train to Tucson the next day, he care- fully scrutinized the other passengers, waiting at the station. He carried his saddlebags over his left shoulder and his holster on his right hip. The young woman, who was at the boarding house last night, was sitting on a bench, just staring straight ahead. The big surprise was the arrival of the large man from the boarding house. It appeared he was going North on the same train as Brown. The others waiting seemed innocuous. There were two families of four each and two Spanish women who appeared to be traveling together. Brown looked around the station for anyone who might be the law, but he didn't see anyone that fit that profession, other than the big man from last night.

There were three scheduled stops on the way to Tuscon. Brown watched as one of families got off at Rio Rico; but no new passengers boarded at this stop. There didn't appear to be any pas- sengers departing at the second stop of Amado nor did anyone board the train there. That is, until the last minute when the young man, who was at the boarding house last night, rushed out of the station and boarded the train as it was moving away from the depot.. Paranoia was creeping into Brown's thoughts. He waited to see if the young man joined up with the larger man, but he didn't. The young man sat with the young woman, who was at the boarding house last night. They entered into a lively discussion, which caused her to cry. The young man put his arms around her as she continued to sob, and just as suddenly, she pushed him away. Brown couldn't hear much of their conversation, other than he distinctly heard her say, "how could you?" Brown instinctively touched his gun to give him a feeling of security. The money wasn't that heavy but it was bulky and could be in the way, if he had to react quickly.

The appearance of the young man changed Brown's plans. As the train slowed for the last stop before Tuscon, Brown got ready. When the train stopped, Brown grabbed the saddlebags, hopped off the train and made his way to the rail car where his horse was tethered. He slid the rail car door open, tossed the saddlebags into the car, climbed up and tied the saddlebags to his saddle and mounted the horse. He'd sad- dled the horse prior to boarding, just in case. He hadn't survived this long without having a backup plan. Brown ducked as he and the horse jumped off the train and rode away from the train depot. He didn't stop to see if anyone was looking.

After Brown cleared the train depot, he headed west. He smiled as he congratulated himself for having the foresight to have the horse on the train with him. He even complemented himself for placing food and water with the horse in the event, he had to exercise this option. This new route would be tedious and rough traveling until he was able to reach a train depot that was safe; Tucson was out of the question now. The next significant train depot was Phoenix. If the authorities guessed he'd go from Bisbee to Nogales and then Tuscon, would they guess that he would go to Phoenix? He decided to stay at least fifteen miles west of Tucson, as he made his way north. Brown wondered where a posse would come from. He'd have to be alert for the next thirty days. That young guy boarding the train at the last stop had to be an omen. He assumed anyone after him hadn't figured on this option. This was just a small set back; he wouldn't be denied reaching his destination, even if it took him longer than he planned.

# CHAPTER FOURTEEN

The twins had a couple of friends over for their sixth birthday party. Naiwa's two children had never been to a birthday party, but they loved the candies and cake. The main attraction for the twins was their big brother Juan, who brought them a pifiata filled with candy. Chatan and Wachiwi participated in all the games as actively as Thomas and Helga. Sarah saw a marked change in their outlook. They were no longer listless and each had put on enough weight: they no longer looked emaciated. Sarah was mesmerized at the positive change in her son. It was as though he changed overnight from a malcontent to a respected member of society. She was sure that Crazy Horse would be proud of his son. For all the concern and heartache Juan caused her for nearly twenty years, he more than made up for it now. It was obvious to her that Tommy Sanchez had a deep impact on her son; it was as though Juan looked upon Tommy as his older brother. The two men were frequent companions, whether on hunting trips or just weekend rides, around the ten thousand acre ranch.

After the visiting parents and children had departed, Tommy poured Sarah and Juan a glass of Chardonnay from their own vineyard "How did the sheriff handle the nine you brought in. Did he accept your word that they confessed?" Juan asked Tommy.

"Whether he did or not is irrelevant. Eight of them confessed to him. Only Meade said he was coerced. I told the sheriff that if I ever saw any of them again, I'd hang them. Are you still concerned that we acted illegally?"

"I've met the owner of the Starr Ranch; his name is Earl Singleton. He isn't someone who'll take too kindly to what you did. The word is that you went onto the Star Ranch and threatened to hang them all."

Tommy smiled. "I didn't exactly threaten to hang them; it was more of an intimidation. I threw ropes over the main beam, fashioned nooses and let their imagination run wild. They were confessing before I took any overt action."

"Being a lawyer now, I can tell you that your intimidation would constitute a threat, in the eyes of the law. If they have a good lawyer, they'll be able to beat the charges. Hell, I could get all of them off," Juan couldn't help smiling.

"Have it your way. To me the only threat I made was to the sheriff. I told him that if they got off, I would hunt them down and hang them. The sheriff filled me in on the bank robbery. You said there were three involved; he said there were two. Were you misinformed?"

"There were two that entered the bank. Witnesses said there was a third man outside holding their horses, but it was three that rode away into the hills."

"Any descriptions of the three?"

'The two inside wore masks but were described as tall and slender, probably over sixfeet tall. The man outside wore his hat low, but was kind of burly and shorter than the other two. He was probably around your height."

"Any hint to who they were?"

"No. What are you thinking, Tommy?"

The sheriff knows this country pretty well. He thinks the posse did a good job because he was with them for a week. They covered every known trail in the hills between Santa Barbara and Santa Ynez. The only thing they found was some unused provisions in the Painted Cave Area. The chaparral made it difficult to track them, but he feels that if the robbers were in the Santa Ynez Mountains, when the posse was there, he would've captured them. He believes someone is sheltering them either in Santa Barbara or Santa Ynez. He asked if I would be interested in going into the mountains to see if I could pick up their trail."

"Why would you want to do that?"

"I don't, unless you accompany me and the sheriff."

"I'd have to touch base with my employer, but I think he'll agree that it's part of our contract with the bank to help bring the robbers to justice. When do you want to go," Juan asked.

"I like to go the day after tomorrow. I agreed to meet the sheriff at the Painted Cave site around noon. We'll have to leave early and we'll be gone three to four days. Would that work for you?"

"I'll get back to you by the end of the day." After Juan left, Tommy was playing tag with Tommy Junior, Helga Elizabeth, Chatan and Wachiwi in the front yard of their home. Sarah was helping Naomi and Naiwa with the laundry when two riders came up their long access road. Tommy watched as they approached, but continued to play with the children. When the riders were near enough to be heard, one of the riders asked, "are you Tommy Sanchez?"

Tommy sent the four children into the house. "It depends on who's asking," Tommy responded.

"I'm Earl Singleton, the owner of the Star Ranch."

"What can I do for you, Mr. Singleton?"

The other man with Singleton held back as though to defer to his boss. He was as tall as Singleton. Both appeared to be at least four inches taller than Tommy. "I assume you're Sanchez. You can start by telling me why you raided my ranch two days ago and took my men.

"Your men were cattle rustlers."

"Who says so?'

"All of your men except Meade, said that they rustled twenty head of my cattle and then took them to your ranch through a hole, in our joint fence. Eight of them signed a statement in front of the sheriff to that effect. Three of the eight worked for me and implicated your men. It didn't seem possible that they weren't rustlers."

"That's because you threatened to hang them."

"Well, I certainly intimidated them, but I didn't threaten to hang them. They could've refuted their confessions when they were in front of the sheriff, but they didn't. They were rustlers alright. Rustling is a hanging offense in this area."

"Did my foreman Meade confess?"

"No, but that didn't mean anything. He's a rustler; in fact he was their leader. Three of my men were involved and they implicated him as did the five you employed."

"What am I going to do? You've taken all my men and I have cattle that must be rounded up and sold?"

"There're plenty of good cowhands looking for work in town. Just go to the hotel in Santa Ynez tomorrow; there'll be a few men hanging around the hotel. They'll help you get others."

Singleton didn't seem to be pacified or appreciative of Tommy's suggestion. He turned to the other man who had his hand on a holstered gun. Singleton turned back to Tommy. "I don't believe Meade is a cattle thief. I've known him for two years. He may be a little rough around the edges, but he's no cattle thief. It's just your word against his."

"I don't appreciate you calling me a liar. I've given you evidence in the form of their confessions to the sheriff; that should be enough for anyone. I suggest you leave now. You're no longer welcome on my property."

"You're pretty tough for someone who isn't carrying a gun."

"I don't need a gun. If you look to your left and then to your right, you'll see there're two rifles trained on both of you. Both individuals are excellent shots. I think it's time for you to leave."

Singleton wanted to have the last word. "This isn't the end of this. We'll meet again and it'll be just you against me."

Singleton and his companion turned and rode back the way they came. Tommy watched them, until they were out of sight.

Sarah came off the porch and walked toward Tommy; she was one of the people who had a rifle trained on Singleton; Raul was the other. She voiced her concern. "Tommy, this guy looks like someone who's going to try to get even. You better have Raul or one of the men with you, when you go into town next time."

Tommy put his arm around her waist and walked her into the house. She was trembling and he could see a tear starting to run down her cheek.

"I'll be careful."

# CHAPTER FIFTEEN

Stanley Rider, the President of White Elephant Western Wear, called his top salesman, Robert Lang, into his office late January. He told Lang that he'd like to expand his business into the southwest part of the country.

"I know you're doing well in your own territory, but you seem to be the type of person, who's up for an adventure. There are quite a few gold and silver strikes that are fueling the southwest expansion. Towns are springing up overnight and within a year their populations increased to over a thousand people. We've got a good business here and our product is reliable, but it's too dam cold. There are days when the snow is so deep, that I can't get out to the barn. I love the summers but not the winters. Although my wife and I grew up here, we don't have to die here. The temperature in Dubuque has been holding at twenty degrees for over a month. It'll be a lot warmer in Tucson or Santa Fe. If you could establish our business in the southwest, we could move our headquarters and manufacturing operation to a much warmer climate. What do you say?"

"Can I think it over?"

"No. You're the one for the job. You're young and single and I'd like you to do it. Tell me what it'll take for you to do this."

Quitting wasn't an issue with Lang. He liked his job; in fact he liked Stanley Rider. "Who's going to handle my customers while I'm gone and what about compensation, for taking on this added responsibility?"

"I'll have Jones fill in for you for a couple of months, while you're away. The two of you will split any commissions on sales in your territory."

"What about an advance for two months while I try to establish our brand?"

"That's acceptable, but I'd like to see if it'll work within thirty days. Once you establish the business, you can decide whether you want to come back to your old territory, or keep the new one. I don't want to abandon Iowa; I just want to see if we can open a new territory and move our corporate office to a warmer climate."

"You've given this a lot of thought. When do you want me to start?"

"Take a couple of weeks to get ready and then take the train to Santa Fe. If you can establish a foothold there, then I want you go to Tomb- stone and see if we can break into that market. Subsequently, I'd like to enter the Tucson and Bisbee markets."

"Why not start in Tucson? That's a bigger market and would give you a better indication, if we can be successful."

"You may be right. But let's do Santa Fe first. It's closer and if that works, then we can decide what should be the next step."

Lang didn't own a house and he didn't have a steady girl friend. But he did have several female acquaintances located throughout the state, he was reluctant to leave that part of his social life behind. Within a couple of days, he was resigned to the move; in fact he was looking forward to it. As far as the girls were concerned, there would be girls in New Mexico.

Stanley Rider saw Lang off on the train to Denver, where he stayed overnight and then pressed on to Santa Fe the next morning. Several days later, he dressed, had breakfast, grabbed his sample case and walked to the first of the two emporiums, located in the Plaza, in down- town Santa Fe. He asked to speak to the owner. He was informed that the owner was in a meeting and wouldn't be available for an hour. Lang decided to look around the store and see what brands of working clothes the store carried. As he felt one of the shirts on a table, he was surprised to find that the fabric of the shirts in the store was similar to that used in White Elephant's shirts. He checked the label. The color drained from his face when he saw the White Elephant label on all the shirts. He checked work pants and found the same label. He didn't know what to think. Was Stanley Rider playing a game on him? No, that couldn't be the case. But how did White Elephant's clothes get here?

The salesman noticed Lang looking at the work clothes and went over to see if he could make a sale. Lang told the salesman that he had to run an errand and would be back in an hour to see the owner. He walked out into the quadrangle that distinguished old Santa Fe and found a bench under the trees in the center of the square. He was an astute individual and immediately felt that something was wrong. He decided to check out the other store to see what brands they were carrying. Just before entering the second emporium, he placed his sample case outside, just under the display window. He approached one of salesmen and asked to see what work clothes the store was carrying. "We sell White Elephant work clothes exclusively," the salesman responded.

"If I wanted a large order for my workmen, say about forty shirts and pants, how much of a delay would there be in filling the order?"

"Let me check with the owner. I'll be right back."

The salesman came back within a few minutes with another individual, who stuck out his hand. "I'm William Green, the owner. I under- stand that you want to place an order for forty White Elephant shirts and pants. Is that true?"

"Well, it depends on the time it takes to supply that amount."

"Well I can wire the order to the corporate office in Denver and have the merchandise here in three days. Of course, I have to know the sizes you want and how you intend to pay for the shipment."

"I didn't realize that White Elephant has an office in Denver."

"Oh yes. They've been operating under the name, Western Outerwear. We've been dealing with them for nearly a year and they're quick to respond. Normally their salesman, Mr. Brown, sends the orders by wire, but I believe he's in Tombstone opening up that territory, for his company."

"If I place an order now, how soon will you require payment?"

"We'd like payment upon receipt."

"Since I'm making a significant order, I think there should be a discount."

"I agree. Here's a list of our prices for White Elephant. For this size order, I can give you a ten percent discount. Is that acceptable?"

"Yes. Yes it is. Here's a list of sizes. Can you place the order now and give me a copy of the invoice?" Lang asked.

"Certainly. Why don't you step over here and I'll take the order down and wire it immediately."

As soon as he received a copy of the order, Lang shook hands with the owner. "I'm going out of town but I'll be back in three days. Thank you for your prompt action." Lang walked out- side and picked up his sample case.

The stage was leaving for Tombstone at seven the next morning and Lang would be on it. He sent a wire to Stanley Rider to tell him he was on his way to Tombstone and would be in touch. He didn't know if Santa Fe was an anomaly, so he decided to see if the same problem existed in Tombstone. Maybe he'd get to meet Wyatt Earp.

# CHAPTER SIXTEEN

The stagecoach trip from Santa Fe took eight hours with two stops along the way. Lang checked into the Birdcage Saloon and Hotel and treated himself to a fine steak dinner on Stanley Rider. After dinner, he went into the saloon, sat at the bar and ordered a scotch and water. There were two salesmen sitting a few stools from him. He raised his glass and nodded in their direction. One was an army agent buying horses for the cavalry; the other was a liquor salesman. Neither of the two men heard of Brown. Three of the working girls joined the men at the bar and the party lasted until two in the morning; they never left the Birdcage

Tombstone was a bustling town with buildings being erected everywhere. There was so much construction that the one lumber yard couldn't keep pace with the demand. Several of the new buildings were framed but had only wooden fronts with cloth sides and rear.

The next morning Lang, with a slight hangover, called on the two general stores in town. Both stores were enclosed with sheet rock and clap board. Like Santa Fe, both establishments were carrying White Elephant shirts and pants. This time his order in both stores was higher but the process was the same and he was given a copy of a telegraph order sent to Denver. Lang thanked the owners and promised to be back in town, three days hence.

It took him four days to return home to Dubuque. On the way, he had a twenty four hour layover in Denver. He wired Stanley Rider and told him there was a scam originating in Denver. He asked if Rider knew anyone that Lang could talk to about Western Outerwear. Rider told him to call on Henry Jones, the president of the First Trust Bank of Denver. He presented Rider's telegram to one of the clerks at the bank and asked to talk to Mr. Jones. Thirty minutes later he was escorted into Jones office and offered some brandy. "Stanley Rider and I were classmates at Andover in Massachusetts. What can I do for you, Mr. Lang?"

"Mr. Rider had been approached by Western Outerwear to see if our company would consider a joint venture with their company in Oklahoma. We're performing our due diligence and wonder if you could tell us something about the owner, his management style, their financial capability and most of all, their reputation. Everything you tell us will be confidential and we'll be discrete."

Thirty minutes later, Lang had a pretty good idea what Western Outerwear's capability was, who Water Reinhart was and the reputation he'd developed. Lang thanked Henry Jones and after visiting the exterior of their headquarters, he spent the night at the Laurel Hotel. He took the train to Dubuque the next day.

Lang met with Stanley Rider within a day of his return. When he related the entire story, Rider just sat there and didn't say anything for five minutes. "You never met Brown?"

"No. I got a description, but that's all. As far as I know, he's in some other town setting up the same scam. From what I was told, by one of the store owners in Tombstone, Brown had gone to Bisbee to open up that territory. There's one other thing I forgot to tell you. When I was in Denver, I saw some Chinese women coming out of the Western Outerwear Building around eight in the evening. I don't know what they were doing there, but my guess is that they're tied to the scam. I didn't talk to them or follow them, because I didn't want anyone to know, that we were on to them, until I talked to you."

"You did right. Make out a list of your expenses and give them to my secretary."

"What are you going to do?"

"'I'll let you know when I figure it out." Rider wasn't truthful with young Lang. He knew exactly what he was going to do, and he knew who was going to do it for him. James T. Jefferson was the regional Pinkerton Agent for the southwest part of the United States. Originally from Iowa, he'd been a high school classmate of Stanley Rider and a life long friend. It took him a week to wind up an ongoing case, before he took the train to Dubuque and met with his friend. Rider and Lang spent over thirty minutes briefing Jefferson on the details of the scam in Santa Fe and Tombstone.

"Did you ever see or meet Brown?" Jefferson asked Lang.

"No. He was described as over six feet tall and weighing about one hundred ninety pounds. He was also described as ruggedly handsome and liked to dress in a black suit, black boots and a black Stetson hat," Lang responded.

"Sounds like a pirate to me. What do you want me to do?" Jefferson asked Rider.

"I want you to gather enough evidence to put Western Outerwear out of business and Brown and Reinhart in jail."

"Well I can do the investigation alright, but any prosecution will have to be by legal authorities."

I know. I know. When can you start?" Rider asked.

"Immediately. I have a contract for services that you need to read. My company requires one month's worth of expenses up front. If you don't have a problem with any of the terms, I'll start getting ready."

Jefferson felt that the case against Reinhart 's company was straight forward. Initially, he'd go to Santa Fe and Tombstone, meet with the owners of the general stores and put them on record. The second step would be finding Brown. Armed with copies of the three invoices, Lang brought back to Dubuque, Jefferson took the train to Santa Fe.

The shop owners in Santa Fe were shocked when Jefferson approached them with the story Lang told. When he produced the invoice from the owner of one of the general stores in Santa Fe, the owner admitted that he knew something wasn't quite right.

"The price was too good to pass up," he told Jefferson.

"Can you give me a description of Mr. Brown?'

"He was about six feet tall and slightly less than two hundred pounds. The oddity was that he liked to dress in black, from top to bottom," the owner responded.

Jefferson needed a sketch of Brown. The one thing Santa Fe wasn't lacking was an abundance of artists and portrait painters. Jefferson hired one of the artists that had set up shop in the quadrangle. Within a few hours, the man was able to draw a likeness of Brown from the shop owner's description. Armed with the sketch, Jefferson made contact with the bank, hotel and restaurants that Brown frequented. Each person contacted, acknowledged that the sketch was the likeness of Brown. From everything he'd been told, Jefferson assumed that Brown had gone from Santa Fe to Tombstone. In fact, the owner of the hotel that Brown stayed in while in Santa Fe, told Jefferson that he met Brown in Tombstone while on business. In fact one evening he had dinner with Brown at the Birdcage.

"What did you talk about?"

"We talked about the social scene and where you could become acquainted with women. We went to one of the saloons he frequented, and met two ladies. Brown doesn't know any homely women.

"Can you give me the names of the women?"

"No, I'm sorry. I don't remember.

"Don't remember, or won't tell me?"

"What difference does it make? I did remember one thing he told me. He said he planned to open up the Bisbee territory."

Jefferson's meeting in Tombstone with the two general stores owners mirrored what happened in Santa Fe. With signed statements of all four owners, he went in search of Brown. All indications were that he moved on to Bis- bee. Rather than present his evidence of fraud against Western Outerwear to the sheriff in Denver, Jefferson took the stage to Bisbee and arrived late at night.

Jefferson found that White Elephant goods had made their way to the two Bisbee general stores. He showed the owners a sketch of Brown. They identified the person in the sketch as Brown, who was the White Elephant salesman.

While going from the hotels and restaurants to the Bisbee National Bank in search of Brown, he learned about their major bank robbery, which had taken place three weeks earlier. Brown had established a pattern in the two towns of Santa Fe and Tombstone. Once he received an order for merchandise, he'd set up an account at a local bank and secure a line of credit. Jefferson asked to speak to Franklin Herbert, to determine if this was the bank where Brown established an account. He was told that Herbert was on paid vacation.

That same day, Jefferson received a telegram from the main office of the Pinkerton Agency, telling him to put the Western Outerwear scam on hold. They directed him to make a quick investigation of the bank robbery at the Bisbee National Bank. Pinkerton had been hired by the major stockholders of the bank. Jefferson immediately summarized his findings of the scam and forwarded it in writing to Pinkerton Central, with a copy to Stanley Rider.

Armed with written direction from Pinkerton Headquarters, Jefferson presented himself the next morning to Jon Southern and Henry Wilcox, the two major stockholders of the bank.

They met at Southern's office, in the Burns Building. The Brown issue had been set aside for the moment. Southern spent an hour covering the facts in the case and asked Jefferson where he wanted to start the investigation.

"I want to start with the two people who were present at the robbery, namely Mr. Herbert and his wife. I understand that Mr. Herbert hasn't returned to work and isn't receiving visitors. Is there anything you can do?"

"I've talked to Herbert just before you arrived and insisted that he cooperate with you. He agreed to meet with you at his home at three o'clock, this afternoon."

Mrs. Herbert greeted Jefferson at the front door to their clapboard cottage, located a block from the Bisbee National Bank. She escorted him into the living room, where her husband was slumped down in a high back chair, just staring out their picture window. Herbert was a man of approximately fifty years olds, slightly overweight with a receding hairline. He acknowledged Jefferson and invited him to sit on the couch to Herbert's immediate right. Kathy Herbert came back a few minutes later with some lemonade and cookies, placed them on the table in front of the two men and left the room. After they exchanged greetings, Jefferson started the questioning.

"Mr. Herbert, I've met with Mr. Southern and Mr. Wilcox this morning and they gave me a summary of the robbery. What I'd like from you is more detail. Southern told me that the robber broke into this house while you and your wife were asleep and woke both of you. Subsequently, you and your wife were forced to go to the bank and open up the vault. Is this true?"

"Yes, that's true."

"Mr. Herbert, I want you to show me where he entered the house and the route he took to your bedroom. Then, I want to retrace the steps you took to the bank on the night of the robbery."
"Is this necessary?"

"I want to understand everything and the best way to do that, is to start at the beginning and follow it to a conclusion."

After Herbert showed Jefferson where the robber entered his home, they walked to the bank and went in the back way. After a series of questions, Jefferson had a good understanding, how the robbery went down.

When they returned to Herbert's living room, Jefferson continued the questioning. "After Brown took the money, he took your wife as hostage. Is that true?"

"Yes."

"As I understand it, he released her several hours later in the town of Naco. For the trip back, the robber gave your wife a gun and some ammunition. Is that true?"

"Yes, that's true.

"That seems odd. Why do you think he took your wife?"

"He said he didn't want me to alert the sheriff, until she returned."

"Is that what happened?

"Yes"

"I also understand that he became quite familiar with your wife in your home, to coerce you into opening the vault."

Herbert's face turned red and he stammered his answer. "That's true."

"It's not my intent to embarrass you Mr. Herbert. I just want all the facts."

Jefferson looked at his notes. "You said the robber was about six feet tall, had a long beard, with worn clothes that smelled. Is that true?"

"Yes"

"Was he familiar to you?"

"No."

Herbert answered very quickly and caused Jefferson to pause, before he asked another question.

"Was he familiar to your wife?"

"Certainly not."

"Did you ask your wife, if he seemed familiar to her?"

"I did not."

"How much money was taken?"

"Fifty one thousand, six hundred dollars."

"Who else has the combination to the safe?"

"No one."

"There must be someone else in case you're ill or incapacitated?"

"Jon Southern and Henry Wilcox, they're the major stockholders in the bank."

"Let's go back to the way he entered. He came in your back door. Did you leave it unlocked?"

"No. I always make sure the doors are locked. He must have picked the lock."

"I checked the door and I couldn't find any marks that a burglar would use in picking a lock."

"I don't know anything about that."

"Don't you think it's interesting that he walked into your house as though he'd been here before? This doesn't appear to be a spur of the moment robbery. He knew that you had the combination to that safe."

"What are you implying?" Herbert was very indignant.

Jefferson ignored the outrage. "Did anyone in town know that you had the combination to the vault?"

"The stockholders and anyone they told."

"Was there someone you told?"

"No."

"What about your wife?"

"I don't like your inference."

"I don't care, but I want an answer."

"I didn't tell her."

"Who else has access to your house?"

"No one."

"You and your wife must have had friends or business associates to your home for cocktails, dinner or a party."

"I can't recall that we ever did."

"That seems strange, because Jon Southern told me that he'd been to dinner parties at your home, on two occasions. Why would he say that, if it wasn't true?"

"Now that you mention it, I do recall the dinner parties. "Herbert seemed to slump a little lower in his chair.

"Could the man who robbed you been a guest at one or several of the dinner parties?"

"The people we invited were the movers and shakers in town. We certainly didn't invite a bank robber."

"I'd like a list of people you invited."

"I don't have a list.

"I don't think you grasp how serious this robbery is. Some people put their life savings in your bank. You don't seem to want to cooperative to me. Why is that? First you don't re- member having people over and now you can't give a list of your guests. Perhaps I can ask Mr. Southern," Herbert turned pale.

"I'll ask my wife if she saved the list of invitees.'

"Did your wife have friends to your home while you were at work?"

"Certainly not."

"That seems strange that a woman who's the wife of the bank president, doesn't have women friends over for tea."

"She may have."

"I'd like to talk to your wife and I'd like a list of her lady friends."

"Why. I've told you everything. "Herbert was glaring at Jefferson.

"I've been hired to do a thorough investigation of this robbery; therefore, I want to talk to everyone involved."

"I want to be present when you question her."

"Why?"

"This whole episode has embarrassed her enough. I don't want to put her through it again. I insist."

"I'll be sensitive to her ordeal, but I want to question her without you present. It can be wherever she desires but I want to talk to her today. I've been tasked by my company and your stockholders to look into this robbery. I don't want to leave any stone unturned. I have no intention of completing an investigation without talking directly to those involved."

Herbert seemed to deflate once Jefferson mentioned the stockholders. Jefferson knew that Herbert had briefed the two major stock- holders about the robbery. They told Herbert that they didn't blame him, but then again, they hired Jefferson to investigate.

"I wonder if there isn't someone you know or maybe an acquaintance that could have com- mitted this robbery. It's easy to grow a beard, put on tattered clothing and disguise one's self. Think hard, and see if you can visualize some- one you know, who could do that. It would take a few weeks to grow the beard. Can you remember if any of your friends or acquaintances was out of town for a few weeks?"

Herbert didn't respond immediately and when he did, he wouldn't look directly at Jefferson. "I really have no idea."

Being sensitive to Mrs. Herbert's ordeal, Jefferson agreed to meet with Kathy Herbert in her husband's office at the bank. Herbert escorted his wife to his office at one PM the next day and then excused himself. He told his wife that he was going down the street to have lunch. Kathy was a pleasant looking woman, about thirty years of age, dressed in a black cotton dress and wearing white gloves. When Jefferson introduced himself, she didn't look directly at him. "Mrs. Herbert, did the robber say anything to you after the two of you left the bank?"

"Not that I recall."

"It took almost two hours to reach the border town of Naco. He must have said something."

"Keep up, is all that I can recall."

"Did he say anything when he let you go?

The sheriff recalls that you said the robber gave you a gun, which was unloaded and handed you some ammunition. Is that true?"

"Yes."

"Why do you think he did that?"

"I don't know. You'll have to ask him."

"Bear with me Mrs. Herbert. As I understand from the statement you gave the sheriff, the only thing you were wearing was a torn night- gown. Is that true?"

Kathy Herbert started to cry, so Jefferson waited until she composed herself and, asked the question again.

"Yes, dam you. Is it your intent to humiliate me more than I've been?"

"No Mrs. Herbert, I'm trying to catch a robber who humiliated you. If that's all you were wearing when he let you go, then you'd be vulnerable on your way back home. Isn't that true?"

"Yes, I suppose I would."

"Then why did he give you a gun with bullets?"

"I told you I don't know."

"I think he gave you the gun to protect you. I also think he wanted to protect you, because he knew you." The color drained from Kathy Herbert's face and she put her face in her hands.

"Do you want to tell me about the robber?" Jefferson asked.

"I don't know anything about the robber. I keep telling you." She seemed hysterical to Jefferson.

"I think you know who the robber is. Tell me about him."

Kathy Herbert glared at Jefferson. "I can't tell you. He'll come back and kill me."

"No he won't. He's on the run and is never coming back here. We need your help to catch him. I insist you tell me what you know."

"If I tell you, what are you going to do with the information?"

"I'm going to use it to run him down and put him away for a long time."

"This will ruin my husband. He didn't do anything wrong."

"Well, I don't know about that, but sooner or later you're going to have to tell me because now I know you know who the robber is."

"It was a salesman named Brown." "You can't be serious?"

As soon as she mentioned the name, it took Jefferson only a few moments to realize it might be the man, he'd been seeking for the White Elephant Scam. He took out the sketch of Brown and showed it to Kathy Herbert.

"Is this the man who robbed the bank?"

"Where did you get this?"

"That's not important. Is this the man?"

"Yes."

"How did you meet Brown?"

"I was introduced to him by my husband.

"Why?"

"He was a salesman, who opened an account at my husband's bank."

"Did you have a social arrangement with Brown?"

"If you mean did he come to the house for dinner a few times, then the answer is yes."

"So Brown was familiar with your home."
"Well he had dinner there twice."

"I think Brown entered your home on the night of the robbery with a key to your back door. Did you give him a key?"

"I did not. Kathy Herbert seemed to be on the edge, but Jefferson was determined to find out the truth.

"So Brown had a disguise that fooled your husband. How is it that you weren't fooled?"

"What do you mean?"

"I think you know what I mean."

Kathy Herbert started to sob uncontrollably; Jefferson waited for her to calm down, but she either wouldn't continue or couldn't continue.

Jefferson now had the identity of the robber. He owed a responsibility to the two stockholders to tell them what he found out, but he didn't have to destroy Kathy Herbert, in completing his objective. She probably was used by Brown and she'd have to live with that. Jefferson was sure her husband knew it was Brown but couldn't divulge the name for fear he'd implicate his wife. It was time to have Brown's description telegraphed to every law enforcement agency in the southwest. But first he had to tell the stock- holders, who the robber was.

# CHAPTER
# SEVENTEEN

**B**rown was in dire need of supplies. He'd been traveling just east of the Santa Rosa Mountains and now was abreast of Tucson Arizona. He'd moved closer to the Tucson, Phoenix Road while making his way north. Being short of food and ammunition, he decided to take a chance and make a quick stop in the town of Marana.

A general store stood out in a row of four or five stores along a dirt road running north and south through the town. Brown's black clothes were filthy and he had at least a week's growth on his face. He wanted to make his stop in the town as short as possible. Luckily, the store had enough to satisfy Brown's needs. Before leaving town, he made a quick check of the bulletin board in the general store, to see if there were any circulars out about him or the Bisbee Robbery; there were none.

As he headed north out of town, he noticed two Mexicans taking an interest in him; he hadn't noticed them, as he came into town. They didn't make any overt move; they just watched him as though assessing any stranger. Brown was definitely paranoia, so he decided to find a place out of town, where he could conceal his horse to see if they followed him. He found a secluded place about two miles on the road north and waited. Thirty minutes later, he saw the two Mexicans, who appeared to be following his horse's tracks. He didn't know whether they were freelancing or were part of a band, but it really didn't matter. Brown made sure his horse was tied down and then broke out his rifle. When the two riders were within one hundred yards, he shot the lead rider, who staggered backward and fell off his horse. The other rider immediately jumped off his horse and pulled it to the ground using it as a shield. Brown cursed himself for being so slow; he now had a big problem. The hunted man may now be the hunter.

Making a run for it seemed out of the question; he had to fight. Brown put his rifle down near his mount and started to crawl on his stomach toward the downed rider. He decided his fate would rest on his revolver and knife. There was a horse standing where the first rider fell, but he couldn't see the other horse or rider. Brown didn't want to raise his head and give away his position, as he made his way toward the standing horse. The sandy soil covered with Chaparral and Manzanita Bushes made the going tough. He crawled within twenty yards of the standing horse, and stopped. The rider he shot was lying next to it, but the other man wasn't in sight, nor was his horse. Brown crawled closer to the standing horse and at that instant was struck from behind. He fell on his face but quickly rolled onto his back. A Mexican was on top of him, lashing out with a knife. Brown tried to fend off the attacker, but was unable to grab the knife, as the attacker slashed at his arms.

With both arms bleeding, Brown was in a fight for his life. The smaller man was alternating pounding him in the face with his left fist and slashing him with a knife, he carried in his right hand. Brown knew that he had to do some- thing or it would be all over soon. He grabbed the Mexican's right wrist in his left hand and simultaneously smashed his right elbow into the Mexican's jaw. It stunned the Mexican long enough for Brown to push the smaller man away. Brown rolled on the ground and came up on his haunches, just as the other man charged him and knocked him down again. But this time, Brown was better prepared. He quickly reversed position, pulled his knife from his boot and drove it deep into the man's chest. He could feel the life running out of the other man as he held onto the knife. When he was sure the Mexican was dead, Brown rolled onto his back and lay there exhausted.

His clothes were covered with blood and his arms stung. He grabbed some water from the canteens the two Mexicans were carrying, took off his shirt and assessed his wounds. There was a serious of flesh wound on his right shoulder and both of his arms had been sliced; all his wounds were bleeding. He ripped his shirt sleeves and used them as a tourniquet, to stop the bleeding on both arms. He was too weak to bury the two men, but he took their firearms and both horses. He'd let their horses go later.

Brown didn't know if the two Mexicans had friends that would follow later. It didn't matter, he needed rest and his wounds had to be tended to. Luckily he had some bandages and ointment with him. He took off the tourniquet and dressed his wounds; the bleeding had stopped. He gave the horses some grain, tied them securely and fell asleep; he didn't wake until early the next morning. After tending to his wounds, he felt that he was strong enough to take care of the two bodies. He tied a rope around the feet of the dead men and used his horse to pull them off the trail. He piled brush over the bodies and broke camp. Most likely, the two didn't know about the bank robbery; they followed him thinking he'd be an easy prey.

# CHAPTER EIGHTEEN

Tommy and Juan met the sheriff at the Painted Cave Site, just south of the San Marcos Pass. "I've got some bad news for you Mr. Sanchez. The attorney for the rustlers petitioned the judge to drop the charges. Each of the defendants signed new statements, saying their confessions were coerced by you."

"I wasn't aware there was a hearing on the charges."

"There wasn't. Our city attorney thought this was a hearing to set a trial date. He was blindsided by the judge."

"Sounds like he might have been paid off or he was flat out incompetent. Where are the rustlers now?" Tommy asked.

"I haven't seen them since their release. I assume they went back to the Star Ranch or maybe they're in one of the saloons near the beach."

"Can we pick them up on other charges?"

"No."

"Who's the judge?"

"His name is Martin Beers; he was an appointee of the governor to fill the vacancy, when the previous judge died."

"What do you think, Juan?" Tommy asked.

"I wouldn't be surprised if some money changed hands. The ruling doesn't make sense. They signed confessions in front of the sheriff. Were you called or did anyone ask you about the confessions?" Juan asked the sheriff.

"No. The first I knew there'd been a change was when their attorney appeared with the court order, and asked for their release. Before I complied, I sent a messenger to the court house, to ask the city attorney what happened. The courier returned with a note from the city attorney, ordering me to release the prisoners. As you can probably guess, Meade and several of his men made threatening remarks about you, after they were freed."

"What are you going to do?" Juan asked Tommy.

"I'll deal with the rustlers after we get back. Right now, I'd like to see what happened to the bank robbers. There are numerous Chumash trails throughout the Santa Ynez Mountains. Some are used on a continual basis; others are covered over with brush and known only to tribe members."

The question for Tommy, Juan and the sheriff was which trails into the Santa Ynez Mountains, would be the most promising. The sheriff had previously travelled over the Tun- nell Trail chasing after the robbers, but found nothing. The three decided to use the Jesuita Trail, this time. The initial part of the trail was clear but when they had gone about five hundred yards, it became treacherous so they dismounted and trailed their horses behind. The three were skilled trackers but Tommy's skills exceeded those of the other two; he took the lead. It took them a few hours to reach In- spiration Point, where they found an old trail leading down the mountains, in the direction of the Santa Ynez Valley.

"It's hard to tell if the robbers used this trail but it's entirely possible that they came this way. There are signs that several horses were walked up this trail and there's a sign that horses were walked down the path, leading to our valley," Tommy was pointing down the slope.

"What do you think we should do?' The sheriff asked Tommy.

"I think Juan and I should continue down the mountain and find out where it leads. We have enough provisions to get us back to our ranch. What about you?' Tommy asked the sheriff.

The sheriff didn't get a chance to respond. Shots rang out and the three dove into the underbrush.

"Do you see where the shots came from?" Juan asked.

Tommy didn't respond. He was already moving away from Juan and the sheriff. The shots had come from down the trail. Someone probably followed them from the Painted Cave. Tommy intended to go further down the footpath and come up behind whoever fired on them. Juan and the sheriff crawled behind a large rock, waiting for their assailants to fire again.

"Where's Mr. Sanchez?" The sheriff asked Juan.

"Don't worry about Tommy. He wants us to stay here while he tries to circle behind them. Don't worry; he's done this before."

Tommy crawled on his hands and knees and sometimes on his stomach. He had gone about two hundred yards back down the mountain, while paralleling the Jesuita Trail. Tommy instinctively knew he was behind whoever fired on them, but he wanted to rest for a few moments. He planned to come up behind, whoever had ambushed them. He checked his revolver, crossed the trail on his stomach and slowly started crawling back up the mountain again. The going was slow because of the many boulders and cactus bushes off the trail. He didn't want to make any noise that would spook who- ever was ambushing them. Soon he could hear three men ahead of him. They were conversing in Spanish, trying to decide what to do. Tommy heard two of those voices before, but he couldn't place them. As he came nearer to their location, he could make out movement. He slowly made his way within ten feet of the three and stood up. It was the men who worked for him and had rustled his cattle.

"If you want to live, put up your hands."

One of his former Vaqueros turned quickly and reached for his gun. Tommy shot him be- tween the eyes. The other two dropped their weapons and raised their hands.

"Who else is up here?' Tommy asked but there was no answer, so he shot one of the vaqueros in the foot. The man fell to the ground and started screaming.

"Tommy turned to the other vaquero, but before he could take any action, the man yelled out in Spanish, There's only the three of us."

"You better not be lying because you'll be the next to die." Tommy responded.

"I swear on my mother's head that it's only the three of us."

Tommy yelled to Juan and sheriff. "Leave your horses and come back down the trail, but keep an eye out, in case there are others up here."

The sheriff wasn't fluent in Spanish so Tommy did the interrogation. Juan bandaged the foot of the Vaquero Tommy shot and helped him to his feet. Tommy addressed the two still alive.

"Who sent you up here to kill us?"

There was no answer so Tommy aimed his gun at the other foot of the one he shot; the man screamed out that it was Meade. "He told us to kill you."

"Where is Meade?"

"I don't know."

Tommy aimed his gun again at the Vaquero's foot and the man yelled out. "Meade said he was going back to the Star Ranch."

"Where are the others who were released?"

"They left with Meade."

"Where are your horses?"

"They're tethered about thirty yards over there." One vaquero pointed in an easterly direction.

"Juan, get their horses." Tommy directed.

"I'll take these two back to the Santa Barbara Jail? And, if it's alright with you, I'm going to deputize you two, in the event you come across any of the other rustlers," the sheriff said.

Tommy looked to Juan who nodded agreement. They tied the two vaqueros and the dead man to their horses.

"What about Meade?" Tommy asked the sheriff.

"I'm going to get a warrant for his arrest but you can pick him up if you find him. If they see you, they may figure that you got these three, so be careful. As soon as I take care of these two and the dead man, I'll head to your place in Santa Ynez, with a couple of deputies."

# CHAPTER NINETEEN

Before leaving Bisbee, Jefferson set up a meeting with the two major stockholders. He gave them a written summary of his findings. He didn't expand on any of the details, but he wasn't surprised when they asked questions, about Herbert and his wife. "Do you think Herbert and his wife were complicit in the robbery?" Southern asked.

"I don't believe they were complicit. I think they were used. Brown made a point of developing a relationship with the couple. His main objective was to rob the bank."

"Do you think they knew that Brown was the robber?"

"I think they both had a good idea who it was. But again, I don't believe they were complicit in the robbery."

"Did Brown have a relationship with the wife?" Wilcox asked.

Jefferson didn't think it was his job to speculate. "I really don't know. She may have known him socially, but I don't believe she was involved in the robbery, other than being used as a hostage."

"It seems to me that Herbert didn't put up much of fight. He kind of laid down on us," Wilcox remarked.

"I don't know what I would have done if an armed individual was molesting my wife. I'm not married, but if I was married, I probably would've opened the vault. I think Herbert did the best he could, under the circumstances. My only fault with him was that he wasn't a good judge of men. He may have spoken too freely with Brown. I found out from some of the employees at the bank, that Herbert and Brown had lunch at least two or three times a month. I don't know what they discussed, but Brown obviously had the bank robbery in mind for some time, "Jefferson said.

"If you want my vote, I think Herbert needs to go," Wilcox seemed to be the aggressor.

"We'll talk about it later." Southern said

Jefferson walked to the telegraph office and wired his office with the results of his investigation and went to the hotel restaurant to have dinner, before retiring for the evening. He intended to leave tomorrow and return to his Pinkerton office. At breakfast the next morning, he was joined by the two stockholders of the bank.

"Good Morning Mr. Jefferson. Do you mind if we have a few words with you?" Southern asked.

"Not at all, please sit down. Why don't you join me? The breakfast fare is very good, especially the poached eggs."

"We've already eaten. The reason for our visit this morning is that we need help in getting back the money that was stolen. We contacted your main office and talked to one of your supervisors. We asked him if you could continue on with the case. You have a very impressive resume."

"What about Brown?"

"We assume he won't give up the money readily. We think you can handle the situation. Do whatever you have to."

"It's up to my corporate headquarters. I'll telegraph them and see what their instructions are."

Southern took out a telegram from his pocket and handed it to Jefferson. "That won't be necessary. I think this telegram is all you need."

The telegram read, FOLLOW BROWN,- AP- PREHEND -RECOVER MONEY.

"A subsequent telegram directed us to advance you three hundred dollars, before you left Bisbee." Southern handed the telegram to Jefferson and an envelope containing three hundred dollars.

"You gentlemen have been busy. If that's what you and the Pinkerton Agency want, I'll get on it immediately. You must understand that I don't know where Brown went. He may have travelled from Naco to the border town of Nogales and then up to Phoenix, but that's only a guess on my part. That's what I would do. I'm going over to the sheriff's office and look at his maps and then decide which way to go. I also want to talk to the Herberts again. Brown may have let slip something we could use."

"We know he's at least three weeks ahead of you, but do you think you have a chance of running him down. Some of the financing was through investors that we knew, but most of the money that was stolen belonged to, Wilcox and me. So you can see why we're anxious to recover the funds, "Southern told Jefferson.

"Pinkerton has a vast network to call upon. If I can guess which way Brown went, then I have a reasonable chance of capturing him. I'll talk to you after I return from the sheriff 's office and hopefully a meeting with the Herberts."

After an hour looking at the most recent maps in the sheriff 's office, Jefferson decided his original guess, was the best avenue to take. The question was how to get there. He was weeks behind Brown, but from his past experience he knew he could recover a lot of that time. Brown would waste time by staying away from populated areas until he got as far as Phoenix or maybe even further. He also had to be very cautious, because he was carrying a large sum of cash with him. Then again, if he went another direction, Jefferson would have a difficult time tracking the man down and recovering any of the stolen funds.

Jefferson walked from the sheriff 's office to Herbert's home. Kathy Herbert open the door and her face turned pale and she stammered a greeting, but she wouldn't look directly at Jefferson. "I'd like to speak to you and your husband, if he's available?"

"Who's at the door?" Jefferson heard Mr. Herbert call out.

"It's Mr. Jefferson. He wants to talk to you and me."

Herbert came to the door. "I thought we finished with the interrogation?"

"I need some help. Since you two knew Brown better than anyone, perhaps he might have divulged to either of you where he was from and where he might be headed."

"I think we'd be the last two persons on earth that he would confide in," Herbert said.

"I won't take much of your time but I would like you to try and remember anything that he might have said."

"One time, he talked about California. He said that was one place he'd like to visit, if he had time. I can't remember any other place that he mentioned," Franklin Herbert said.

Jefferson sent the sketch of Brown to all law enforcement agencies throughout Arizona, New Mexico and California. He identified Brown as a bank robber who was armed and dangerous. Jefferson assumed that Pinkerton and White Elephant felt that they had enough evidence to proceed against Western Outerwear and Rein- hart. But to be sure, a series of telegrams went back and forth to the main office of Pinkerton which eventually relieved Jefferson of any further work on that case. If follow up was needed, Pinkerton would send another agent. Apparently, legal proceeding had already been initiated against the company and its president.

Now if Jefferson apprehended Brown that would be a win-win situation, all around.

Three days later Southern met with Franklin at his home. "Franklin, we've decided it would be better if the bank went forward without you as their president. If you don't make a fuss, we'll give you two month's salary as a severance. Since the house you're occupying belongs to the bank, the stockholders wanted it vacated in sixty days."

"But I've cooperated with your investigator and I didn't have anything to do with the robbery. I think you're being totally unfair."

"Think it over for a few days. My offer still stands. I'll show myself out."

Kathy Herbert came home from shopping and saw that the house was dark inside; all the shades had been pulled down over the windows. She went looking for Franklin and found him in his office. "What's the matter Franklin?" she lit the kerosene lamps.

"The bank fired me and told me we have sixty days to vacate the house. I'm ruined. Everyone in town will know. They'll probably think we were in on the robbery"

After her eyes adjusted to the shadows in the room, Kathy saw the gun in Herbert's hand. "Franklin, that's not an answer to our problem. Let me have the gun, please."

"It's better this way. I'm too old for you and that's why you became acquainted with Brown. You didn't think I knew, but I did. I hoped you would grow out of it, but you seemed mesmerized by him."

"Franklin, I was bored and made a mistake. It was just something that got out of hand. I didn't realize until later how wonderful you are. Please let me have the gun."

Franklin sat back in his chair, but didn't relinquish the gun he held. Kathy knew what she had to do.

"I was a fool Franklin. You're more a man than Brown could ever be. Don't let it be too late for us to put this behind us and go on with our lives. I want very much to be your wife; it's not too late to start a family. You're an intelligent man. Your life isn't over and you can do any-thing, you set your mind to.'

"It's too late. I'm too old to start over. No one will hire me. The word will be out, that I may have been involved in the robbery. No one will trust me. I have some money set aside, but not enough to support us for more than a year."

"I wrote my father and told him everything that happened with Brown and the robbery; I didn't leave anything out. He suggested we come to Tucson; he'll let you manage the hard- ware store our family owns. That's just to help us out in the short term. He's always wanted a bank. While you're running the hardware store, he'll put together the investors for a bank in Tucson. He wants you to be the president of that bank. He's always admired you. Now please give me the gun and let's not talk about this anymore. I don't want to go on without you"

Kathy sat on Franklin's lap and mussed his hair and kissed him hard. She ran her hand down inside his pants. Soon, he handed the gun to her. There were tears in his eyes.

# CHAPTER TWENTY

With enough supplies to last another week, Brown pressed on to his destination. The longer he took to get there, the greater the chance he'd be found by bandits, or some sheriff trying to make a name for himself. By now, someone had probably found the two he killed outside Marana. So when he was south of Phoenix, he turned west with the intent to pick up the train in Gila Bend. He knew that added another two weeks to his trip, but he felt it was necessary. He continued to travel just north of the foothills of the Cimarron Mountains, camping by day and traveling by night.

The main street of Gila bend consisted of a dry goods store, saloon, livery stable, boarding house/hotel, barber shop, a train station and a stagecoach station. Though travel by stage- coach to the major towns had ceased, it was still an important part of passenger transportation for those towns, not serviced by the railroad. Brown made up his mind that he wouldn't travel by horseback anymore; he'd face whoever may be after him, here in Gila Bend.

The first order of business was to offload the horses. He hated to part with the large bay. It had been a good companion over the past month and gotten him through some tough times. Brown didn't want to spend too much time hassling over the price, so he took what the livery owner said he'd pay and walked to the boarding house. The proprietor said he had one room left, so Brown paid in advance and asked about a bath. He was told there was a bath in the barber shop. He put his bedroll in the room and took the saddlebag containing the stolen money, his suit, shirt and boots with him.

There were no patrons in the barber shop, so Brown treated himself to a hair cut, shave and then a bath in the back room. The barber cleaned and pressed his suit, polished his boots and steamed his shirt, while Brown was having his bath. He kept the saddlebags close and his gun even closer. Later, he didn't recognize him- self, when he looked in the mirror. He gave the barber a two dollar tip.

Dinner was at five that evening. Before sitting down, Brown put his saddlebag in the boarding house safe. The proprietor assured Brown that there were no other valuables in there. But, he would immediately notify Brown if another guest wanted to place items in there. He was hungry and in dire need of a good meal; hardtack and beans had been his staple on the trail. There were four other people present as he sat down at the head of the table. A man and a woman sat to his right while two young men sat to his left. As soon as the first course was served, a large man entered the dining room and sat down at the end of the table facing Brown. The same man had been at the boarding house in Nogales, when Brown was there. Brown felt trapped, but decided to see how this played out. He felt confident that he could kill the man, if he had to.

The conversation at the table was limited to the demise of the stagecoach lines and how hot it was outside. The big man didn't enter into any of the small conversations nor did he take much notice of Brown, who decided to take the initiative "Don't I remember you from the boarding house in Nogales, about a month ago?" Brown asked.

"I was there."

"What type of work are you in?" Brown asked.

"Not anything that would interest you."

The message was clear, so Brown didn't try to converse with the man anymore. He shifted his attention to the two young men sitting to his left and found out they were dry goods sales- men, on their way to Yuma. He smiled to him- self, as they told him about their wares. Every once in a while, he'd look at the woman sitting to his right and wondered who she was, but she wouldn't maintain eye contact.

Once dessert was served, the large man left the dining room. Assuming that the large man went to his room, Brown strolled across the street and walked into a dim lit tavern. It had a potbellied stove in one corner and a pool table at the far end. This was one of five drinking establishments in Gila Bend. He looked around to see if there was anyone he recognized. His eyes caught the silhouette of the large man from the boarding house, leaning on the bar having a beer. Brown took a table on the near wall, sat down and ordered from the bar maid. While keeping his back to the wall, he kept one eye on the man at the bar and his other eye on the two girls working the room. He knew the strain of the past month was getting to him, as he self consciously touched the revolver, he carried on his right side.

The large man drank his beer and left the saloon, with not even a nod in Brown's direction. Brown knew at that moment that he was going to kill him. He wouldn't do it in Gila Bend, but if he was on the train tomorrow, he was a dead man. He bought a beer for one of the girls, who sat down at his table but after another thirty minutes, he got up and walked back to the boarding house.

Brown retrieved his bag from the safe and went directly to his room on the second floor. "It's protected here. There's no need to take your saddlebag to your room. I'm on duty all night and besides I'm armed," Brown ignored the night manager and walked to his room.

The bureau was sturdy, so Brown moved it in front of the door in case someone might try to lighten his load, while he was asleep. But he couldn't sleep. He could do that on the train. In the morning, Brown cleaned up, threw the bedroll into the trash and took his saddlebag with him. He joined three others for breakfast; the large man and one of the dry goods sales- men were missing. After breakfast, Brown walked to the train depot and bought a ticket to Yuma. He'd arrived an hour early, because he wanted to see if the large man would be on the same train. He wasn't disappointed. About thirty minutes before the train departed, the man approached the ticket agent and bought a ticket. He then went inside the station. But that wasn't as much of a surprise, as the man and woman who walked up and bought a ticket fif- teen minutes prior to departure. It was the man and woman, he saw in Nogales, at the boarding house. But they weren't at the boarding house last night. Brown wondered where they stayed.

It'd been nearly a month, since he was in Nogales. Anyone that got on the train with him in Nogales should be in California by now. Why were they all here? Could they collectively or individually be looking for him? It was likely that news of the Bisbee Bank robbery was well known by now, but would these three be the ones that would be looking for him. Their presence on the train was too much of a coincidence for him to ignore. Well he'd come this far; the die was cast. If they were after him, they wouldn't like what would happen to them, if they made any aggressive move in his direction.

Behind the engine, was a baggage car and then three passenger cars. The only restroom facility was located in the rear of the third passenger car. Most of the passenger seated themselves in the first passenger car, with a handful in the second one. The young man and woman from Nogales were in the first car and the large man was in the second passenger car; Brown made his way to the third car and sat down mid- way in the car, facing the door he'd just come through.

About an hour after they left Gila bend, the large man went back to use the restroom. Brown was the only one in the car. He waited until the restroom door closed and then he made his way to the rear of the car. He opened the exterior door and stood on the platform, so that he'd be hidden from the large man, when he exited the restroom. When that door opened, the large man walked out and stared in the direction, where Brown had been sitting. Brown quickly opened the platform door and thrust his gun in the small of the big man' back

"Don't make a sound," Brown said.

The large man paused as though trying to assess his options. Brown held the door open and stepped backward onto the platform. "Keep your hands up and step back slowly onto the platform; we need to talk."

The man turned to look directly at Brown before stepping out onto the rear platform. Brown signaled him to the side. "Why are you following me?" Brown asked.

"Who the hell are you and why do you think I'm following you? I'm an Arizona Marshal and you've made a serious error. Now hand that gun over before you get into more trouble."

"I saw you in Nogales and a month later I see you in Gila Bend. You have to be tracking some- one. I think it's me"

"You must have done something big to think I'm after you. The only thing I can think of that big is the Bisbee bank robbery. So you're the one they're all looking for. Hand over your gun; you're under arrest."

There was a look of disbelief on the man's face when Brown shot him in the chest. The big man clutched his heart before he fell onto the platform. Brown felt for a pulse, but the man was dead. Brown looked in the passenger car see if anyone heard the shot but the noise of the train probably muffled the sound. Turning the large man onto his back was difficult and at one moment, Brown fell onto the corpse. He recovered a badge and identification for Horace Short, an Arizona Marshal in his left inside pocket. There was a reward poster for Pearl Hart in a side pocket of his western style jacket. She was wanted for robbery in Gallup, New Mexico. Brown yelled out in frustration and immediately turned to make sure he hadn't alerted anyone, to what he'd done. Pearl was in jail the last he knew. Why was the Marshal looking for her here? Was she in this area? Brown suspected that Short thought Pearl might be on this train heading to California. This put a crimp into Brown's plans. Pearl could recognize him and that wouldn't be good.

Marshall Short had sixty dollars in his wallet; Brown pocketed the money and then cleaned out all the dead man's pockets. When he was satisfied that he recovered everything important from the lawman, he pushed the marshal off the platform. The body hit with a thud and slid down the embankment. Brown waited a few minutes and then pocketed the circular and threw the marshal's personal effects over the side.

# CHAPTER
# TWENTY-ONE

From Inspiration Point, Tommy and Juan slowly made their descent down to the Santa Ynez Valley. The footing was treacherous, so they trailed their horses behind and stopped many times before they reached bottom. The route had been traveled recently but Tommy didn't find anything that would lead them to believe that it was the Santa Barbara bank robbers, who used the route. It was near five o'clock, so they decided to camp overnight at Gidney Creek, near the Forbush Homestead, which was only ten minutes away.

"What are you thinking?" Juan asked Tommy.

"It seems like a big coincidence that Meade is back in town and we have a bank robbery and cattle rustling. I'm wondering what really goes on at Star ranch."

"You think Singleton is involved?"

"I don't know what his involvement is but he certainly has created an atmosphere on his ranch that allows these things to happen."

"You think Meade is involved in the bank robbery?"

"I don't know. I just know that Meade is a bad actor. He and the others at Star Ranch rustled our cattle and some of the same group tried to ambush us back on the trail. There's also your description of the third man in the robbery. Matches Meade, don't you think?" Juan nodded his approval.

Juan found some trash from a previous camp site near where they set up camp, but nothing in the trash gave them a clue to the bank robbers' identity. It was still daylight as they made their way to the Forbush Homestead. They wanted to make Frank and Jessie Martin, the owners, aware they were in the area and ask them whether any cowboys had traveled near their homestead, in the past month.

Frank Martin saw them coming from a distance. He had a rifle in his hands as he greeted them. To Tommy's question about others that travelled near his place, he responded." I remember seeing three men camped out near the creek about three weeks ago, but I didn't recognize them. Two were tall and thin while the other was on the burly side. I didn't approach them. I just watched them until they left."

"Did you see which way they went?" Tommy asked.

"They took the trail toward Santa Ynez."

Martin asked them to come to his adobe and have coffee. "We can only stay for a few minutes, Frank. We need to get to our camp before it gets too dark."

Jessie Martin greeted them at the door to the one room adobe, and gave Tommy and Juan a mug of hot coffee. "Is this is the first time you've been inside?" Jessie asked.

"First time for me, it's pretty cozy, "Juan said. They left the Martin Adobe before dark and made their way back to their camp. Early the next morning, Tommy and Juan travelled west until they intercepted the Santa Ynez River. As they were traveling along the bank, Tommy signaled Juan to hold up. They dismounted and led the horses behind a large bush. Coming along the bank on the other side of the river were six riders; Ed Meade was in front.

"Do you think they saw us?" Juan asked.

"I don't know. Let's see what they do. They may be on their way to the Star Ranch. Then again, they may be looking for us. We'll let them pass and then follow them, at a distance."

Tommy and Juan maintained a reasonable distance behind the six riders until they reached a wide bend in the river, where it ran north and south. Tommy again signaled Juan to stop. "I've lost them and I don't like it. Follow me," Tommy said.

When he was about forty feet away from the river and in a tree line, Tommy stopped. "You hold the horses, I'm going to scout ahead and see what I can find."

Tommy slowly made his way, paralleling the river, until he came upon a rise where he could look down on the river, for some distance. He crawled another fifty yards and came over the rise, but didn't see anything. He remained where he was while continually looking first on one side of the river and then on the other through binoculars, until he saw something move. It took some time, but finally Tommy saw six men in pairs of two, behind boulders on the opposite side of the river. They were spread out about ten feet apart. Tommy was sure they were waiting to ambush him and Juan. Not only were he and Juan outnumbered, but the location Meade and his riders chose made it impossible for him and Juan to get around them or come upon them, without being seen. His only choice seemed to be to disperse them, if he could. If that didn't work, he and Juan would go into a Guerrilla mode and employ hit and run tactics on the six.

Tommy aimed at the two men behind the most southerly boulder and fired three quick shots. The men broke cover and appeared to be going for their horses. The two most northerly pair moved to Tommy's right and as though they were trying to outflank him. He hit one of those two men in the upper right thigh and his fellow rider pulled him to safety. Tommy waited until all six left their positions, then he crawled back and made his way back to where Juan was waiting.

"I heard the shooting. What's up?"

"They apparently spotted us and set up an ambush behind some rocks on the other side of the creek. I just tried to disperse them. I hit one. Maybe they'll make their way to the Star Ranch. In any case, we have to get out of here. I suggest we go south for a ways and then cross the river and try to pick up their trail.

"Could they leave some of their men behind to look for us?" Juan asked.

"I think we better be alert for it."

"Don't you think they'll take the wounded man back to their ranch?"

"I wouldn't count on it."

Finding a way over the creek was time consuming because of the steep banks on either side of the river. Eventually, they found an area that wasn't too steep and went across. They travelled perpendicular to the river for about two miles, before they headed north again.

After they rode another thirty minutes, Tommy raised his hand." Let's stop here. You go east and I'll go west for about two hundred yards and then come back together in kind of an arc. I'm not sure we lost them. Are you comfortable with this? Your mother would kill me if anything happened to you," Tommy said.

Juan Smiled, "it's like old times."

They left the horses tied to some small Birch Trees and made their way through the brush. Tommy didn't see any sign of the riders, so he slowly made his way back to their rendezvous. He waited about ten minutes and when Juan didn't return, Tommy walked in the direction Juan took, but not directly. He made his way a little further east than Juan was supposed to go and then came back to where he thought Juan should be. As Tommy made his way through some thick brush, he could hear noises up ahead. That's when he saw Juan tied to a tree and two of Meade's riders were slapping him in the face and punching him in the stomach. Tommy didn't want to chance a shot so he took out his knife and crawled on his stomach until he was within ten yards of the two men. They seemed to be enjoying the abuse they were inflicting on Juan and were oblivious to him.

As Tommy straightened up he stepped on a dead branch. The sound alerted the two men and they turned toward him. But Tommy was in full attack mode. He leaped at the two, stabbing one in the heart and knocking the other to the ground, with a body block. The fallen man started to get to his feet but Tommy was too quick and too angry. He grabbed the man from behind and slowly chocked him to death. Tommy retrieved his knife from the fallen man and cut the ropes around Juan.

"What happened?"

"These two were waiting for me. I'm sorry Tommy. My instincts are not what they used to be."

"Don't worry about it. Is this the only two you saw?"

"Yes. I get the impression that the others went looking for you. We may not be out of it yet."

"What did they say?"

"They wanted to know where you were."

Tommy turned over the two men. They were two of the rustlers he grabbed at the Star Ranch. "You go directly back to where the horses are tethered and I'll wait to see if anyone picks up your trail. Let's remember this location. I'll notify the sheriff where the two bodies can be found. That is,if anything is left of them when he finally gets up here. You okay to move with- out help." Tommy said.

"I'm not hurt; I'm mad. "Juan responded. "Keep your eyes open. These guys mean to kill us."

"I wasn't mad before but I'm sure as hell am now. I just hope we get another chance. "Juan said.

"They seem to want us pretty bad."

Tommy didn't want to use Juan as bait but he had to split up because they were outnumbered. He waited five minutes, and then picked up Juan's trail. The ploy worked because he came up behind two of the other riders, just before they were to spring another trap on Juan. After both men were disarmed, Juan tied them to a tree and Tommy started questioning them, but they wouldn't answer any of his questions. "Juan, grab your rifle and keep an eye out, I'm going to really ask them some questions, so don't be concerned when you hear some screaming."

Tommy took two knives out of his saddle-bags and stood in front of one of the riders tied to a tree. He asked him where Meade and the wounded rider were. When there was no answer, he threw one of the knives straight at the man; the knife hit the tree about three inches above the man's head. The man screamed in terror. "Where are the other two?" Tommy asked the man again.

"They went back to the Star Ranch. Meade took the wounded man back," was the man's response.

"Why have you been tracking us?"

"Meade wanted you dead. He told us to kill you and then come back to the ranch."

"What do you want to do with these two?" Juan asked Tommy.

"Since we have some manpower, we'll have them bury the dead and when they're finished, we'll take them back to our ranch. The sheriff said he'd be up in a day with some deputies and a warrant for Meade. That's when we'll go over to the Star Ranch and pick up Meade and the wounded one. In the interim, we'll hold these two until the sheriff arrives. We'll let Meade worry about the four he left for us."

The two were tied to their horses and Tommy kept them in front of him and Juan, in case they were ambushed again. They came up to the main house through the south entrance to the ranch. Sarah was waiting on the porch, but when she saw the bruises on Juan's face, she wanted to know what happened. "We had an encounter with some of Meade's men. Juan got beaten up a little but he's okay and I settled that score. These two are going back with the sheriff, when he arrives."

Raul came up to the four as Tommy got off his horse. "Take these two, tie them securely and have someone watch them, I don't want them to escape. They tried to dry gulch Juan and me. The sheriff is going to take them back when he arrives. Two of the Star Ranch riders were killed and one is wounded. I want at least six guards out and strategically placed throughout the ranch. I wouldn't be surprised, if they might try to retaliate tonight."

Raul took the two riders while Juan, Sarah and Tommy went into the house. When Juan saw the frown on Sarah's face, he knew that he was going to have to put up with some motherly concern, for at least a day, and maybe more.

# CHAPTER TWENTY-TWO

Jefferson followed Brown's trail to the border town of Naco and found out about the miner, who boarded a horse there for a week. The description of the miner matched that of the bank robber. So the question for Jefferson was, where did Brown go from Naco? He was sure that Brown would head south of the border and then resurface back on the US side, sometime later.

Jefferson had no intention of going south of the border, so he returned to Bisbee. Prior to going to Naco, he'd wired Brown's description to the sheriffs in all the towns on the US side of the border. Three days later, he received a telegram from the sheriff in Nogales Arizona. Brown had stayed at a boarding house in Nogales and left town on the train to Tucson. Jefferson checked with his office and let them know, he was on his way to Nogales, via Tucson.

The Nogales sheriff was chasing a rustler when Jefferson arrived in town and wasn't expected back for two more days. Jefferson decided to speak with the proprietor of the boarding house and showed him the sketch of Brown. The proprietor identified Brown as a person who stayed at the inn. Jefferson asked who the other boarders were at the time Brown stayed there and was furnished a list. Jefferson looked over the names and was surprised to see that Horace Short was at the boarding house. He didn't recognize any other name on the list.

"Was Short a large man who looked liked a lawman?"

"Yes, how did you know?'

"He's an old friend of mine. I wonder what he was doing here. When did he leave?"

"He left the next morning on the train to Tucson as did Brown and a woman on that list I gave you."

Jefferson looked at it again. "Was the woman's name, Mary Stills?"

"Yes. Her husband owned a livery stable in Rio Rico, which is about five miles north of here. He was killed during a robbery, the morning she left for Tucson."

The revelation that the owner of the livery stable in Rio Rico, just north of Nogales was murdered while Brown was in Nogales, made Jefferson pause. No one saw the crime commit- ted, though someone saw a white man trailing three horses as he rode north toward Phoenix. Jefferson wondered if Brown was responsible for that crime as well. Could the wife and Brown have carried out the robbery and killing. He wired his office with the information.

"Does anyone know who killed the husband?" Jefferson asked.

"Not as of this date."

"Could you tell if Brown and the wife traveled together?"

"No."

The odds were that Brown arrived in Nogales by horseback. Jefferson went to both livery stables in town and found out that an old miner, who resembled the Bisbee bank robber, sold two horses to the livery stable owner. Jefferson received confirmation that Brown had been here when he talked to the barber and showed him two sketches. The first one was a sketch of the bank robber. The second was of Brown.

"He looked like a down and out miner in the first sketch, when he came in here. But after a shave and a bath he looked like the man, in the other sketch."

"Was there anyone with Brown in either disguise?"

"I didn't see anyone."

Jefferson stayed three nights at the boarding house waiting for the sheriff to return. When the sheriff finally did return, he wasn't in a good mood. Jefferson recounted the Bisbee bank robbery, showed a picture of Brown and then had to listen to the sheriff recount his last three days tracking horse rustlers. At the end of the day he was glad that he was patient, because the sheriff filled him in on the elusive Mr. Brown.

"The information I'm about to tell you is not confirmed by anyone; it's just supposition on my part and may or may not be true. If Brown has been posing as a down and out miner who robbed the Bisbee bank, then how did he get here? I think he travelled south of the border from Naco and ended up here. I know a down and out miner sold two of his horses to the livery stable owner and then walked to the barber shop, got a bath and a shave. That miner then became a businessman named Brown and stayed at the boarding house down the street."

"I'm aware of most of that. "Jefferson responded.

That little dialog must have gotten the sheriff's juices flowing because he went on to tell Jefferson some of things that happened while Brown was in the area. "A number of bodies were uncovered in a single grave about two miles south of here. We had a doctor examine them; it looks like they were dead about a week. They belonged to a gang that preys on people travelling south of the border. I wonder who killed them?"

"Then there's the murder of Henry Still, the owner of a livery stable in Rio Rico. The description of a white man leaving the livery stable with three horses, prior to Still's body being found, could fit the description of Brown. Two of those horses were sold the same day to a rancher near Tupac, which is five miles north of Rio Rico. The only thing the rancher can re- member about the seller was that he was white and wore a black suit. My problem is how did Brown kill Henry, sell the horses north of there, come back and eat breakfast at the boarding house and then get on the Tucson train? I don't think he could've pulled that off without help; it doesn't fit."

"And there's the mystery involving the wife of the dead livery owner. Mary Stills was her name. She was a pretty little thing and someone saw her get on the same train as Brown. So why was she leaving at the same time her husband was being murdered? And what really makes this all interesting is that Brown got off the train one stop before Tucson. He left with the horse he'd placed in a rail car. Mary Stills didn't go with him. What do you think about that?"

Jefferson reached in his pocket and took out the list the boarding house proprietor had given him. There was Mary Stills name right next to James Clevenger. "Who's James Clevenger?" Jefferson asked.

"He's a clerk in our bank."

"He was having dinner at the boarding house with Mary Stills the night before her husband was killed. I wonder if Clevenger left on the Tucson train with Mary Stills. Or did she get on the train with Brown, and he dumped her?" Jefferson asked.

"I don't know, but I know where we can get an answer." The sheriff responded.

The Sheriff and Jefferson walked back to the Nogales boarding house and asked for the proprietor. When he came downstairs, the three men went into the dining room and sat down.

"Tell me about James Clevenger, "the sheriff asked the proprietor.

"He works as a clerk in the bank and is a permanent boarder here. Or at least he was, until he left that morning when the other three got on the train for Tucson."

"What do you mean he left?"

"As I recall he left early that morning and didn't come back for breakfast. I assume he meant to leave because his clothes were gone from his room. Lucky for us his room was paid until the end of the month."

The sheriff and Jefferson went to the railroad station and checked the company's records. They wanted to see who boarded the train the morning Brown left. Of the five names on Jefferson's list only

Short, Mary Still and Brown had boarded the train that morning. Again, Jefferson wondered if Stills and Brown had been traveling together. But when did they meet?

Back at his office, the sheriff added something else. "Sometime after Brown jumped the train, a man travelling alone, stopped in Marana. The town is a couple of stops up the line toward Tucson. After he purchased sup- plies, two of the local thugs followed him out of town. Their bodies were recovered two days later by some of their friends. If the man who stopped at Marana was Brown, he's probably long gone by now and probably bypassed Tucson and Phoenix. He's going to put as much distance between himself and Bisbee as he can. He could be on his way to California. If that's his plan, he'll probably stop at Gila Bend."

Jefferson telegraphed Gila Bend, but after waiting a day and not receiving a response, he made his way to Gila Bend by train, via Tucson and Phoenix. At each stop along the way, Jefferson got off the train and showed the sketch of Brown to the barber, the workers at the livery stables and the manger of the boarding houses. No one along the way remembered seeing Brown, but Jefferson got lucky in Gila Bend. A man resembling Brown, sold horses at the livery stable, got a shave, bath and had his black suit pressed by the barber. He stayed overnight at the boarding house.

The boarding house manager provided some more interesting information for Jefferson." There were five other people who stayed with us the night you mentioned. "

The manager got out his register and showed Jefferson that the five were Hiram Short, Frank Cassidy, Joel Hughes, Mrs. Grace Teller and Mrs. Joan Fields, in addition to Brown. "There was one other thing. Mr. Brown stored his saddle- bags in our safe during supper, but he retrieved them right after supper and took them up to his room. I told him I'd be on duty and I was armed, but he wouldn't listen; he just asked for his bags."

Jefferson was trying to process all this information. Short and Brown had stayed at the boarding house in Nogales as well as the one in Gila Bend. He also wondered if Short was on to Brown for the Bisbee bank robbery or was he following up on the livery stable murder, or could he be looking for someone else.

Jefferson wired the Arizona Marshal's Office in Tucson and asked what case Short was pursuing. The response two hours later indicated Short was trailing Pearl Hart, who was wanted for a robbery in Gallup, New Mexico. She was presumed to be in Arizona. Jefferson went back to the sheriff 's office. "Do you have a circular on a Pearl Hart?"

The sheriff fumbled around his desk for a minute. "Here it is. It says she robbed a stage- coach outside Florence with a male companion and served two of a five-year stretch in Yuma. The male companion was never identified."

This was becoming a puzzle, so Jefferson made his way to the railroad station and much to his surprise found out that Brown, Short, Clevenger and Stills had boarded the same train for Yuma. What is this all about, Jefferson wondered. Mary Stills, Brown and Short leave Nogales on the same train. Mary Stills" husband is murdered and now she, Short, Brown and Clevenger, who were at the boarding house in Nogales on the same night, leave on the same Yuma train. Why? Jefferson wondered how Clevenger fit into all this

Jefferson wired the sheriff in Nogales and asked him to find out why Clevenger left No- gales, and where he might be headed. The next day he received the information. Clevenger had quit his job as clerk in the bank, the day before Henry Stills was murdered. No one knew where he went, though he always talked about California. Jefferson was chasing Brown for the Bisbee robbery. Short was chasing Pearl Hart for the Gallup robbery, but who was following up on the Henry Stills murder?

# CHAPTER TWENTY-THREE

**W**ith the Marshal no longer a threat, Brown sensed a feeling of security. Killing someone wasn't something he enjoyed, but he showed no concern about killing anyone, when he was threatened. He thought about the couple in the forward passenger car and what he should do about the flyer that Marshall Short was carrying.

They had travelled three hours from Gila bend when the train stopped to refuel and take on water. The passengers had an hour stop to stretch their legs and get a sandwich at the kitchen of the Mohawk Depot. Brown took his time getting off at this stop. He carried the money with him in a saddlebag, hanging from a strap around his shoulder. This allowed him enough flexibility to reach for his gun, which he carried in a holster on his right hip. The young couple got off the train and made their way to a restaurant on the other side of the depot; yet, Brown kept them in sight. He sat at a table inside the restaurant near enough to them and tried to listen in on their conversation. The woman was crying while the young man was trying to console her. Brown could only make out parts of their dialog, though he distinctly heard the young man say to her, "we have enough to make it to California."

After the couple stepped outside the small restaurant, Brown followed them at a reason- able distance. He heard the woman say she was going to the privy.

Brown slowly walked up to the young man. "Is your wife ill?" he asked.

The young man turned toward Brown abruptly and looked at him defensively, before he spoke. "No, the length of the train ride is get- ting her down. She'll be okay."

"How far are you traveling?" Brown asked trying to sound friendly and yet keep the dialog going.

"We're going to visit relatives in California."

"I've been to California, tell me where they live?"

The young man hesitated before responding. "I really don't know. My wife's relatives are meeting us in Los Angeles. Please excuse me; I need to attend to my wife."

Brown didn't press it and stepped aside to let the young man join the woman, who was returning from the outhouse, behind the depot. Well if Short was following up on a three week old circular, surely someone must be checking up on a five week old bank robbery in Bisbee. But who would that be? Certainly not the young man, but where did the woman fit in? Brown had assumed that Short was following him. This presented a problem for Brown. He knew that Kathy Herbert wouldn't tell the authorities about their affair but she'd let them know it was Brown, who robbed the bank. Sooner or later a description would be waiting for him at the next stop. The chances that a lawman would be waiting at Yuma were fifty-fifty. He didn't like the odds.

Before the train departed, the conductor walked up and down the three passenger cars, collecting money from the new passengers. He was also confirming that those on the train were paid commuters. Brown knew that the conductor could've done that with one pass through the three cars; he was probably looking for Marshall Short.

"Did you see a large man get off the train here in Mohawk?" The conductor asked Brown.

"No, I didn't. But to be honest, I really wasn't paying any attention. Is he someone important?"

"He's an Arizona Marshal and I have a telegram for him."

"Sorry," Brown said.

The conductor left the car and the train started to roll about two minutes later. Brown fancied that the telegram had a description of the couple in the other car, but he knew that not to be true. He'd have to make a move before they reached Yuma.

He started looking at all the possible scenarios. If it was the couple in the first car that were the subject of the telegram, then their presence on the same train decreased his chances of getting to California. Even if the authorities weren't looking for him initially, the reality was that if someone was chasing the couple, they might have another circular with Brown's description. He didn't like the possibility that he might have to shoot it out to get away. He just couldn't be on the same train with this couple. Either they had to go or he had to. He didn't want to chance another killing so he planned to leave the train at the next stop. It was the town of Wellton, about twelve miles from Yuma.

When the train stopped at Wellton, Brown waited in the rear car until most of the passengers got off the train to stretch their legs or have something to eat. Wellton was a small town; yet, it had a livery stable. After the passengers returned and the conductor checked tickets, Brown grabbed his saddlebags containing the stolen money and stepped off the rear platform, just as the train got underway.

The livery stable was near the end of the main street, so Brown walked to it and approached the owner about buying two rideable horses. After a spirited negotiation, Brown settled on another roan that looked sound. That was the only horse the owner had available. Brown needed another horse. There was a combination saloon and general store a few buildings from the livery stable, so Brown walked to the store and purchased enough food and provisions for three days. He checked the bulletin board for any flyers and then bought some riding clothes, boots and a canteen. When the storekeeper saw the amount of Brown's purchase, he couldn't be more helpful. The only problem was that he'd remember Brown if the authorities asked; that wouldn't be good. Killing some bandits or some local toughs wouldn't concern most people, but killing a store keeper, minding his own business, could be Brown's downfall.

# CHAPTER TWENTY-FOUR

The sheriff and two deputies arrived at the ranch in Santa Ynez around noon and were invited to have lunch inside the house. Tommy had two of his vaqueros take care of their horses and told them to have them ready at a moment's notice. The sheriff and his men were pleased and a little embarrassed as Sarah and the two other women waited on them. Each personally thanked Sarah, Naomi and Naiwa as they left the dining room. The two deputies stayed back as the others went out onto the porch. They wanted to help Naiwa clear the table and wash the dishes. Naiwa had blossomed into an attractive woman. She had fixed her hair and wore it in a pony tail which accentuated a very pretty face. In addition, she'd discarded her Indian garb and was now ac- customed to wearing bright dresses that Sarah purchased in Santa Ynez.

Juan, Tommy and the sheriff stepped out onto the front porch. They waited until the two deputies joined them and then discussed what action they were going to take. "Mr. Sanchez, I have warrants for Meade and six others. I'd like you and Juan to accompany us to the Star Ranch. I also have an affidavit appointing you and Juan, as temporary deputies."

"I thought the judge said that Meade and the others were innocent and he dismissed the charges. So how did you get warrants?" Juan asked.

"My brother is a member of the city council. After he heard what the judge did, he went to the courthouse and told him that if he wanted to continue being a judge in Santa Barbara, then he better let the sheriff do his job or else. I think that's what he said or words to that effect," the sheriff smiled as he related the story to Tommy and Juan.

"Is this a blanket warrant or do you have separate warrants for each of the six?" Juan asked as he looked over the documents.

"Why do you ask?" The sheriff asked.

"Well, there were originally nine that Tommy took to Santa Barbara. Of those, you took two back and a third is dead. That leaves six. We killed two, wounded one and captured two. They're being held by Raul. That leaves Meade and a wounded vaquero. I think you need a warrant for each, "Juan responded.

"I see what you mean. Though I have a blanket warrant, the judge set it up so that I could add any John Does that are incidental to serving the warrant. I think we're okay."

Sarah joined the men on the porch. The sheriff got up and offered her his chair. She declined. "I know you're going to the Star ranch. The problem is that they'll be waiting for you Tommy. Do you think you have enough men to take them all in?"

"There are five of us here. I can have Raul bring along three other vaqueros, if you'd feel more comfortable."

"Juan is not going with you, is he?"

The question was more of a statement and Tommy understood the maternal instincts of Sarah and agreed, but it was going to be difficult telling Juan he couldn't come. Tommy was trying to find the words, when Juan spoke up.

"I think that's my decision. I know you're my mother but I'm an adult and can make my own decisions. "I'm going with Tommy and the deputies, and I don't want to hear any more about the subject. "Juan was angry.

Sarah looked to Tommy for support, but he wouldn't make eye contact.

"My goal is to assist the sheriff in serving the warrants. That's my responsibility as a citizen, but I agree with my wife's suggestion that we take more men, so Raul and two vaqueros will accompany us. But I also want to safeguard the women and children on this ranch in the event Meade and his men double back, while we're at the Star Ranch. Juan, I want you and four vaqueros to guard the ranch. You stay at the house and have the other four spread out so they can alert you immediately, if there is an attack. This satisfies your mother and it also satisfies me. There's no one I'd trust more with my wife's safety than you, "Tommy looked directly at Juan.

"I've always respected you as an older brother, but I can't spend the remainder of my life, hiding behind your coattails. I want to go; Raul can stay with the four Vaqueros."

Tommy knew he had a problem. Sarah was wrong, but she was his wife and he wasn't going to defy her. She had to make the decision. Tommy looked at her and shrugged his shoulders. He could tell she was conflicted. "I'm sorry Juan. You're correct. I've overstepped. I won't stand in your way, if you want to go with Tommy," Sarah said.

Juan leaned back in his chair and smiled at his mother. Finally, the cord had been broken.

Tommy sent Juan to get Raul. When they returned, Tommy explained everyone's role.

"I, the sheriff and his two deputies will go down the main access way to Singleton's house. Juan, you and three vaqueros will come up the back way, similar to the route, we took that night we visited Meade. I know you didn't come with us that night, but the three vaqueros that'll be with you, know the way. I don't want you to take any chances. They could expect us to come from the south and not the main entrance. If you encounter Meade or any of his men, fire three shots in rapid succession and we'll join you."

The sheriff and his men mounted their horses and waited for Tommy who was taking to Sarah. "Thank you Tommy. At least I was heard. Please watch out for him. I couldn't love you more than I do at this moment."

After Tommy said goodbye to the children and Sarah, he and the others saddled up and made their way to the Star ranch, which bordered Tommy's and Sarah's spread on the east side. The entrance for the Star Ranch was along Santa Barbara Road, nearly two miles away.

The main house for the Star Ranch sat back four thousand feet from the entrance along Camino Real, which connected Santa Ynez to Santa Barbara. As they approached, Tommy could see cattle grazing but didn't see anyone, until they neared the house. Tommy could see Singleton and two men come out on the porch. Each wore a six gun on his hip; each carried a rifle. It wasn't lost on Tommy that the man standing to Singleton's right was tall and slim and the one to his left was short and squatty. Tommy assumed there might be others in the main house; they'd have to be careful. He let the sheriff and his two deputies ride slightly ahead of him, but all four came abreast of the porch, at the same time. They were face to face with Singleton and his two men.

"Mr. Singleton, I'm Sheriff Hollis. I have warrants for the arrest of Ed Meade and one of your riders, who was wounded."

Singleton didn't move. "What's the charge?"

"Cattle rustling, though I suspect we'll add attempted murder once we bring them back to Santa Barbara."

"Those charges were dropped."

"Well they've been reinstated and warrants were reissued and signed by the judge, who mistakenly dropped the charges. Is Meade and this man here?" After the sheriff read the names of the two men out loud, he handed the warrant to Singleton.

"There not here. What's Sanchez doing with you? He's not a deputy, "Singleton sneered at Tommy.

"He is now. Do you mind if we look around to see if Meade and the other four doubled back."

"I certainly do mind. I told you they weren't here. That should be good enough for you."

Just as the sheriff was trying to decide what his next course of action would be, three shots rang out in rapid succession. Everyone looked south toward the creek, separating the two ranches. That is everyone except Tommy. He drew immediately and aimed his gun at Single- ton and his two men. "You three stay right here while the sheriff and his deputies investigate those shots."

The sheriff and his two deputies immediately galloped toward the sound of the shots, past the main barn and bunkhouse, while Tommy kept his attention centered on Single- ton and his two men.

"I don't think you can get all three of us. I suggest you ride out of here while you still have the chance, Breed."

Tommy could see the three were assessing their chances. The man on Singleton's left seemed ready to challenge Tommy. It didn't take him long to make up his mind. As he dropped his right hand to grab his gun Tommy shot him in the right leg. The man on Singleton's right then made a move and Tommy shot him in the left leg. Both men fell and were writhing in pain on the porch. Singleton was turning left and right looking at the two men. He then looked directly at Tommy.

"If you holster your gun, I'll show you how it is to face a real man."

"Put your gun on the porch. "Tommy directed Singleton.

When Singleton didn't move immediately, Tommy asked him, "do you want it in the left or right leg?" Singleton dropped his weapon on the porch.

Tommy got off his horse and grabbed the three guns and put them in his saddlebag. He ordered Singleton to lead him into the house. He figured that the two moaning on the front porch were neutralized.

"I want you in front of me in case there's someone inside."

Holding on to the back of Singleton's shirt and keeping him in front at all times, Tommy checked all five rooms in the one story home. When he was satisfied there was no one else in the house, he directed Singleton to go back on the porch.

"What are the names of your two men?"

"Charlie Simmers is the tall one and Frank Hodges is the shorter one."

"You can tend to your men now."

"The next time we meet, it's going to be different. I promise you," Singleton snarled at Tommy.

By this time the sheriff, his deputies and Juan returned with one of the rustlers. "Meade got away; this one surrendered, after we shot him in the arm. He's the one that you shot in the leg at the river. Other than him, no one was hurt."

The sheriff didn't say anything about the vaqueros, so Tommy didn't ask. He assumed they went back to the ranchero. One of the deputies was assisting the two fallen men. The bullets went through their legs, so he bandaged the wounds and suggested that Singleton take them to a doctor. The sheriff however wasn't satisfied. "You told us Meade and the other rustler wasn't here, when in fact, they were on your property."

"You asked me if they were here. I assumed you meant in the house, so I said no, which is true. If you wanted to know if they were any- where on the property you should have asked that question. I can't read your mind. You may be the law in this county, but I have friends. I'm going to file charges against you and Sanchez as soon as I see to my friends. If you have nothing else, get the hell off my property."

Tommy was off to the side and signaled Juan to join him. "Juan, does the name Charley Simmers or Frank Hodges mean anything to you. They along with Singleton meet the description of the bank robbers."

"I went to Santa Barbara last week and talked to a friend of mine who works in the bank. I asked for some information about the robbers and the two guards on duty that day. I'm waiting for him to get back to me."

The two men that Tommy shot were still being treated by the deputies while the one, his vaquero shot, was tied to a horse. Both of his wounds seemed minor. Tommy, the sheriff and his two deputies were starting to mount their steeds when Tommy sensed some movement to his left, where Singleton had been standing. Tommy turned just as Singleton shifted his weight, leaned on his back foot and threw a hard punch. Tommy ducked, positioned his weight on his left side and leaned down. Singleton punch went over Tommy's head and pulled the bigger man slightly past Tommy, who struck out with the heal of his right boot into the back of Singleton's right leg, just below the knee. Everyone turned and looked at Singleton. They could hear Singleton screaming and saw him thrashing on the ground. "I guess that was the next time you mentioned," Tommy said.

"Mister Sanchez, you are one lethal son of a bitch," the sheriff was laughing.

"What condition do you think I'd be in if that punch of his had landed? Take a look at Single- ton and the two I shot, lying on the porch. Don't you think they match the description of the three bank robbers, you've been chasing?"

"You're right. Proving it may be a problem, since they were wearing masks."

"Well if they file suit against us, they'll have to go to Santa Barbara. Maybe you can put them in some sort of line up with masks on, to see if the people in the bank think they match the de- scription. That would take the wind out of them and you never can tell, one of them may confess and try to make a deal. It wouldn't hurt to have that as an option," Tommy replied.

Tommy, Juan, the sheriff and his two deputies went back to Altura Prado with the wounded man. The three vaqueros, who went with Juan, met them and took their horses and the wounded man. Tommy asked the vaqueros what happened while they were at the Star Ranch.

"Meade and another man saw us as we got near the bunkhouse so I fired the three shots you directed. Meade and this man started to ride off, so I shot at them and hit this one. I think Meade made his way south. Once the sheriff joined us, Juan decided we should go back the way we came. Did we do right?"

"Absolutely. Put this one with the other two. Raul, have one of the vaqueros take a look at his wounds and see if he needs more patching up. Don't take any chances. Let's double the guard tonight. I think the stakes are higher that we'll be attacked, after I knocked Singleton down. The sheriff 's taking the three back to Santa Bar- bara tomorrow. He and his men need a place to bunk tonight. Can you take care of that?"

"Ci, patron."

The next morning the sheriff said his goodbyes and he and his deputies escorted the prisoners back to Santa Barbara. Before he left, he spoke to Tommy and Sarah. "Meade probably escaped to the hills. He's not going to be happy and may make a move against you or your family. I can leave one of my deputies here to help out, if you need him. I think Singleton and his two hands are neutralized for now, but they're going to come after you sometime, probably when you least expect it. They're that kind"

"I think we can handle it here. We have enough men to handle Meade, Singleton and his men."

# CHAPTER TWENTY-FIVE

**J**efferson had an adequate view of the railroad depot across the street from his hotel window in Gila Bend. He watched as two cowboys picked up supplies at the general store and two children with books make their way to school. Just then the telegraph operator ran across the street toward the sheriff 's office. Jefferson finished washing up, put on his jacket and walked downstairs. On a hunch, he walked to the sheriff 's office, presented his credentials and asked the sheriff if there was any significance to the telegram he just received.

"They found Marshall Short lying along the tracks about thirty miles from here. He'd been shot in the heart. They're bringing the body back here tomorrow. Did you know him?"

"We go back a long way. He was a good man. I sent a description of a bank robber that I'm chasing, to this office. Did you receive it?"

"I read it when it came in. It's got to be here someplace."

The sheriff sorted through some of the papers on his desk before he found it. "Here it is. Do you think he's involved?"

"He was on the same train as Short. In fact, they were at the same boarding house in No- gales about ten days after a major robbery in Bisbee. Brown may have thought Short was on to him, and may have eliminated a potential threat. Brown seems to leave a trail of bodies wherever he stays or goes."

"That train stops at Yuma. We could telegraph the sheriff and see if Brown is still in the area." The sheriff said.

"If you wouldn't mind, why don't you write the message and sign it. I'm going to the telegrapher on another matter and I'll have him send it."

The train to Yuma was tomorrow at four in the afternoon. Jefferson went back to the hotel and caught up on some paperwork, before having dinner and then turning in for the night. Jefferson arrived in Yuma the next evening and immediately went to the sheriff's office. The sheriff was out of town and his deputy didn't know anything about the killing of Marshall Short or whether the sheriff had found Brown.

"I'm looking for a telegram sent to the sheriff, asking him if an individual named Brown was still in the area. Do you know if it arrived?"

"I'm sorry but I really don't know."

"When will the sheriff return?"

"Probably tomorrow, but I can't be sure."

The telegraph office was five doors down from the sheriff's. Jefferson was told that the telegram from the Gila Bend sheriff had arrived and was delivered to the sheriff's office; the deputy obviously wasn't going to be helpful. Jefferson needed a place to stay until the sheriff returned. The only hotel in Yuma had one room available for a two night minimum. Jefferson paid four dollars in advance and went up to his room. He'd start checking on Brown tomorrow.

Armed with the sketch of Brown, he made his way to places he assumed that Brown would frequent, namely the barber shop, the boarding house and the train station, where Jefferson was at this moment. No one there remembered seeing anyone that fit the sketch of Brown. Trying to trigger the station manager's recollection, Jefferson mentioned that Brown was on the same train as Marshall Short, who was found murdered. This helped the station manager remember who the conductor was on that train. He lived in Yuma and this was his day off. Jefferson received directions and walked to the man's home. He was sitting on his front porch smoking a pipe when Jefferson approached. He showed him a sketch of Brown.

"I remember him. He sat in the rear passenger car. I made two passes through all the cars on the Gila Bend to Yuma leg. On the first occasion, I had a telegram for a Marshal Short. I remember asking the man in the sketch, if he saw him. He said he didn't. On the second occasion, I was checking tickets and he wasn't there. I made some inquiries of the other passengers. One man said he saw him get off at Wellton just as the train got underway. The only things in Wellton other than the depot that might interest a man, are a saloon and a livery stable. I don't know what happened to him; he may still be there."

"What was in the telegram you wanted to give to Marshal Short?"

"I don't know. I gave it to the sheriff when we stopped in Yuma.

"How far back is Wellton?"

"About ten miles."

"When's the next train back to Wellton?" "It's the day after tomorrow."

Jefferson didn't want to waste any time. He was catching up, but was still at least a week behind Brown. He hired a horse and carriage and after getting direction, rode off toward the small town of Wellton. The conductor wasn't kidding. The depot sat at one end of a short dirt street. The livery stable was at the other end, with the saloon in the middle. He tied his rig to the rail out front and walked into the livery stable. There was only one person attending the stock inside the stable. He told Jefferson that he sold a Roan to the fellow in the sketch.

"He wanted two horses, but I only had one to sell so he took the Roan and went to the saloon," The livery stable owner said.

The next stop for Jefferson was the saloon. There were two customers sitting at the bar as Jefferson walked in. He showed the bartender a sketch of Brown. "Did this man come into the saloon about five or six days ago?"

"He came in but didn't stay long," The bartender responded.

"Is he still in the area?"

"Why do you want to know?" The bartender responded as he cleaned a couple of glasses.

Jefferson didn't have time to waste so he leveled with the man. "He robbed a bank in Bis- bee and was using the train to escape."

"Is there a reward of some kind?"

"I'll pay one hundred dollars for information that I can use."

"Can you pay it now?"

This interchange was being listened to by the two customers at the bar, who now turned on their stools and looked directly at Jefferson, as if to size him up. Jefferson reached inside his jacket and took out a revolver, he carried in a shoulder holster. He laid the gun on the bar and then took a hundred dollar bill out of his wallet and placed it next to the gun. "I'm a Pinkerton agent and I can use a gun. As you can see, I have a hundred dollars. What do you have that I can use?"

"He walked in here and asked if he could buy my horse that was tied up out front. I didn't want to sell the horse so I said you can have it for two hundred dollars. He reached in his pocket and laid the money on the bar in front of me and started toward the door. I said, I changed my mind. I want two hundred and fifty. He walked back and pulled back his coat. I could see a revolver in a holster on his right side. He just stood there as though waiting for me to say something more. I saw the look on his face and told him, "two hundred was the deal."

"Did he say anything else?"

"He asked if there was a way around Yuma, without being seen."

"So he was on his way to California?"

"I assume that's where he's headed, but I wasn't going to ask anymore questions than necessary. He looked like someone who could really handle himself."

Jefferson left the money on the bar but held the revolver in his right hand and walked over to the two customers at the bar. "I've had a long day and don't want any company. Do you under- stand me?"

Both men didn't say anything as they looked away and started drinking their beer.

# CHAPTER
# TWENTY-SIX

The horse Brown bought at the livery stable was a sound animal; the one he bought from the saloon owner was only good for hauling supplies. Bypassing Yuma without being recognized would be difficult. Riding around in a black suit and tie would attract the wrong people, especially if they thought he was carrying fifty thousand dollars in his saddlebags. He had to get supplies and another change of clothing. It took him three hours of riding before he was directly north of Yuma. He had to continually check to see if he was being followed. Though the train was the preferable way to go to California, he still could pick it up at another stop west of Yuma. Chances were that there'd be descriptions of him at every stop along the route to San Diego and maybe as far as Los Angeles. Another problem was that the state of Arizona sent a marshal with a warrant for Pearl Hart. Now with the marshal dead, there'd be more of an effort to find out who killed him Brown decided to take the ferry across the river and stop at Jaeger City, California, about a mile from Yuma. The town had been partially restored after the great flood of 1862, but with population decreasing, many of the building were allowed to return to nature. The Butter- fields Overland Mail Company still had an office and station there. In addition, the town had a blacksmith shop, a hotel, two general stores, a livery stable and numerous houses for the in- habitants of the town; many were vacant.

After watering and feeding his two horses, Brown left them at the livery stable for the night. He went to the hotel and took a room. Half of the rooms were available. The town wasn't on the main route to California and would soon become one of the many ghost towns that the desert eventually swallowed up. He ate a quick dinner in the hotel bar and washed it down with a couple of beers and went up to his room. He locked the only window in his room and moved the bureau up against the door and went to sleep, with his colt in his right hand. Around one AM, he woke. Someone was trying to open his door. Brown sat up straight in bed and aimed the gun at the door. Then he heard laughing and someone say, "that's the wrong room. She's in the one at the end of the hall."

Sleep was out of the question now. He cleaned up and sat in the only chair in the room, until the sun rose. The next morning over breakfast, he reviewed his options. The train was out of the question. Going south to Mexicali and west along the border would be as bad as when he went from Naco to Nogales. Bandits could be shadowing him and ready to pounce, whenever he let his guard down. He couldn't forget the gang of six that waited for him south of Nogales. Now the bandits south of the border may not know about the bank robbery in Bisbee, but as a lone rider, he would be vulnerable to whatever outlaw faction, he'd encounter from here to San Diego.

Brown looked out the window and his gaze fell on the two Butterfield Overland Stages that were gathering dust, on a lot next to their office. He paid for breakfast, grabbed a cold beer and walked across the street and into the Butter- field office. "How many stage runs do you have daily?" Brown asked the local manager.

"We have a couple of mail runs, one to Braw-ley and another to El Centro, some passengers runs to the small towns in the area, without rail, but nothing big. Our company is drastically cut- ting back. The train is upon us."

"Is it possible to hire one your stagecoaches for a trip to San Diego or even to Los Angeles?"

"Hell, yes. If you've got the money, I can set that up for you."

"How much do you need?" Brown asked.

"The price is dependent upon what you want. I'll give you what I think you need and you can scale back, if you think it's too much." You'll need two drivers, an extra team of horses, which can be trailed behind the stage. That's because we don't have any stations from here to San Diego and therefore can't change horses. I suggest you stop when necessary and get your own food. I have to carry some extra wheels and pay the drivers for a round trip. I think one thousand dollars would be about right."

"That's too much. I'll pay eight hundred or I'll look at other options. If you can live with eight hundred, I'll want to interview the two drivers."

"It's a deal, but I want six hundred up front and the balance in San Diego. Should you decide to go further, I want a hundred and fifty dollars a day extra. Is that's okay."

"I think a hundred and fifty a day should do it." Brown shook hands and asked to meet with the drivers.

At noon, the Butterfield Manager showed up with two former drivers for Brown's approval. Both were anxious for the work. Neither was very big and didn't appear to be a threat. After a few questions, Brown said he was satisfied and wanted to know if they could leave early the next morning. Everyone agreed. Brown paid the advance and the drivers got the stagecoach and two teams together. That afternoon, he practically gave away his two horses to the manager of the livery stable. He and the two drivers were on their way at five the next morning.

# CHAPTER TWENTY-SEVEN

With a two hour head start, Pearl was confident she'd be able to cross over into Arizona, before any New Mexico, peace officer apprehended her. She was dressed as a young cowhand and avoided any significant towns, until she reached Holbrook Arizona. She stopped in the town to purchase provisions, but didn't stay long so as not to create any unwanted attention. About four in the afternoon, she camped five miles out of town off the road to Flagstaff. She carried a 38 pistol in her saddlebag, but had never fired the weapon in anger. She wondered if she could defend herself, if stalked and challenged by anyone. Throughout her flight from Gallup, she was unwilling to put herself in a position to find out what her capability was. Around six that evening, a rider appeared at her camp and asked for some food. Pearl was apprehensive. The tension of the last few days was wearing on her nerves.

"I don't have much food. I can give you a couple of biscuits, but that's all, provided you take them and leave. "Her voice was shrill and she was extremely nervous.

"You're a woman aren't you? I saw you in Holbrook and wondered why a woman was traveling as a man and alone. Was I wrong?" the stranger asked.

"You can have the biscuits and leave, or you can just leave. Whether I'm a man or a woman is my business. "Pearl was starting to get some of her confidence back. She reached into her saddlebag and grabbed her revolver.

The rider started to get off his horse. Pearl stood up and pointed her gun at the stranger. Pearl pulled her revolver from her saddlebag and pointed it at the stranger. "If you don't leave, I'm going to shoot you."

The stranger sat back on his horse, turned the reins to the left and exited the camp. Pearl knew she'd weathered her first encounter but still wasn't sure if she was safe. Sleep was out of the question. She found a spot against a large rock and sat down with her revolver in her lap. In the back of her mind, she knew she wasn't safe. She kept the fire burning and placed her bed roll near it. Someone looking into the camp would think that she was asleep by the fire. Two hours later, she heard movement to the left.

Pearl squeezed up closer to the rock and pointed her gun out in front of her. She saw the man, who'd asked for food, cautiously approach the bed roll. As he was about to pounce, Pearl shot him in the back and he fell forward landing on her blankets. Pearl walked slowly to the fallen man and turned him onto his back with her foot. She jumped back when she saw the amount of blood gurgling from his chest. The man moved slightly, convulsed and died.

She sat down and cried. Why had this had happened to her, she kept saying over and over to herself. The event seemed to paralyze her for over an hour, before she realized that the body had to be buried. There was only three dollars and some change in the man's pockets, but no identification. Pearl checked the area and found the man's horse and led it into her camp. There was a small shovel attached to his saddle and a poncho in his saddlebag. She dug a small trench, yet deep enough for the man and wrapped the body in the poncho, before rolling him into the grave. She piled dirt over the corpse doused the fire and cleaned. When the embers were out, she took both horses and rode toward Flagstaff. She was still numb. This couldn't be happening to her. Killing someone, even if she felt justified, wasn't anything she wanted to repeat.

There were now two states either not wanting her in their jurisdiction or actively seeking to prosecute her for a crime. She needed to get to California, the most expeditious way possible. While in the Yuma prison, Pearl spent some time looking at the existing maps of California and Arizona. The guards, whom she favored, were more than willing to slip them into her cell for as little as a kiss, a quick feel or a look at her breasts. Though she wasn't able to retain any of the maps, she memorized the routes through the state of Arizona. For her situation, the route to Flagstaff and then on to Phoenix, seemed to be the most realistic.

Maintaining her previously method of traveling, she continued to avoid populated areas and any gathering of people. As she neared Flagstaff, she realized that she could do without sleep and still survive, when confronted.

Three weeks later she was on the outskirts of Phoenix. She found a livery stable, sold both horses and saddles and then rented a room in a cheap hotel. She locked the door and fell asleep. The next morning, still in male attire, she bought a ticket to San Diego and the next day, she boarded the train.

# CHAPTER TWENTY-EIGHT

Jefferson didn't encounter any problems on his way back from Wellton. Since he'd already paid for his room, he returned the rig and went back to his hotel. The next morning he waited outside the sheriff's office until the man returned, Jefferson introduced himself as the sheriff dismounted in front of the jail. He asked about the telegram that the conductor said he couldn't deliver to Marshal Short.

"Give me a few minutes to wipe the dust off and I'll look for it."

Five minutes later the sheriff returned and opened a locked drawer in his desk. He took out the telegram and handed it to Jefferson. The telegram read, "Henry Stills murdered in Rio Rico... have warrant for James Clevenger...Clevenger on train to Yuma...apprehend."

Jefferson wrote down the message and asked about the telegram the sheriff from Gila Bend, had sent. "I got it just after the train arrived from Gila Bend. I went to the depot, but Brown wasn't on the train; he'd gotten off at Wellton, The only reason for him to get off in Wellton was that he sensed he was being followed. I assumed that he was looking for a horse, so he could bypass Yuma. I know all the trails around here, so I went out and tried to track him down. That's where I was when you came to town. I found some tracks but I couldn't be sure it was him. If he got around Yuma, he's probably in Jaeger City on the California side. Just so you know, there's a Butterfield Station there. You never can tell."

Jefferson notified the Pinkerton's main office that Brown was probably heading to San Diego or Los Angeles and may be on a Butterfield Stage. He also informed the company about Pearl Hart, who Marshal Short was trailing and about the telegram reflecting that James Clevenger, who was traveling with Mary Stills, was suspected of killing Stills' husband. Finally he notified them that he was on his way to California

# CHAPTER TWENTY-NINE

Sarah and the other two women decided to take the four children on a picnic, to one of the south pastures. Tommy had developed a man made pond and stocked it with fish, soon after he and Sarah married. School was starting the next month and Sarah thought this would be an ideal time to bond with her two grandchildren and her daughter. Naomi and Naiwa prepared the picnic basket and Tommy had Raul get the buckboard out and hitch up the horses. "Sarah, I'm comfortable if Raul goes along. There's still some wild game in the south pastures. I think one of the vaqueros spotted a mountain lion last week, near where you plan to picnic. I know you can take care of yourself and Naiwa and Naomi can handle the children, but Raul can be an extra set of eyes."

"You know that he and Naiwa are sort of keeping company."

"No. What do you think of that?"

"I've encouraged it. Their only problem is the language. He speaks mostly Spanish and she speaks only Lakota. I've been giving her English lessons and sometimes Raul is in the class, so to speak. They like to go for long walks at night. They're adults, so I don't pry."

"Do her children know what's going on?'

"I think so. I can see them communicating with their eyes when Raul is around. Mostly they have to come to grip with the relationship between the two cultures. The children had very little contact with white people. In fact, the only white people they came in contact with at the reservation told them what to do and where to go. I'm a little apprehensive about school. I don't believe there'll be any Indian children in their class. I know some of the white children will single them out for being different. I'm having Helga and Thomas look out for them. I know they'll feel uncomfortable initially. How long it lasts will be the problem. This is one of those things you can't control. I know that many people resent us for either having Indian blood or for being married to an Indian. Thomas and Helga were asked many questions by their class- mates last year, but their fair looks seem to be giving them a pass so far."

"I've dealt with this prejudice all my life, but I didn't know you were being subjected to it as well. But it sounds like you have everything under control. We'll just have to wait and see. Today, I want you and Raul to carry rifles with you, just in case, "Tommy said.

"You don't really think there's danger, do you?"

"I just like to be careful." With Raul driving and Sarah up front, the eight made their way south to the fish pond while Tommy went back to reviewing the books, for both the wine operation and the cattle business. The vineyard was in its infancy and though they had a good harvest last year, profit was at least two years away. The cattle business had a lot of fluctuations but they still managed a significant profit the last two years and projected an increase in revenue the next three years. He and Sarah had healthy financial statements; hers was primarily in income property back east and in San Francisco.

The number of improvements to the ranch and the purchase of five thousand additional acres from Don Ortega, had forced them to be a little judicious. Tommy still had money coming from his land investments and rail car venture in San Diego and there was ten thousand acres of buildable land remaining in the partnership. Carlos sent a check every six months and he and Sarah were putting that aside for the children. Tommy hadn't seen his friend since Sarah and he were married. He made a note to write to him this week. Tommy realized how fortunate he'd been; nearly everything he invested in, was profitable.

The children picked a spot overlooking the fish pond and the adults spread out blankets, laid out the food while the children played "tag". When they were called for lunch, the children raced over and competed with each other to see who could eat the most. Chatan easily won that contest. He'd been suffering from malnutrition when Sarah and Tommy brought him to their home. Though, a little small for his age, Chatan was assimilating into his new life. He and young Thomas had become good friends and were constantly playing together. Wachiwi was more of a problem. Helga and she were good friends, but Wachiwi was somewhat with- drawn. Sarah set a goal to bring the girl out of her shell.

The four adults sat on the blankets. Naomi, who could speak three languages, told everyone of her life before Sarah found her on the street, penniless and hungry. She'd married a Sioux Brave, who was killed in a raid by American soldiers. After his death, she found work on a small farm caring for three children, but after a long drought, the family's finances were stretched thin and Naomi was without a home. Sarah found her living on the street begging for handouts and took her home. Naiwa shared some of her life at Camp Robinson with Sarah and Juan. She told them how she met her husband at Camp Robinson and their trek to Pine Ridge Reservation. She lived at the reservation for eight years, before her husband was hung for stealing cattle. They had been hungry for most of their married life. The last five years of their marriage were strained. Her husband was always depressed because he couldn't get any work to pay for food.

Raul told the group about his early life in Guadalajara, where he learned to ride. When he was sixteen, he left home with his only possession, his horse and made his way across the border to New Mexico. Because of his riding skills, he was able to find work immediately. Gradually, he made his way to this valley and was hired by Sarah. The two Indian women and Raul raised their wine glasses to toast Sarah. They were thinking of packing up and heading back home, when Thomas came running up. "There're some men on the other side of the hill moving our cattle," he pointed in that direction.

"They're probably my wranglers, but I'll go take a look," Raul said.

"We'll pack up anyway. Naomi, call the children back. I want them to help put the stuff in the wagon, "Sarah directed.

Raul came running back to the wagon. "They're not my men. I can't be sure, but I think its Meade and three others."

Sarah grabbed her rifle and told Naomi and Naiwa to finish packing up. "Raul let's go take a look."

"Mrs. Sanchez, I'm more comfortable if we leave now. I'm not afraid, but I don't want to take a chance with you and the others. I don't think they saw us. They were more interested in stealing some of our cattle."

"Grab the binoculars and your rifle. We're going to take a look."

Raul and Sarah made their way to the top of the knoll overlooking the valley. Sarah asked Raul for the glasses. She could see Meade and two others moving about ten head of cattle through the gate. Sarah fired a few shots at the three but she was too far away to have any effect.

"I know you're not afraid, but I think its best that we go right now," Raul said to Sarah.

She and Raul made their way back to the wagon. Sarah told the children that some bad men were over the hill and for them to keep quiet, until they were near the ranch house. They drove an hour without incident and pulled up in front of the ranch house as Tommy came out. "Boy that was a quick picnic. You barely had time to eat before you came back," Tommy said.

As soon as he uttered the words, Tommy knew something was wrong. "What happened?" Tommy asked Sarah.

"The kids saw some men herding our cattle on the south pasture and Raul and I went to investigate. It was Meade and three others," Sarah answered.

Tommy looked to Raul who acknowledged in Spanish, what Sarah had said. "Raul, saddle my horse and get another vaquero. I know it may be too late, but the three of us are going to the south pasture to see what's up."

Tommy put on his holster and grabbed his rifle and extra ammunition. "What are you going to do?" Sarah asked.

"I'm going to investigate."

It took Tommy, Raul and the other vaquero thirty minutes to cover the distance to the fish pond. When they came over the rise and looked down in the valley where Raul and Sarah saw Meade and the others, there was nothing there, no men and no cattle. "How many head were down there, Raul?"

"There were ten when I saw Meade and his two men."

"Let's see if we can see where they went." Tommy said.

It was easy to track the cattle and find where they went through the fence." It looks like they may be heading back to the Star Ranch. Okay, I've seen enough. Let's head back to the house. I'll figure out what to do."

Sarah was waiting when the three returned. Raul and the vaquero took the horses to the barn and went back to the bunkhouse.

"What did you find?" Sarah asked.

"There were tracks leading to the Star Ranch, through the same hole in the fence."

"What are you going to do?"

"Let's have supper and I'll tell you what I'm going to do."

Dinner time was especially active this evening. The children were all exited about the three men who rustled the cattle. All four children wanted to know where the cattle were taken and what Tommy was going to do. "Are you going after them?" Thomas asked his father.

It was last year at school, that Thomas and Helga learned from the other children that their father was a famous gunfighter and a half breed. They also learned that their mother had been married to Crazy Horse. They were taunted constantly about their Indian ancestry. Tommy and Sarah talked to them as candidly as they could about their past. It seemed to satisfy both children, but the addition of Naiwa and her two children could raise some of the same issues. It wasn't lost on Helga and Thomas that their parents spoke Sioux to Chatan and Wachiwi.

"Since Tommy didn't answer his son, the boy asked him again what he was going to do about the stolen cattle. "I'm going to get the cattle back," Tommy responded.

"But what if they won't give them back?" Thomas pressed.

"This the last word on this subject, I'll get them back."

Around eleven that evening Tommy slipped out of the house wearing moccasins, riding pants and a poncho. His head was covered with a dark handkerchief and his face was painted black; he was carrying two knifes. After riding south for a mile, he tethered his horse to a tree and hopped over the fence, leading to the Star Ranch. He knew the layout of Singleton's home, because he went inside with Singleton when he and sheriff tried to serve warrants on Meade. Tommy was also aware that there were two dogs roaming outside at night. When he was within fifty feet of the house, the dogs sensed his presence and started to growl. Tommy threw them some meat laced with a sleeping potion and the dogs leaped at the morsels and devoured them quickly. Tommy waited five minutes and the dogs lay down. He knew they 'd be out two to three hours, which was enough time for him to accomplish what he wanted.

He assumed the two small bedrooms were for the two men he shot in the legs. Equipped with a potion that the Indians used to subdue their victims, Tommy made his way to one room and then the other. He put both Simmers and Hodges to sleep and then tied them to their headboards. Neither gave him any trouble, so he made his way to where Singleton slept.

The man was lying on his back, snoring. Tommy tied one wrist and then the other to the bed post, before Singleton woke and struggled to move. "I want you to be quiet while Ito talk to you. If you make a sound, I'll slit your throat," Tommy said.

"You can't get away with this."

"I already did. If I tell you to shut up one more time, I'll really slit your throat. Now, I want you to listen to me and don't talk until I'm finished. Do you understand?" Tommy put his knife to Singleton's throat and Singleton eyes got big, but he nodded that he understood.

"My wife and I are tired of being harassed. Today Meade stole ten head of our cattle. I want them returned." Singleton started to speak and Tommy cut the skin around his throat, and a trickle of blood formed. Tommy put some blood on his finger and showed it to Singleton.

"I don't think you intend to be a good neighbor, no matter what you say. So I'm going to teach you a lesson."

Tommy poured some water on Singleton's hair and when it was soaked enough, he shaved Singleton's scalp and left the hair on the pillow. Singleton didn't move a muscle. Tommy put a gag in Singleton's mouth and cut off the lobe of his left ear. Singleton struggled violently and tried to cry out but the gag in his mouth pre- vented that. Tears flowed from his eyes when Tommy put a solution on the lobe, to stop the bleeding.

When Singleton finished struggling, Tommy spoke softly to him. "I want my ten head of cattle back no later than the day after tomorrow. I also want Meade fired and I want him to leave this area. I want you and your men to leave me and my family alone. Now if you don't do what I say, I'll come back another night and cut off the other lobe. There's no way you can protect yourself. I got in here tonight and you have two men in the house and two dogs outside. I can get in any time I want. Do you want to wait the rest of your life for me to show up? I want you to nod that you understand everything I've said." Singleton nodded his head five times.

"If you think that after I'm gone, you can refuse to return my cattle, I'll find you and cut your throat. Do you understand?" Singleton nodded his head again. Tommy left all three men tied up for the housekeeper, who lived in a shack near the bunkhouse.

Tommy slipped out the front door, checked on the two dogs. They were breathing normally, so he went over the fence joining the two properties. He picked up his horse and rode back. Sarah was waiting. "How did it go?"

He picked Sarah up in his arms. "Want to make love to an Indian?"

"I thought you'd never ask."

# CHAPTER
# THIRTY

**P**earl waited until the train made its last stop before Los Angeles, to change into a dress. She fixed her hair, put on red lipstick and discarded her male clothes. She was going to face whatever was waiting for her, as a woman. She was tired of posing as a man. Pearl Hart had finally made it to California. She had nineteen hundred dollars left from the money she stole from the cattle buyer. She wanted a new life.

Waiting for all the passengers to get off the train, increased her anxiety. Finally, she stepped off the train and looked around to see if anyone was watching her. When she realized that everyone was in a hurry and no one noticed her, she relaxed and walked into the train station. Although there were policemen in the station, none seemed to be particularly interested in her; they were just milling around. Horse drawn cabs were lined up outside the station. Pearl cautiously approached the first cab in line. She asked the driver if he could recommend a nice hotel for a single lady.

"I'd recommend the Clareton on Spring Street, Lady."

"Take me there."

"Is this your first visit to Los Angles?"

"Yes."

On the ride to the hotel, Pearl saw automobiles, bicycles, an electric trolley car and horse drawn vehicles moving side by side on the downtown streets. Iron rails were embedded in the street for the electric trolleys to ride on. Plastered on the side of one of the electric trolleys, was an advertisement for Buffalo Bill's Wild West Show.

The driver carried Pearl's bags into the hotel and told the receptionist that the lady was looking for a room. Pearl was in awe of the magnificent wood paneling, the huge chandeliers hanging from the ceiling and the assorted upholstered chairs and couches in the lobby. After Pearl signed in, the receptionist hit a bell and a young man showed up. He picked up her two bags and carried them up to her room on the second floor. The room had a view of Spring Street and what amazed Pearl was that she had her own bathroom. "Dinner is served at eight in the main dining room. I can have the desk make a reservation for you, if you want?" the bell boy said.

"I wonder if I have suitable clothes for the hotel dining room?" Pearl asked the porter.

"What you have on miss, is suitable."

"Is it suitable to be an unescorted female in the dining room?"

"Yes. Some of our guests are unescorted females." Pearl tipped the boy a dollar.

After she was comfortable with her appearance, Pearl walked down the stairs into the lobby and over to the registration desk. Several brochures were neatly stacked along the long desk. Pearl picked a few that outlined the attractions of Los Angeles. There was a separate advertisement for

Buffalo Bill's Wild West Show, promising a ten cent discount for Clare- ton Hotel Guests. Pearl was more exited about the wild west show than the steak dinner she ordered in the dining room. She carried all the brochures up to her room and read them two more times.

The next morning she hired a horse drawn cab to take her to the fairground and bought a ticket for the afternoon show; she wasn't disappointed. There was a reenactment of the Battle of the Little Big Horn and the crowd booed the Indians, when they shot the actor, who was playing George Armstrong Custer. Two patrons hopped onto the arena grounds and tried to help Custer's men. They had to be restrained and were escorted out of the complex. After a brief intermission, there was a reenactment of a wagon train being attacked by Indians. The crowd cheered when the Indians were repulsed by the arrival of the US Cavalry. But the main attraction was the target shooting contest be- tween Buffalo Bill Cody and Annie Oakley. After twenty shots at four different targets, Annie Oakley emerged as the winner. Pearl stood and clapped until her hands hurt.

After the show Pearl walked around until she found Buffalo Bill's tent. He was alone when she walked in. "I'm sorry Miss, but the show is over. You can come back tomorrow if you'd like, for just half price."

"Are you hiring?"

"It depends on what you can do and maybe who you are. We need to sell tickets, you know."

"Well I'm Pearl Hart. I'm the only woman who ever robbed a stagecoach. In fact, I'm the last person to rob a stagecoach."

"I've seen your picture in the Gazette. I thought you were in jail."

"I was, but my sentence was reduced, though they asked me not to come back to Arizona. New Mexico might not be too healthy either."

"Are you wanted?"

Pearl lied. "Not that I know."

"You know we travel a lot. We go to Europe nearly every year. Does that interest you?"

"It does. I'd like a job with your show, Mr. Cody."

"It'll take me a few days to figure out how we can use you, probably a stagecoach robbery. Come back tomorrow around ten in the morning, bring your stuff and we'll have you fill out an application. You can room with Annie Oakley until we get squared away. Is that okay?" Pearl was too stunned to say anything; she nodded her head twice.

Pearl stayed another night at the Carleton and the next morning reported to the fair- grounds. Buffalo Bill was sitting in a chair in the middle of the arena. He asked her to sit down in one of chairs next to him. "I think I've got it figured out. We have the Custer battle; the wagon train battle and I think the stagecoach robbery would work this way. We'll have the robbery on one end of the arena and you, dressed as a man, rob the stage. Then, you and your partner ride off and go into the saloon on the other side of the arena. The sheriff will ride up and ask the passengers what happened. They'll point toward the saloon and he'll come after you; I'll play the sheriff. When I come into the saloon, I'll say hands up and your partner will go for his gun. I'll shoot your partner and when I learn you're a woman, I'll turn to the audience and ask them what to do with you. What do you think?"

"I'm all for it, when do we start?"

It'll take us about a day to set it up and another day to rehearse the scene. As far as compensation is concerned, we share every- thing around here. I get three shares, Annie gets two shares and everyone including you, gets one share each. Should we bring in someone to pump up sales, we'll pay them as if they were a contractor. After we clean up and all expenses are paid, we split what's left. Some days we make a lot; other days we don't get anything. Do you have a problem with the arrangement?"

"I'm all in." Pearl couldn't control the smile on her face. She was elated.

Just as Bill finished laying out the scenario for Pearl, a tall man walked into the tent and sat down next to them. He was blond, lean and good looking. "This is Casey Puller. He'll be your partner in the holdup."

Pearl took one look at the good looking young man and her heart skipped a beat; she nearly wet her pants. She wondered if her luck had changed.

Moving out of the Carleton and into the wild west community was like a dream come true for Pearl. Her new tent mate, Annie Oakley, had her quirks but she was fun to be around. The rehearsal went smoothly, so they decided to see how it worked with a Friday Audience. Pearl was nervous, but Casey told her not to worry; it would come out all right. So at noon, the stage- coach came into the arena and Pearl and Casey hid behind a false rock and held up the stage. Pearl reenacted the scene where she gave back the dollar to the passengers, and the audience clapped. When she was captured by Buffalo Bill, playing a sheriff, the audience voted to let her go free. Some days, the audience voted to have her put in jail.

In October the show took the boat to England; Pearl met the queen, who came to see the show. After the evening show there was a reception and a receiving line for the queen. When it was Pearl's time to be presented, the queen asked, "so you're the woman who robbed the stage in America?"

Pearl blushed and could barely speak, but she curtseyed and blurted out, "yes mum."

# CHAPTER THIRTY-ONE

**I**t took nearly thirty hours to reach Los Angeles by stagecoach. Brown spent that time reviewing his options and finally decided to bypass Los Angeles. He told the drivers to continue to Ventura. He wasn't sure what kind of welcoming committee was waiting for him in the big city, so he decided to be extra careful. The two drivers were elated. They'd been working part time for a year and were delighted to make some solid money for a change. In fact, if Brown had asked them to take him to San Francisco, they would've been happy. The only request they had for Brown was to telegraph their Butterfield Office and get their concurrence. "I'd rather let your company know after I arrived some place, instead of telling them where I'm going. If that's not okay with you, we'll part company now."

Both drivers said that was okay with them as long as they got paid for the extra time. Ventura, circa nineteen hundred was enjoying a major influx of immigrants from the east coast. Fueling the migration was the climate, the arrival of the Southern Pacific Railroad Station, natural resources and specifically a burgeoning oil industry. Construction was going up every- where, with most of the new construction being performed by immigrant Chinese laborers. Consequently, there was a major block of Chinese living in the immediate area, which created a backlash with the white settlers. Though the Chinese were needed for construction and other menial jobs, their presence was considered a threat to the community. Eventually, they were restricted to four blocks within the city.

The town was named San Buenaventura until eighteen hundred eighty nine, when the post office made the decision to change it to Ventura. About this time, seventy percent of wooden buildings were converted to brick. Almost all of the main streets went through a significant upgrade.

The stagecoach drivers dropped him at the Rose Hotel on Main Street. He released the two drivers, once he was assured that the hotel had a room available. Brown paid the drivers a bonus and asked them not to let their company know where they dropped him, until they got back to Jaeger City. It was Sunday evening and his first order of business the next day was to find a bank that would take cash. He was tired of not sleeping at night, because he had to watch the money. Ventura wasn't that far from his final destination. He was confident from his many talks with Herbert that money could be moved from bank to bank, which meant he didn't have to be in the same city, as his nest egg.

Brown met with the president of two different banks the next day to see which one would be easier to deal with. He wanted to be sure that he wasn't creating too much attention, if he deposited nearly fifty thousand dollars into a checking account. He made up a story about selling a herd of cattle in Los Angeles and taking cash in lieu of a bank draft. Neither banker seemed too concerned, about the amount of cash being deposited in their bank. But Brown wasn't comfortable with either, so he decided to wait until he reached Santa Barbara.

Back at the hotel, Brown had a lunch of crab cakes and a bottle of Chardonnay and thought about his situation. He didn't want to chance using the train to get to Santa Barbara, so he decided to take the steamer boat, "The Pride of California". He bought a new black suit, black Stetson, white shirt and had his boots polished before he embarked on the short trip north. He'd made reservations at the Arlington Hotel for two nights and had a carriage waiting for him, when he arrived at Stearns Wharf. It was a short ride to the hotel.

The next day he interviewed the presidents of two of the largest banks in town. He felt comfortable enough to deposit twenty four thousand dollars each, into checking accounts in their banks. No eyebrows were raised; both bankers seemed to act like this was a common day occurrence. Brown felt that a load had been lifted from his back. He celebrated with a steak and a bottle of Merlot at the Arlington. He wanted some action and was referred to a couple of night spots down State Street, but declined. He could always come back another time.

Train service north still was some way off, so he booked a seat on the stagecoach to Los Olivos the next morning. Brown hadn't felt this relaxed since the Bisbee robbery. He boarded the stage along with two other passengers and looked forward to the trip. Half way to Santa Ynez, there was an hour stop at Cold Springs Tavern. The delay was only an hour and the passengers could stretch their legs, get a fine meal served by Mrs. Kinevan and the driver could change horses. The stagecoach had just come over the San Marcos Pass, when Brown felt the stage come to a complete stop. He wondered if they were at the stagecoach stop. Just then, he heard someone shout, "get out of the stage and put your hands in the air."

Brown and the other three passengers stepped out of the stage and faced two men with guns pointing at them. He and the other two were quickly disarmed and told to clean out their pockets. They put their valuables including any jewelry into a hat the bandits had placed on the ground. Brown tried to bluff his way through the situation by telling the robbers, he wasn't carrying any money. One of the robbers hit him alongside the head and Brown fell to the ground. His wallet with nearly two thousand dollars was taken from him. With that much cash, the bandits were in a good mood and didn't abuse the passengers, as was common when a stage was robbed.

Brown got to his feet in time to see the two bandits ride down the hill toward Santa Ynez. Although the bandits wore masks, Brown knew he'd recognize their horses, if he ever saw them again. His gun had been thrown in the bushes alongside the road by one of the bandits. Brown asked the stagecoach driver if he saw where the gun was thrown. The driver led him to the spot and Brown picked up his pistol. He was bleeding freely from the gash on the side of his head, but he was alert and especially angry.

"I'm worried about the wound on your head. Mrs. Kinevan is good at fixing wounds and getting the bleeding to stop.Let's all get in the coach and head to Cold Springs Tavern," the driver told Brown and the other two passengers.

When the coach arrived at the stagecoach stop, Mrs. Kinevan got out her medical kit, and gave Brown a half glass of whiskey. He drank all of it and when he was numb enough, she put five stitches in the gash on the side of his scalp. "Don't worry honey. It doesn't look too bad. You can take the stitches out in a week. I don't think you'll have a scar. Even if there is one, the ladies will like it," she laughed.

"Can someone loan me a horse. I'm not going to let someone hit me on the head, steal my money and take my gun."

"It's too dangerous. Let the sheriff handle it," Mrs. Kinevan said.

Brown reached in one of his boots where he'd hidden a diamond stick pin. The robbers weren't looking in his boots, after they found all that cash in his wallet. "I'll let you hold this stick pin until I return the horse. In addition, I'll give you fifty dollars just for the use of the horse," Brown told Mrs. Kinevan.

"If you want them that bad, I'm not going to stand in your way." Kinevans had two horses in a corral out back with a saddle hanging over the fence. Brown saddled up one of the horses. "Anybody got an idea where the two might have headed?" Brown asked the people at the stage- coach stop.

"I've heard that a lot of bandits hang out in a shack on Paradise Road about three miles from here. It's kind of a saloon. You don't want to go there by yourself. Why don't you wait for the sheriff? You can stay here a couple of days until he gets here. I think you could use the time to let your head heal,"Mrs. Kinevan tried to talk Brown out of it, but without much success.

"I'm going as soon as I have some lunch."

The stagecoach driver gave Brown directions to the shack on Paradise Road, and off he went. About a mile and a half down the stagecoach trail, Brown found the cutoff that the stagecoach driver said would take him to the shack. Initially the trail was all downhill and then it leveled out. Ten minutes later, Brown could see the cabin like structure ahead. As he got closer he saw the horses the robbers used, tied to a rail. But there were four other horses next to those two. Brown wasn't sure what awaited him inside the shanty, so he decided to wait until some of the other patrons left, or the two robbers came outside. He tied his horse to some brush and sat down under a tree. He was sure he couldn't be seen from this location, but could see anyone who entered or exited the cabin. He wasn't feeling well. His head hurt and there was still a trace of blood coming from his wound. Two hours later, four men came out, mounted their horses and rode off to the east.

Brown made his way to the porch of the old building and looked over the cafe doors leading inside. He could see a small bar in the right corner of a large room and two men, who he assumed were the robbers, standing at the bar, each with one foot on a rail. A bartender was pouring one of the men a drink when he looked up and saw Brown. "Come on in and have a drink, stranger."

The two men looked up and appeared to be in shock as they saw Brown come through the door with his gun pointing at them. The two robbers looked at each other. It appeared to Brown that they were trying to decide what to do. One of the men reached for his gun and Brown shot him in the shoulder. The other man raised his hands while the bartender just stood, and watched.

"I've come for my money. Either hand it over or I'm going to kill you right where you stand. "

"Now, you can't do that," The bartender said."

"Shut up or I'll shoot you too."

Brown walked up to the bar and addressed the man with his hands up. "I want my money and I want it now."

"He's got it. " He pointed to the man on the floor."

"Drop your gun on the floor and then get my money. Don't even think of doing anything foolish. I just as soon kill you."

The robber dropped his gun on the floor, retrieved Brown's wallet and handed it to him "We spent some money in here, but the rest is there."

"How much did you spend in here?" "Maybe, a couple of hundred."

Brown turned to the bartender. "Give me what they spent, unless you want me to put a slug in your leg."

The bartender reached under the bar and took out two one hundred dollar bills and handed it to Brown. "That's considered robbery in these parts mister."

Brown turned to the two bandits. "I'm keeping your horses. Maybe that'll make up for the stitches I have in my head."

After counting the money and finding that he had nineteen hundred dollars left, Brown slowly made his way to the door. "If anyone follows me, I'll kill them. Do you understand?" The bartender nodded as did one of the bandits. The other man was thrashing on the dirt floor clutching his wound. Brown mounted his horse and took the robbers' horses with him.

He had a choice to make. He could ride twenty miles to Santa Ynez or go back to the stagecoach stop and take the stage tomorrow. He decided to ride to Santa Ynez. Going back would raise a lot of issues and may get the sheriff involved. He'd rather ride the twenty miles.

# CHAPTER THIRTY-TWO

It took Brown the remainder of the day to reach Santa Ynez, book a room at the Central Hotel and stable the three horses in the local livery. The next morning, he went back to the livery stable and sold one of the two horses he took from the robbers. He also made arrangements with the owner to have the horse he borrowed, returned to the owners of the Kinevan Kitchen, along with fifty dollars. In his note to Mrs. Kinevan, he asked that she return his stick pin. Brown went to the barber shop where he had a shave, a haircut and a bath, while they cleaned and pressed his suit. After the barber shop, he strolled along Sagunto Street peering into the windows of the seven or eight shops along one side of the street. It was noon by then, so he went back to the hotel for lunch.

When Sarah was twelve, she discovered that she liked to draw pictures of the livestock on their small farm in Pennsylvania. Six months later she started to work on portraits and had her older brother James, pose for her. When she was captured by the Sioux at the age of thirteen, her entire outlook was one of survival. It wasn't until she was married to Crazy Horse, that she renewed her interest in her art. Most of her subjects initially, were the Indians in her village. Later, she concentrated on the tribal leaders wearing ceremonial dress, braves on horseback and the many women in the village who worked so hard. Her first efforts were using charcoal to sketch; when she was able to obtain canvas and oils, she translated the sketches to oil.

After her brother James visited her at Camp Robinson and told her that she was semi wealthy, she joined him in Harrisburg. Later, Sarah enrolled in an art academy in Philadelphia and subsequently was able to make a reasonable living, painting portraits. When she moved to San Francisco, she concentrated on sailing ships, especially since her love at the moment, owned a sailing ship. When her lover was drowned at sea, she turned inward and started to paint in earnest. Surprisingly, she looked to the past and painted colorful portraits of the Indians and the villages where she was a captive.

When Sarah moved to the Santa Ynez Valley, she placed her artwork on consignment with Mattei's Tavern. The paintings were displayed in a room off the lobby where she and Naomi spent most of their days. Subsequently, Sarah purchased a parcel of land from Don Ortega, built her home and moved her paintings to the Central Hotel in Santa Ynez, because it was so much closer. Her marriage to Tommy Sanchez and subsequent motherhood had taken all her free time and she neglected her art. But that changed after the family returned from Philadelphia. Over the past year she'd completed five paintings, which were hanging in the lobby of the Central Hotel. Management was more than glad to show her work. Not only was Sarah a talented artist, but she and her husband were some of the original investors in the hotel.

Once a month, she and Naomi travelled to Santa Ynez to view her works and see whether any paintings were sold. Today, they would take Naiwa with them. Her daughter was still self conscious about being around white people and Sarah was trying to take her out in public more often. Naiwa needed to gain confidence and practice her English. But Naiwa was reticent and wouldn't try to engage, even though her English was improving; the adjustment would take time. One of the vaqueros drove the three women to town. While the women were at the hotel, he picked up supplies at the general store and then waited for the women in the carriage outside the hotel.

The hotel manager rushed up to Sarah as she and the two women entered the lobby."Mrs. Sanchez, we sold one of your painting last week and I have a bank draft for the purchase price."

The picture was a portrait of Red Cloud. Sarah planned to send the proceeds of the sale to the Pine Ridge Reservation. Naiwa didn't understand why the manager was so happy, so Sarah told her in Lakota what happened. Naiwa smiled and hugged Sarah.

When Brown entered the hotel, he saw a very attractive blond woman with two Indian squaws looking at the paintings in the lobby; he was interested. The hotel manager was with the three women and when he saw Brown, he invited him over to meet Mrs. Sarah Sanchez and look at her paintings, that the hotel was fortunate to display in their lobby.

"I admired these paintings last night when I arrived and now I have the pleasure of meeting the artist." Brown tipped his hat as Sarah smiled. She was flattered but apprehensive, as she looked at the handsome stranger.

"I can see that they're exclusively of Native Americans. Do you do landscapes or impressionists?" Brown asked Sarah.

"I did when I was back east, but this is what I like to do."

"I especially liked this one." Brown pointed to a colorful painting of an Indian Warrior, who appeared to be in full battle dress.

It's s one of my favorites. It's a picture of Crazy Horse, just before the battle of the Little Big Horn." Brown couldn't help notice the sparkle in Sarah's eye, as she told him about the painting.

"I'm familiar with the story. This seems to be one of your favorites. Had you ever met Crazy Horse?"

"Yes, but I painted this from memory."

"How much are you asking for the painting?"

"The listed price on the back is, four hundred dollars."

Brown turned to the manager. "I'm going to buy this painting and I'd like you to put it in my room. But the sale is condition on you three ladies having lunch with me in the hotel dining room. I hear the chef is the best in this area."

Sarah was a little flustered and turned to Naomi and Naiwa, who gave no indication of their preference. Sarah was torn, but Brown seemed so charming and he did buy one of her paintings. She didn't think there'd be a problem. "We'd be delighted Mr. Brown, lead the way."

As they were being seated, Brown turned to Sarah. "The clerk said you were Mrs. Sanchez. Where is Mr. Sanchez?"

"He's home tending our twins."

"I haven't been introduced to these two women. "Brown said looking first at Naiwa and then Naomi.

"Naomi has been my companion for nearly eight years and Naiwa is my natural daughter. She and her two children have come to live with us." Brown didn't ask, but he assumed that Crazy Horse might be more than a figure in a painting.

"Were you a captive of the Sioux?"

"Yes. I was a captive for five years before I married into the tribe."

"Was Crazy Horse your Indian husband?"

"How did you know?"

"You seem to be very fond of the painting that I bought. Do you live close by Mrs. Sanchez?"

Sarah knew that Brown was flirting with her but she'd had a glass of wine and didn't think Tommy would be jealous. "My husband and I own Altura Prado Ranch, about two miles from here. The English translation for the ranch is High Meadow. Enough about me, what are you doing in the Santa Ynez Valley?"

"I had some free time between projects and had always wanted to visit California. Luckily, I found this valley; it's beautiful. I have a cousin living here that I haven't seen for years. I thought I'd look him up and then decide how long, I'll be here."

"What's your cousin's name? I know most people in the valley."

"Earl Singleton."

When Sarah and the two women left, Brown approached the manager. "I didn't realize that you allowed Indians into the hotel?"

"Normally, we don't. But since they're with Mrs. Sanchez, the hotel doesn't make an issue of it. Besides, her husband is one of the hotel owners. I can't ask her not to bring the two women and keep my job .

"How close do the Sanchez' live to my cousin Earl Singleton?"

"The Sanchez own Altura Prado Ranch. It's a ten thousand acre parcel just south of the town, with the entrance about two miles from here. Your cousin's place borders it on the south end."

"What's the husband like?"

"He's always been pleasant to me; he owns substantial real estate holdings in the area. The sheriff uses him at times to help with tracking outlaws; Sanchez is probably the best tracker in the area."

"Is Sanchez Mexican?"

"I can't say for sure but the rumor is that he's half white and half Sioux. He's not large in stature but he's someone that you don't want to cross. I was on Sagunto Street five years ago when he was braced by three men in the street. They goaded him into putting on his guns. After he put on his guns, he walked up to the three men and shot their hats off. He drew faster than any man I've ever seen. It was just a blur. If I hadn't seen it, I wouldn't have believed it. It was so amazing. Then one of the men challenged him to take off his guns. The man was much bigger than Mr.

Sanchez, but that didn't seem to matter. Mr. Sanchez took off his guns beat the man badly in front of many of the town's people and told him and the other two to leave town."

"What was the man's name he beat and told to leave town?"

"Ed Meade. He works for Earl Singleton,"

# CHAPTER THIRTY-THREE

**B**rown was one of the most elusive criminals that Jefferson had ever encountered. The man seemed to have an uncanny sense when to move to another locale or when to alter his plans, when he sensed that he was about to be caught or was in danger. When Brown perceived a threat, he either tried to avoid it or eliminate it, and that took time. But Jefferson had one thing that made him unique. He had a history of tracking all kinds of outlaws. He knew that some would try desperately to gain as much distance between themselves and the pursuer. But there would be some criminals like Brown, who wouldn't make a move, without giving it a lot of thought. Jefferson knew that Brown was probably a week ahead, but traveling by train would narrow the advantage that Brown had built up. When Jefferson reached California, he knew he'd only be two or three days behind, perhaps even less.

Jefferson had spent thirty years of his life with the Pinkertons and was a master detective. Coming out of the civil war at the age of eighteen, he was already a man and a crack shot. He started as a stagecoach guard for Wells Fargo and slowly progressed to assisting more experienced Pinkerton Detectives in tracking down wanted fugitives. He earned his first spur when he ably assisted Frank Geyer in the capture of H. H. Holmes, the country's first serial killer. Geyer had gotten a tip that Holmes was holed up on a small farm in Knob Knoster, Missouri. He asked Jefferson to assist him in the capture. In order to confirm that Holmes was in a shack on the farm, someone had to crawl up to the house, look in the window and make sure that Holmes was there. Jefferson was volunteered.

After crawling one hundred yards, he stood up and looked in the window. Holmes was lying on a couch in the parlor. He immediately signaled Geyer, who burst through the front door and captured the fugitive. Later, he became an assistant to James McFarland who would infiltrate the famous Molly McGuires' and arrest the ringleaders. Jefferson also backed up McFarland, when he arrested Harry Orchard for trying to assassinate Governor Steunenburg of Idaho, supposedly on orders of the labor union.

Jefferson was astute enough to know that the Pinkerton Agency had changed over the years and in many ways, not for the good. Yet, he remained loyal to the company and was a personal friend of Allan Pinkerton, until the man died in eighteen hundred ninety four.

The Pinkerton Agency started out inauspiciously working with the state and federal government, in preventing crime and capturing wanted outlaws. Many agents served as bodyguards to well known businessmen and even worked for President Abraham Lincoln during the civil war as spies, infiltrating the confederate army. After the civil war ended, the orientation of the company shifted to penetrating labor unions, acting as strike breakers and supporting big business against labor. Still, they had a law apprehension division, in which James T. Jefferson earned his stripes.

In the eighteen nineties, Pinkerton, or the Pinkerton National Detective Agency, as it was later called, was a formidable company, with twenty offices in the major cities of the United States. They had two thousand active agents and thirty thousand agents in reserve. They were such a potential force that the state if Illinois wouldn't issue them a license, for fear they could muster the thirty thousand into an army, and take over the state.

The sheriff was correct when he suggested that Jefferson go to Jaaeger City. He found the Butterfield Stage Office and quickly learned that Brown had rented a stage, two drivers and two teams of horses. They'd left for Los Angeles four days earlier.

"Were there any other arrangements, such as keeping the stage for a longer period of time or going to another city, other than Los Angeles?" Jefferson asked the station manager.

"What I do know is that we settled on a daily fee for any extra time he wanted the stage and drivers. My sense is that he was going to California, but not necessarily to Los Angles or San Diego. It's just a hunch on my part. My men will inform me just before they start back."

"Have your men notified you where they were in the past few days?"

"No."

"I'd like to stay over tonight and see if you get a telegram in the morning. The train leaves at two in the afternoon from Yuma to Los Angeles. Can I get a ride back to Yuma in the morning?

"Yes. We'll take you there. I suggest you leave no later than ten thirty tomorrow morning." Jefferson stayed overnight in the same hotel, probably the same room as Brown. He had breakfast the next morning at the same spot as Brown, days earlier. He was packed, had his two suitcases already on the stage and was just waiting on the hotel porch to see if a dispatch would come, before he had to leave. He wasn't disappointed. At ten o'clock, the Butterfield manager walked across the road, sat down on the porch next to Jefferson and handed him a message, "Leaving Ventura Cal today for home." Jefferson couldn't suppress a smile as he got up. He walked across the street and boarded the stage.

When he arrived in Yuma, Jefferson bought a ticket for Los Angeles. He wired the Pinkerton office in Los Angeles and asked them to send someone to Ventura to follow up on Brown. Jefferson planned to be in Los Angeles tonight and take the train to Ventura tomorrow. Well Mr. Brown, we're going to be seeing each other very soon. Don't spend all the money, before I get there.

# CHAPTER THIRTY-FOUR

It took Brown only thirty minutes to reach the entrance of the Star Ranch on Santa Barbara Road and five more minutes to ride to Singleton's small framed house. The place seemed deserted, but soon the house-keeper appeared. Brown explained what his relationship was with Singleton. She told him that Singleton and two cowhands went looking for stolen cattle two days ago; she didn't know when they'd be back. "There are two wounded men inside who were shot by Mr. Sanchez, When Mr. Singleton returns, he has to take them to a doctor."

"I'll stay in the bunk house until Singleton returns, if that's okay?"

"It's okay with me. Do you want something to eat? We have plenty."

Brown could tell that Sarah Sanchez was somewhat older than he, but the woman was a beauty. Brown was determined to have her with or without her husband's permission. The Central Hotel Manager told him that Sarah came into town twice a month on a Friday to do shopping. Normally, only one of Indian women accompanied her. He smiled anticipating their next encounter.

Jefferson stayed overnight in the Parkway House in downtown Los Angeles. The next morning he met with the resident Pinkerton Detective and two of his associates. Jefferson asked if they'd been able to determine if Brown had stopped in Los Angeles or had just bypassed the city in favor of Ventura.

"We know that the Butterfield Stage carrying Brown bypassed Los Angeles and Brown ended his journey in Ventura. We interviewed the two drivers. They couldn't swear to it, but both thought he took the steamer north, probably to Santa Barbara."

"Have you made any inquiries into the towns north of Ventura?" Jefferson asked.

"We sent two men to Santa Barbara with a sketch of Brown and here's what they uncovered. A man matching Brown's description took the steamer to Santa Barbara and the next day took the stage to Santa Ynez. That stage was robbed at San Marcos Pass. Subsequently, the passengers were taken to Kinevan's Kitchen, which is the stagecoach stop, near the pass. Brown had been struck in the head by one of the robbers and Mrs. Kinevan put in five stitches to stop the bleeding. Brown decided to go after the robbers. He borrowed a horse from the Kinevans, with a promise to repay them and return the horse. Later that day, a man matching Brown's description wounded one man at the shack on Paradise Road, about five miles from the stagecoach stop. Brown took their horses and wallet. Though the two who robbed the stage were masked, the two wounded men were probably the stagecoach robbers. Kinevan's horse was returned by the stagecoach driver two days later, along with fifty dollars from Brown, who was in Santa Ynez."

"Do we know of any connection that Brown might have in Santa Ynez," Jefferson asked.

"None, that we can find."

Before the meeting adjourned, Jefferson asked about the other two cases he'd wired the Pinkerton office about. "We know that Pearl Hart is in town and working in Buffalo Bill's Wild West Show. Since the warrant on her is a state warrant, we didn't do anything. I don't in- tend to approach her unless there's federal war- rant. The show is leaving for London, by boat in October. I assume she'll go with the troop," the Pinkerton Detective responded.

"What about Clevenger and Mary Stills? He's a suspect in the Stills murder. I don't know how the wife fits in, but she's not with her husband. I can only assume that she knows that her husband's dead"

"They came in on the train and were picked up by Mr. and Mrs. Henry B. Filman, who own a ranch near San Bernardino. I'm sorry, but we were shorthanded at the time they arrived and we couldn't follow up. As far as we know the two are still at the ranch. We'll send a couple of agents to interview him. What are your plans?"

"I'm going to Santa Barbara first and then on to Santa Ynez to see if I can find Mr. Brown. I have two acquaintances living in Santa Ynez. Their names are Tommy and Sarah Sanchez. You can contact me at their Altura Prado Ranch.

"We have an agent living in Santa Barbara, who you may want to contact. He's somewhat older, but he's a good man. His name is George Howard."

Jefferson smiled. He'd known Howard for thirty years. It would be good to swap some old stories or maybe some small lies with a colleague. Before he left on the steamer from Los Angeles, Jefferson sent two telegrams. One went to Santa Ynez to let Tommy Sanchez know he was coming to the valley. The other was to George Howard, suggesting dinner at eight the following evening at the Arlington Hotel, where Jefferson would stay in Santa Barbara.

Jefferson could've taken the train north to Santa Barbara, but he opted for the steamer. The trip was without incident and the boat docked at Stearns Wharf around six in the evening. Jefferson took a carriage to the Arlington Hotel. After he checked into his room and freshened up, he went down to the lounge to have a drink and wait for Howard. He wasn't disappointed. Although a little older, Howard looked the same when he and Jefferson were guards on Wells Fargo stage lines. Howard had become a town marshal, then a railroad detective before be- coming a Pinkerton. He'd been married twice; both wives had passed away. He'd been living in the foothills of Santa Barbara for the past five years. After two drinks, they were driven to a fish house near the wharf where Jefferson had docked this afternoon. They both ordered crab cakes and red snapper. After dinner they came back to the hotel and went to the lounge to have a nightcap. Jefferson filled Howard in on what he knew about Brown and the bank robbery in Bisbee.

"Everything tells me that he unloaded most of the bank funds somewhere between Ventura and The San Marcos pass, where he was robbed of nearly two thousand dollars. Brown recovered about seventeen hundred from the two possible stage robbers, and two hundred from the bartender. If he had the entire fifty one thousand with him at the time of the stage robbery, they would've taken it. So where is it? My best guess is that he deposited the money in one or more banks, either in Ventura or Santa Barbara. I suggest we talk to the banks in Santa Barbara first. We can always take the train back to Ventura, if we strike out here. What's your take?" Howard asked.

"I think you're right. Let's talk to the bankers in Santa Barbara tomorrow and show them Brown's sketch. Now they may not want to tell us anything, because the deposit of fifty one thousand dollars makes them look good, especially to their stockholders. But I can read men pretty well and I'll be able to tell if they're holding back anything from us," Jefferson said.

He and Howard met the next morning at the Arlington and formulated a plan. They'd visit only the three banks in Santa Barbara that had sufficient assets. They assumed that Brown wouldn't leave his hard earned loot, with a bank that could possibly go out of business. The three were The First National of Santa Barbara, the Cattlemen's Bank and the Pacific Trust bank.

Jefferson and Howard visited The First National bank and learned about their bank robbery two months ago. The bank manager was more than glad to meet with the two men, but when Jefferson showed the sketch of Brown, the manager seemed to have developed amnesia. He couldn't remember ever meeting the man. His eyes shifted from Jefferson and then Howard, but he wouldn't look either man in the face." I'm sure you know it's a federal crime, if you accept stolen money," Howard said.

"I have nothing to say. Now if you'll excuse me, I have another meeting," the manager said. Jefferson and Howard left, but they knew that they had one candidate for the stolen funds.

Cattlemen's Bank assured the two Pinkerton men that they had no knowledge of Brown or the stolen money. Jefferson and Howard believed them. It was at the Pacific Trust where they were positive that Brown had deposited some of the funds. The bank manager was so evasive that the two Pinkerton's found it difficult not to tell the man, he was a down right liar.

Back at the Arlington, they consolidated their notes. "I'll bet that he deposited half of the loot in the First National Bank and the other half in the Pacific Trust Bank. That's what I'd do if I were him. That way he'd feel safer. He could always come to Santa Barbara and recover all or half, if he needed money. I don't think we need to go to Ventura," Howard said.

"I agree. Let's check in with the sheriff and give him a copy of the Brown sketch. You never can tell, Brown may want some money and come to Santa Barbara and save us the trouble of going after him," Jefferson responded.

The meeting with the sheriff was interesting. "If the First National Bank Manager is willing to look the other way and accept stolen money, what about the robbery at their bank several months ago? Did they know the robbers or were they complicit in the robbery. I've got a cousin who works in the bank. I'll show him Brown's sketch and ask him to let me know when Brown comes into the bank. Now if all the money is in the Pacific Trust, I can't help you there, but I'll certainly help you any way I can. Since you're on your way to Santa Ynez, there's a man who lives there by the name of Tommy Sanchez. I suggest you tell him about the stolen money. He may be of some help," the sheriff said.

"I know Tommy Sanchez and his wife. I helped them several years ago to find her son, Juan."

"Juan is an attorney now and one of his clients is the First National Bank. It's a small world. You may want to contact Juan as well. Both he and Mr. Sanchez helped me track the bank robbers. Juan was roughed up a little but he's okay now. Give my best to the Sanchez' and their son."

Howard provided Jefferson with a horse and the two rode to the San Marcos Pass where the stagecoach robbery took place. Then they rode on a meandering road through heavy tree cover- age to the Cold Springs Tavern built in 1861 by Chinese laborers. The complex included a rest stop, a kitchen run by Mrs.Kinevan and three small cottages for overnight guests.

Jefferson was only two days behind Brown at this time but he wanted to interview the Kinevans and then go to the shack on Paradise Road and interview the store keeper. Mrs. Kinevan confirmed what Jefferson had been told. After a quick lunch at the tavern, he and Howard rode to the shack on Paradise Road. Surprisingly, one of the suspected robbers, a man named Morley, was at the bar talking to the bartender, when the two Pinkerton men walked in. Jefferson showed each man a sketch of Brown and both confirmed that Brown was the one who shot Morley's partner and stole both their horses.

"So he came after you and your partner and recovered some of his money."

"I don't know what you're talking about.
That was our money we saved up punching cattle."
Morley said.

"I see. Then how come you haven't filed charges with the sheriff. If he stole my hard earned money, that's what I'd do."

"We can take care of Brown ourselves."

"I'm sure you can take care of yourself. Just look at you."

"Well, it's my business isn't it?"

It was getting late, and they didn't have time to bother with Morley, so Jefferson and Howard rode back to the stagecoach stop and stayed overnight. Cold Springs Tavern was rustic with only three small cottages for overnighters. But Mrs. Kinevan's did more than make up for the austere surroundings, with a special dinner for the two Pinkerton men. After dinner, they adjourned to a small bar in the corner and met two other individuals, who were staying in one of the cabins.

Over breakfast, the next morning, the two other men shared with Jefferson and Howard their experience travelling by train from Los Angeles to Santa Barbara, and then the stage to get here. Both men planned to spend some time hiking the Chumash trails in the mountains south of Cold Springs, before they continued north to San Francisco. They charmed Jefferson and Howard with stories of bear hunts and tracking mountain lions. They weren't boasting, they were just commenting on things they did or observed. It wasn't until Jefferson was leaving did he learn that he had breakfast with the famous John Muir, the naturalist, and his friend William S., Davey Brown the equally famous bear hunter.

# CHAPTER THIRTY-FIVE

Tommy Sanchez came in from the vineyards with a few grapes in his hand and sat down at the kitchen table with Sarah, who was having a cup of coffee. "Can I get you anything Tommy?".

Tommy showed her the handful of grapes he picked this morning "I think we're going to have a good harvest this year. I'll need to bring in more laborers to supplement our work force and I need to do it soon. What have you scheduled today?' Tommy asked Sarah.

"I was going into town to do some shopping, why?"

"What time are you heading there?"

"I planned to leave around ten."

"I'm going to town a little later and see if there are any men available. We could meet for lunch at the hotel around noon, if you like."

"I would. I'll take Naiwa and Naomi with me and when we're finished shopping, they can go back home with the vaquero. I can return home with you. Would that work?"

"Yes."

"How many men are you going to hire?"

"I'd like to hire ten but I'll be satisfied if I can find eight that are suitable. Why?"

"Well, I'll buy more food supplies and bedding for around ten."

Raul hitched up a wagon for Sarah and the two women and a rig for Tommy. Sarah left at ten with the two women and one of the vaqueros while Tommy followed an hour later. While Sarah was picking up supplies at the general store, Tommy was hiring ten men who hung out near the hotel. All spoke a Chumash dialect which wasn't familiar to him, but several of the men could converse in Spanish. and were able to translate for the others. When Tommy was satisfied, he told the men to get their gear together and meet at this same place tomorrow morning at seven. He'd have someone meet them and take them to the ranch. The men would be hired for three weeks and they'd be given lodging in the bunkhouse, on the ranch. It was noon when Tommy finished with the laborers and he went to the hotel to join Sarah.

Sarah finished up at the general store at eleven thirty and had the supplies put in the wagon. She told Naomi and Naiwa that the vaquero would drive them home when they were ready. She wasn't going back with them; she was going to have lunch with Tommy and would meet them at home in a couple of hours. Sarah walked into the hotel dining room and ordered a glass of house chardonnay and waited for Tommy. "How nice to see you again Sarah, may I join you?"

Sarah looked up and saw Jason Brown standing at her table. "Nice to see you Mr. Brown. I'm sorry, but I'm waiting for my husband, who'll be here any minute."

Sarah was surprised that Brown didn't leave. "Perhaps we could have lunch another time, say next Friday at the hotel here?"

"I appreciate the invitation but I'm married. I don't make appointments with other men. You understand?"

"I was hoping our relationship could get beyond just having lunch." Brown smiled.

Sarah was flustered. She wasn't accustomed to so overt a proposition. The smiling asshole in front of her was enjoying himself, at her expense. "You've got a lot of nerve coming on to me this way. I'd appreciate it if you would leave. Good day Mr. Brown."

"I heard you're more partial to Indians. Perhaps if I was an Indian, I could curry your favor."

No sooner had Brown uttered the last word when he was grabbed from behind and flung to the floor, knocking over a table and two chairs. Standing over him was Tommy Sanchez. Brown reached for his gun but before he could reach his pistol, he was staring at a colt forty five in Tommy's hand. "If you want to live, I suggest you put your gun on the floor. It makes no difference to me whether you draw or put your gun on the floor."

Brown knew he was looking at death in the face and decided to withdraw. He'd have an- other chance. He was amazed at how fast the smaller man hovering over him, was. He laid his gun on the floor, got to his feet and dusted off his coat. When he reached for his gun, Tommy said. "Leave it there. We'll be in town for a couple of hours and I don't want to worry about you back shooting us."

"Who the hell do you think you're talking to?" Brown was enraged.

"I really don't care. I expect an apology to my wife and if I were you, I wouldn't try to contact her again or I'll kill you."

Brown tipped his hat to Sarah but wouldn't apologize. So that was Tommy Sanchez. He was as fast as the hotel manager said he was. Brown didn't want a shootout with the man here or any other place, but there would be other ways. He wanted Sarah Sanchez and nothing was going to stop him.

# CHAPTER THIRTY-SIX

On the way back to the ranch, Tommy asked Sarah if she ever met the man in the hotel before. "His name is Jason Brown. He's the one who bought one of my paintings last week. It was the one of Crazy Horse. Naomi, Naiwa and I had lunch with him after he purchased the painting. I didn't think anything in having lunch with him, but he seemed to think it was something special. I'm sorry Tommy. I didn't think."

"You didn't do anything wrong. Having lunch with someone who bought one of your paintings seems perfectly normal. I wonder where this guy came from and better yet, why is he still here?"

They drove down the entryway to Altura Prado and saw that there were two horses tied to the rail on the side of their house. Two men were sitting on the porch; one looked familiar. James T. Jefferson came off the porch to greet Sarah and Tommy and introduce his friend George Howard. Tommy shook hands with both men and Sarah hugged Jefferson.

"What a surprise. I hope you're staying for dinner." Sarah said.

"We'd like that and wonder if we could stay with you for a couple of days, while we complete our business?" "We'd be delighted to have you. Now if you'll excuse me, I'll tell the ladies that we have company for dinner." Sarah left the three men on the porch and went inside. Tommy led the two men and their horses to the bunkhouse and asked Raul to take care of them.

"Why don't you two relax and then come up to the house. Dinner is at five and I think we're having steaks tonight. So bring your appetite."

Sarah had send word to Juan that Jefferson was having dinner with the family that night. She asked if he could come. At dinner, Jefferson reminisced about the last time he saw Tommy. "We were sitting outside that little saloon in a cow town in Nebraska waiting for Juan and his buddies to show up. Jefferson looked over at Juan and smiled. I really didn't know what to expect. When Juan finally arrived with his bud- dies, Tommy went inside, while I came through the back. Eight of them were drinking at the bar and they were looking for trouble. There were only two of us and I was worried. That's when Tommy gave them all a shooting exhibition. I think you convinced Juan that he'd better change his course in life or he was going to meet someone like you and it wouldn't be good. I hear that you're an attorney now, Juan."

"I can honestly say that my life changed right there, in that saloon, on that day. We didn't have a clue what we would do next. All we seemed to be good at is shooting up some saloons and scaring little old ladies. I knew better, but I was still angry. I was angry at my father for dying and I was angry at my mother because she was white. We were having a few beers and getting ready to shoot up the place when this breed walks in and tells us to knock it off. He shot Little Bear and Charley Shoots in the shoulders, who were dumb enough to draw on Tommy. I think you would've shot me, but I sobered up and I'm grateful Tommy. Without you and my mother, I'd be dead. Thank you," Sarah broke down crying.

"Tommy was overwhelmed with the confession that Juan made, but he decided to change the subject. He looked at Jefferson and asked, "are you still with the Pinkertons?"

"Yes, and so is my friend George. I've come from Bisbee, but George is assigned to Santa Barbara. We met the sheriff and he said to send his regards."

"Are you looking for someone in our area?"

"We're looking for a bank robber, He held up the Bisbee National Bank several months ago and I've tracked him here. He's a killer. Here's a sketch of him." Jefferson showed the picture to Tommy and Sarah.

Sarah gasped. 11It couldn't be. What's the man's name?"

"Jason Brown."

"0h Tommy!" Sarah gasped.

"We had a run in with Mr. Brown in the Central Hotel dining room at noon today. I took away his gun because he was getting too familiar with Sarah," Tommy said.

"He's a cousin of Earl Singleton, who's stolen some of our cattle. His ranch borders ours on the south. Their entrance is on the road to Santa Barbara," Sarah said.

"You didn't tell me that Brown is a cousin of Singleton?"

"I'm sorry Tommy. I just forgot," Sarah responded.

"You think he's staying at Singleton's?" Jefferson asked.

"I hadn't given it much thought until now, but he may be. Sarah said he'd been staying at the Central Hotel in Santa Ynez, but I guess he could've moved on to the Star Ranch." What's your plan?"

"George and I'll go to Santa Ynez and see if he's still at the hotel. If he's not there we'll go to the Star Ranch."

"We've had problems with the owner of the Star Ranch and his men. I took nine of them to Santa Barbara for trial because they rustled my cattle. Recently, I gave Earl Singleton two days to return another ten of my cattle that were rustled, by one of his men. He hasn't returned the cattle and he's not at his ranch. I've got a busy morning with the grape harvest just starting, but I could send a couple of my really good vaqueros with you, if you'd like."

"I think we're fine. If we need help, I'll call on you."

If you're not back here by four tomorrow afternoon, I'll send some of my men to look for you. That's a bad lot on the Star Ranch, don't take any unnecessary chances," Tommy said.

# CHAPTER THIRTY-SEVEN

Singleton and two of his new hires searched two days before they stopped in the shack on Paradise Road. They learned from one of the patrons, that there were cattle grazing in a small valley north of here. Luckily, Singleton had his two cowhands along when they came upon the cattle. Meade was sitting under a tree, smoking a cigar with a rifle laid across his knees, when they approached. To say that he was reluctant to give up the steers, was an understatement.

Singleton got off his horse and approached Meade. "Those are Sanchez' cattle, aren't they?"

"I've changed the brands. No one can tell that they're not mine. I'm going to take them to Santa Barbara and sell them. Why?"

"We're taking them back with us. Sanchez paid me a visit in the middle of the night and cut off the lobe on my left ear. He said if I didn't return his cattle, he'd come back and cut off the other lobe."

"He did the same thing to Don Ortega and had him fire me. Why don't we go back and kill the son-of-a-bitch right now? We can get there by dark. I know how to get close to his house. I've been there a few times by myself."

"I'll take care of Sanchez when he least expects it. Now are you going to give me his cattle or are we going to take them?" The two men with Singleton had their hands on their pistols and seemed to be waiting for Singleton to give them an order.

"I'd like to get paid for my effort. Why don't you give me fifty dollars and you can take them with you."

"Not a chance. I'm not paying you for stealing cattle."

"Singleton turned to the two cowhands, but he kept his hand on his gun. "Start rounding up the cattle. We're taking them back to my ranch, with or without Meade's permission."

Meade didn't want a fight with Singleton. He could always go back and rustle some cattle from Sanchez, at a later date. "Ok, I'm not going to battle with you. You can take them. Sanchez really has you buffaloed, doesn't he?"

"Ed, if I were you, I wouldn't press your luck. You're not Sanchez. But at least you were smart enough to give up the cattle, because I would've taken them. You've been gone a few days, where are you staying?" Singleton asked.

"In a cave at Lizard's Mouth about eight miles west of here. It's not quite enclosed but no one has looked for me there. You owe me some wages. Why don't you bring it by this week? I'll be home."

It took the better part of the day to bring the cattle back to the Star Ranch. Singleton planned to wait until tomorrow to deliver the steers to Sanchez. He was surprised when the housekeeper told him that his cousin was staying in the bunkhouse. It'd been nearly ten years since they last met. They'd always been on good terms, just not great friends. Singleton remembered that Brown wasn't anyone to fool with.

He walked into the bunkhouse and found Brown in the foreman's room. The two men shook hands. "What brings you to the valley?" Singleton asked.

"I'm on the run and thought this valley would be a good place to hide out and maybe settle in. You have any problem with that?"

"No. I welcome you as long as the law doesn't come after me."

"What I did was in New Mexico, so the locals won't have any reason to come after me. I'm just not sure about the federals or the Pinkertons."

"You can stay in the foreman's quarters as long as you're here; he won't be coming back. My two pals and I have the three bedrooms in the ranch house, but you can have the run of the house. Is that okay with you?"

"I'm fine, but what happened to your ear?"

"It's a sore spot with me, but one of my men rustled some cows from next door. The neighbor paid me a visit late at night, drugged the two guys inside and cut off my ear lobe. He said if the cows weren't returned, he'd come back again and cut off the other lobe."

"You got to be kidding. Who's the neighbor?"

"Tommy Sanchez."

"That son-of-a-bitch. I had a run in with him today. He hit me from behind, threw me to the floor, drew down on me and took my gun. I owe him big time. Why don't we go over to his place tonight and cut off his ear," Brown said.

"Not tonight, but maybe one of these nights we'll pay him a visit. My two pals have a score to settle with Sanchez as well. He shot both in the leg and they've been laid up since. I'm taking them in the buckboard to Santa Ynez tomorrow morning to have their wounds checked. When I come back, we'll talk some more about Sanchez."

"It was a forty-five that Sanchez took. I wonder if you have an extra gun around that I could carry, until I buy another."

"You can use this forty-five. I have another" Singleton removed the gun from his holster and handed it to Brown."

The two men that Tommy shot at the Star Ranch were hobbling and need help into the buckboard the next morning. Singleton could ride, but he limped when he walked. He might as well have the doctor look at his leg while he was intown. He owed Tommy Sanchez bigtime. Maybe he and cousin will visit Sanchez and re- turn the favor.

The doctor examined the bullet wounds and said the two men were progressing satisfactorily. He changed bandages and told them to take it easy and come back in a week. He wasn't sure about Singleton leg. "There may be some ligament damage to the knee. Try it for a couple of more days and if you're still lame, we'll put a splint on it to keep it immobile."

Singleton and his two compares went for a late breakfast at the hotel. When they entered the hotel, they could distinctly hear one of two men, standing at the front desk, ask the clerk about a man named Brown. They were showing the clerk a drawing of he man they were seeking. While his two friends made their way to the dining room, Singleton walked over and looked at the sketch. One of the two men, who Singleton assumed was a lawman, turned and asked him if he recognized the man in the sketch.

"What do you want him for?"

"He's wanted for bank robbery and murder."

"I'm sorry, but I don't recognize the person in the sketch. Now if you'll excuse me, my friends are waiting for me."

After Singleton left, the manager told Jefferson and Howard that the man in the sketch was a cousin of Earl Singleton, who they just talked to. "Where does Singleton live?" Jefferson asked.

"He owns the Star Ranch here in Santa Ynez. You can access it on the road to Santa Barbara."

Jefferson and Howard left the hotel and walked across the street to the Crazy Girl Saloon. They sat at a table by the window, had a beer and watched the hotel front door.

Singleton joined his two companions, who were already seated in the restaurant. When the two lawmen left the hotel, Singleton told his two sidekicks that they had to leave immediately. "Why?" One of the men asked.

"I'll tell you on the way."

When they were out of town, Singleton told his two pals that two lawmen were circulating a picture of Brown, who apparently had robbed a bank in New Mexico and killed at least eight men."

"He'll bring the law down on us, that's for sure," Charlie Simmers told Singleton.

When Singleton came out of the hotel with his two friends, they immediately got in their wagon and left. Howard and Jefferson finished their beer, got on their horses and followed Singleton and his friends at a distance.

Sensing that the two lawmen might visit the ranch looking for Brown, the three hurried back hoping to give Brown enough time to get away. Brown was sitting on the porch cleaning his Colt, when the three rode up. Singleton got down off his horse, called one of his vaqueros over and told him to help his two friends into the house. "After that, take care of the horses and buckboard."

Singleton sat on the porch next to Brown. "We may have company. There're two lawmen in town circulating your picture. You're wanted for bank robbery and murder. I think you need to get out of here as fast as you can saddle your horse," Singleton said.

"I'm not going. This is it. If they want me they're going to have to take me and I'm not going to be easy to take. Can you lend me a rifle or if you want, I'll pay for it."

"Alright, but get out of sight. I want you to stay in the bunkhouse. I'll take care of the two if they show up; we don't want any killing here." Singleton went inside his house and came out with a Winchester and handed it to Brown.

Jefferson and Howard could see Singleton and the two men enter Star Ranch and ride down toward a house. They thought they saw another man on the porch, but couldn't tell where he went. They rode up to the house and looked directly at Singleton sitting alone on the porch. The two Pinkertons didn't know where the other two men were, so they remained on their horses. Both had their hands resting on their pistols "My name is Jefferson and this is George Howard. We're Pinkerton Detectives. I've been on the trail of a bank robber by the name of Jason Brown. We have reason to believe he's staying at this Ranch."

"Who says so?" Singleton asked.

"The manager of the Central Hotel." Jefferson responded.

"Never heard of this man Brown," Singleton said while barely looking up at Jefferson and Howard.

"That's interesting since we've been told by two different people that he's your cousin."

"Even if he is, and I'm not saying he is, he's still not here."

"Do you mind if we look for ourselves?" Jefferson said.

A man could be seen coming out of a building that Jefferson assumed was a bunkhouse.
He had a rifle in his hands. "I do, unless you've got a warrant. I suggest you both leave and don't come back." Singleton stood up and there was an edge to his words.

Jefferson looked at Howard and nodded to the man standing near the bunkhouse; he looked familiar. Jefferson knew that this could be tricky. He and Howard had to be careful. "We'll just wire the sheriff and get warrants to search your place. From what I was told by the sheriff, he's already visited you about cattle rustling and hiding fugitives. If he comes up here with the warrant, I assume he'll arrest you as well. Why don't you just cooperate with us and make this a whole lot easier on all of us."

Two shots rang out and Howard fell off his horse. Jefferson was hit in the upper part of his left shoulder, but he was able to dismount quickly and train his gun on Singleton. Howard was lying on his stomach and Jefferson didn't know if he was alive.

Another shot rang out and Jefferson slumped to the ground. His gun fell from his hand. He was bleeding heavily from a wound in his right side. Brown ran up and was about to shoot the two wounded men, when Singleton intervened. "No more shooting. We had this handled. They couldn't search the property for you, without a warrant from the sheriff and he's in Santa Barbara. We're not wanted for anything and now you've made us part of your problem. I want you saddle up and get the hell out of here. We don't need this."

"What are you going to do with these two?" Brown asked Singleton, while pointing to Howard and Jefferson.

"We're going to take them to the doctor in Santa Ynez. They're not going to die here.

You're wasting time. I want you to leave. My suggestion is that you go through our fence on the south part of our property and head for the hills. Ed Meade is hiding out at Lizard's Mouth. I'll have one of my men show you the route to Lizard's Mouth; my housekeeper will fix you up with three days provisions. You can have an extra horse to carry the provisions, but I want you gone and I want you gone now. Relative or no relative, I'm not going to swing for what you did. I hope I never see you again."

Singleton turned to one of his men who came out of the bunkhouse, when shots were fired. "Jose, I want you to lead Brown out the south part of our property, Then I want you to come back and help us with the two on the ground."

# CHAPTER THIRTY-EIGHT

It was after four in the afternoon and Jefferson hadn't return, so Tommy, Raul and two of the vaqueros rode to Sant Ynez looking for Jefferson and Howard. Their first stop was the Central Hotel; the manager was still on duty. He remembered talking to the two Pinkerton detectives and suggested that they'd go to the Star Ranch to look for Brown. "I told the two men that Brown said he was Earl Singleton's cousin."

Tommy and his men left the hotel and walked down the street to O"Hara's Saloon and looked inside, but didn't see either of the Pinkerton men. As they were walking back to their horses, Earl Singleton and his two of his men rode into town in their buckboard. Tommy could see there were two men lying in the back of the wagon. Singleton pulled up in front of the doctor's office. He and his companions lifted one of the men out of the wagon. They took him through the side door of the doctor's. Tommy could tell it was Jefferson, so he walked over and asked Singleton what happened. "Both men are wounded. The doctor's waiting, why don't you help us?" Singleton said.

They lifted Jefferson onto the table in doctor's operating room and the nurse cut off Jefferson's shirt. Then the four went back out and carried Howard in and laid him gently on the floor. The nurse covered him up with a blanket and put a pillow under his head. Once the doctor determined that Jefferson's wounds were not life threatening, he began to examine Howard. "Let's exchange places between the two wounded men. The one on the floor is more serious and needs immediate treatment."

Once the exchange was made, the doctor addressed Tommy and the others

"It's too crowed in here to work, so why don't you men go outside. I'll call you after I get the bullets out of both men," he said.

Raul's and the two vaqueros were watching the horses, as Tommy, Singleton and his two men walked out of the doctor's office. Tommy again asked Singleton what happened to Jefferson and Howard.

"They came out to my ranch looking for Jason Brown. Someone in our bunkhouse shot them with a rifle," Singleton said.

"Who was it?"

"We don't know."

"I don't buy that for a minute. You had to know who was in your bunkhouse and you had to see who shot them."

"Well, we didn't."

Singleton was touching his left ear, when Tommy drew his weapon with blinding speed and shot off the other lobe. Raul, who was nearby, drew and had his gun trained on the other two men. Singleton was crying out and tried to draw his gun, but Tommy knocked it out of his hand. "I want to know who shot them. If you don't start talking I'm going to start on your feet."

"It was Jason Brown. We didn't have any-thing to do with the shooting. We brought them in for treatment."

"Where is Brown now?'

"I don't know where he went. That's the truth."

Tommy shot Singleton in the right foot and Singleton fell to the ground, grasping at his foot and crying. "Don't shoot me again. I'll tell."

"We gave him some provisions, two horses and a map to Lizard's Mouth. That's where Meade is holed up. Jose rode with him through our south gate"

Tommy turned to Jose. "What do you know about any of this?"

Jose responded in Spanish that he didn't understand the question, so Tommy spoke to him in his language and repeated the question. "All I did was guide him through our gate to the south and show him the way to Lizard's Mouth."

Tommy stared at the man. His lips twitched while he kept looking away and wouldn't make eye contact. Tommy drew again and shot off his ear lobe. The man clutched his ear and the scream he let out could have waked the dead. "I told you everything."

"I don't think so. What else did you tell him?"

Jose was squirming on the ground while holding his ear, but he knew he had to answer. "He kept asking about your ranch, how many men you had on the ranch and where the house was."

"What else?"

"He wanted to know how to get to your house without anyone on the ranch seeing him."

"What else?"

"He asked about your wife."

"What else? If you don't tell me everything, I'm going to shoot off every one of your toes."

"I told him how to get up close to your house without anyone seeing you."

"How would you know how to do that?"

"Meade and I went to your house a couple of times."

"You miserable pig. If anything happens to my wife or my family, I'll come back and kill all of you."

Tommy turned to Raul. "Get Juan and tell him what's happened. See that these two get patched up by the doctor and take all three to our ranch tonight. Have them guarded by at least three men and then take them to the sheriff tomorrow morning. And take someone with you who speaks English. I'm going back to the ranch to be sure that Brown didn't try anything there."

Before he left, Tommy checked with the doctor, but it was too early to tell how Jefferson and Howard were making out

# CHAPTER THIRTY-NINE

As they exited the Star Ranch,, Brown questioned Jose about Sanchez and his wife. "Tell me Jose, If you wanted to sneak up on the Sanchez Ranch and take a good look at Mrs. Sanchez, how would you do it?"

Jose smiled. "I'd wait until it was almost dark and then stay as close to the common fence line as possible. When I was within a couple of hundred yards of the house, I'd leave my horse tied to one of the Sycamores and walk the rest of the way. The bedrooms are to the south and generally there're no lights in the bedrooms."

"Sounds like you've made the trip before."

"Me and Meade went up that way a couple of times. We wanted to see what Mrs. Sanchez really looked like. It was too dark the first time, but we weren't seen by anyone, so we went back again. The second time we got closer and there was candle light in the bedroom and we could see Mrs. Sanchez without any clothes, but Sanchez came out and walked around the house. He even looked in our direction. We thought he spotted us, but luckily, he didn't. I think Meade was scared because he didn't want to go back again. He remembered how well Sanchez could shoot. Are you going there?"

"Not tonight. Maybe some time in the future." But Brown fully intended to go. He didn't quite have a plan in mind. He was just going to see what might happen. He owed Sanchez big time for throwing him on the floor and making a fool of him. There would be payback, and it was going to be tonight.

Following Jose suggestion, he got within a hundred yards of the Sanchez' house and waited until it was dark. He didn't think there would be any vaqueros behind the house and surprisingly, there were no dogs. He made his way to the back of the house and could see into the kitchen. Sarah, the two Indian women and four children were sitting at the table. The young blond boy got up from the table and came outside to the pump and filled a bucket with water. As he turned to go back in, he saw Brown and yelled. He started to run toward the house without the water, but Brown was too quick and grabbed the young man around the waist and held him tight. Sarah came out the door with a rifle in her hand and aimed it at Brown. "Put my son down or I'll blow your head off."

"I don't think so, Mrs. Sanchez." Brown placed his gun against young Thomas' head and smiled.

"If you want your son to live, then drop the rifle. I'll trade you for the boy."

Reluctantly, Sarah lowered the rifle, placed it on the patio and walked over to Brown, who released the boy. "Tell everyone in the kitchen to stay where they are and call your husband and tell him to come out."

"Why?"

Brown backhanded Sarah across the face and she fell to the ground. She was slightly stunned as Brown pulled her to her feet. "I said call your husband."

Sarah glared at Brown defiantly, and said, "Tommy, stay inside. Brown has a gun on me, but he's not going to shoot me. If he does, kill the bastard."

Brown was angry and wanted to beat the hell out of her, but he called into the house, "Sanchez, if you want to see your wife again, you'd better come out and I don't want to see a gun."

Five minutes went by before it dawned on Brown that Sanchez wasn't home. Sarah laughed. "He's not home, but he'll be back shortly and if you value your life, you better get out of here and never come back."

"In that case, I'll just settle for you Sarah."

"What do you mean?"

"I'm taking you with me. We'll let your husband come to me. Maybe you and I'll have some fun while we're waiting for him to catch up. I'm going to find out if you're as good as you look."

"If you touch me, my husband will catch you and skin you alive. You're going to wish you never stopped off here and then you'll wish that you were dead. The best you can hope for is to get out of here now and pray that he doesn't catch up with you."

Brown grabbed Sarah's arm. "Tell everyone inside to stay where they are. If you yell for the vaqueros, I'll kill you. I don't want to, but I will. You and I have some fun times ahead." He laughed

"I'm not going to say anything. You're on your own. I can't wait until Tommy catches you. I'm going to enjoy it."

Brown pulled and when necessary dragged Sarah to where the horse was tethered and threw her onto the saddle. He grabbed the reins, hopped on back of her and rode off the way he came.

# CHAPTER FORTY-ONE

It was dark by the time Tommy reached the ranch. He tied his horse to the rail on the side of the house and walked into the kitchen. Naomi and Naiwa were hysterical; the children were crying. It took nearly five minutes before Tommy was able to get a coherent statement from Naomi. "The man took her."

She made that statement over and over again. Tommy took out the sketch of Brown he carried in his pocket and showed it to the two women. Neither could say that Brown was the man who took Sarah. It was young Thomas who pointed to the picture and told Tommy, "that man took my mother."

How long ago was he here?"

"Twenty minutes." Naomi said.

Tommy blamed himself. Sarah didn't deserve what happened to her. If he'd been a better husband, he would've protected his family by not going off looking to help a friend. He knew what he had to do and he had to do it quickly. What he wanted was stored in the barn. He recovered the trunk from the storage area in the barn and took out the contents. He donned leg- gings and calf high moccasins. After putting on the head band he wore as a young brave, he took some charcoal and put smudges under his eyes and down his cheeks. The last two things he put on were the metal breastplate his father, Sitting Bull, wore at the Battle of the Little Big Horn and a poncho

Red Cloud had worn into battle.

Tommy looked at himself in a mirror and the person who looked back at him was a sixteen year old, who'd been selected by his father, to perform a mission for the village. The Pawnee were their traditional enemies for over a century. It was not unusual for each to raid the other's camp, at least once a year. The two nations stayed in a perpetual state of war. On their last raid, the Pawnees took twenty horses and six women. This was to be Tommy's initiation to become a Brave. He would not fail. He was to infiltrate the Pawnee Camp, neutralize the exterior sentries and signal Sitting Bull when they could attack.

Getting close to their camp by the river was easy. Putting the sentries out of commission would be more difficult. He snuck up behind the first sentry on the river bank, which was the eastern edge of the village and slit his throat. He pulled the Brave into the brush and went looking for another sentry. He made his way. to the tree line on the western border of the camp. That's where he found the second sentry. Tommy nearly gave his position away when he stepped on a dry limb, lying on the ground. But he got lucky when the Brave took his time to investigate. Tommy was able to recover and hide behind some brush. When the Brave walked by, Tommy hit him in the head with his axe and pulled him into the brush.

The last sentry was near the northeastern edge of the encampment, hidden behind some brush. The only reason Tommy found him was the Brave got up to relieve himself and gave away his location. That was the Brave's undoing. Tommy made quick work of him and signaled Sitting Bull. They caught the entire village asleep and slaughtered over one hundred fifty people. People remember that event as, "Massacre Canyon".

Tommy moved away from the mirror and walked back into the house. Initially, the children were startled and shunned away from him, but Naomi and Naiwa smiled. He went into his safe and withdrew an envelope and handed it to Naomi. "In the event I don't return, there are instructions here for you and sufficient money to keep you going, but don't worry, I'll be back with Sarah."

Armed with two knives, a cartridge belt, his gun and holster and a bow and quiver of arrows, he made his way out the front door. He hadn't shot the bow in earnest for some time, but he was confident that his skill would not desert him tonight. He'd given his horse extra grain and water when he arrived at the ranch and within fifteen minutes, he was on his way south. He was sure Brown would take Sarah to Lizard's Mouth, a cave complex in the mountains south of their ranch and high in the hills overlooking Santa Barbara. But it didn't matter. He'd find them no matter where Brown took her.

For over twenty five years, Sarah lived the life of an Indian. She had learned to live off the land, she had learned how to be patient and she had learned not to be afraid. In essence she had learned to survive. Tonight she had to stay alive until Tommy found her. She knew that he was an exceptional tracker. He'd assisted the sheriff on many occasions to track outlaws or escaped inmates; he was always successful. Just because she was Brown's captive, that didn't mean that she couldn't do things that would assist Tommy

They had gone about two hundred yards off their ranch when Brown took the right hand fork. Sarah unhooked the locket from around her neck, and placed it on a branch along the trail. Tommy would easily recognize the locket, because he gave it to Sarah, when he was courting her.

Sarah was in front and Brown sitting behind her . It was Sarah who had the reins. "I'm not going to let you hold us up. You're going to keep up a steady pace or I'll tie your hands behind your back and you won't be able to control the reins." Brown yelled at Sarah.

She was startled out of her thoughts when Brown yelled, but she recovered quickly. She knew she had to stay alert and keep Brown's attention on what Tommy was going to do. "What difference does it make? Tommy is going to find us within a couple of hours. He's trained in tracking men. You have no chance," Sarah said.

"Shut up or I'll gag you as well." This time Sarah noted a change in Brown's tone. It was as though he was starting to realize it wasn't going to be so easy, so she decided to keep the pressure on.

"Your only chance is to ride off by yourself."

Sarah pulled up the horse and turned sharply to her right as though she heard something and Brown grabbed the reins and took out his pistol. "What did you see?"

"It was probably a coyote. I think it ran off." While Brown was distracted, Sarah who had been working on the white, lace cuff on her right sleeve, finally got it off and dropped it over a limb.

They had travelled for an hour when she told him she had to relieve herself. "I don't think you need to go. I think you're just trying to slow us down. I'll stop now, but this is the last time be- fore we get to where we're going to stay tonight. Don't think of running off. I'm going to be right by you all the time."

"You can't be serious."

"I am. It's your choice."

Sarah threw her leg over and dropped down to the ground. She walked off the trail a few feet and squatted down with Brown watching her every movement. As she was rising and adjusting her clothing, she turned toward the trail and yelled out. We're right over here Tommy. Watch out, he's got a gun."

Brown grabbed Sarah by the arm, turned quickly and fired two shots in the direction Sarah was looking. It took him a few moments to realize no one was there. It was only a ploy on the part of Sarah to distract him, and signal her husband. He put his gun in the holster and backhanded Sarah across the cheek. She nearly fell but Brown had hold of her arm and she remained upright. Through tears in her eyes, she said, "I'm going to enjoy watching my husband cut off each one of your toes, before he skins you alive. You're already a dead man."

Brown dragged Sarah to the horse and forced her into the saddle. He tied her hands to the horn." When we stop tonight, I'm going to take care of you."

# CHAPTER FORTY-THREE

**H**e found the necklace and smiled. He knew he was on the right track. About an hour later he found the lace cuff on the tree limb and put it in his pocket next to the locket. In each case, Tommy put new markers out in the event that Juan and some of vaqueros would come after him and Sarah. Tracking humans at night was difficult. Normally, Tommy would look fifteen to thirty feet in front of him as he tracked a man, but tonight his eyes were looking ahead only five feet. He'd been over all the trails in these mountains many times and was comfortable with the footing. He'd even found some of the old Chumash Trails, that were hidden by overgrown brush and new trees. By all appearances, Brown and Sarah were on their way to Lizard's Mouth. Tommy was aware that Meade might be there as well. He'd have to be more careful.

There was an easier route to Lizard's mouth by going south on the stagecoach trail and then on to West Camino Cielo, but Tommy had to be sure that Brown wouldn't change his mind and go someplace else. So he followed the trail Brown made as best he could. Sarah's life depended on it.

He'd been tracking them for over four hours on horseback, when he decided he could make better time without the horse. He dismounted and led his horse to a small pasture that was about thirty feet off the trail. The worst that could happen would be that the horse would find its way home. From here on he could travel by foot and probably make better time. He slung the quiver of arrows over his shoulder and carried the bow in his right hand. The horse carrying Brown and Sarah made enough of a mark on the trail for him to follow, even in the dark. Only a few times, did he have to backtrack to pick up their marks and then continue on. As the hours passed, he could see the length of the horse's hoofs slowly decreasing, indicating the animal was getting tired, carrying two people. Tommy also saw where Brown and Sarah had stopped. The prints were smudged as though there was some action at that spot. Tommy didn't want to think what may have happened; he just concentrated on going on.

Painted Cave was to the east as he neared San Marcos road and headed down a path the Chumash named West Camino Cielo. His destination was Lizard's Mouth, eight miles further on. That's when he noticed the second lace cuff snagged on a bush. Sarah was doing her part, now Tommy had to do his.

# CHAPTER FORTY-FOUR

It was nearly midnight, but the moon was full and Brown could see the outline of what could be a cave or better yet a large outcropping of rocks, outlined by the light of the moon. He could also see some light emanating from inside those boulders. Rather than  come in unannounced, Brown called out to Meade. There was no answer. Brown pulled on the horse's reins and moved closer. "Meade, its Jason Brown. I'm a cousin of Earl Singleton."

"I don't know you. I've got a rifle trained on you, so my advice is to move on or I'll blow your head off," Meade said.

"I've got Sarah Sanchez with me and I need a place to stay overnight. Her husband is probably coming after us."

Meade stepped out from where he was concealed, cocked his rifle and looked at Brown and Sarah. "Is she here of her own volition?"

"You can't be serious. Why would I ride with this scum to visit a pig like you?" Sarah said.

"Shut up bitch or I'll do you right here," Brown said.

"You must be crazy to kidnap her. Do you have any idea what her husband is like? He'll find us both and skin us alive and enjoy it. Get the hell out of here. I don't want you here."

Brown dismounted and pulled Sarah off her horse. "I'm here now and I need a few hours of sleep, after I have some fun with little blondie. You can have some of this after I'm finished with her. If you want to shoot, go ahead but I'll get off at least one shot. So, what's it going to be?"

"Okay. But I don't want any part of her. I've seen her husband in action. I won't be here in the morning."

Brown pulled Sarah into the rock like cave and threw her against the wall. "As soon as I take care of the horses, I'll be with you bitch," Brown said.

"Where can I tether the horse for tonight? I brought along some water and grain."

There's a small clearing where you can tie the horse." Meade pointed in the direction, where the clearing was located.

"There're some mountain lions in the area, but I haven't had any problems for the week that I've been here." Meade said.

"Watch her while I take care of the horses. I'll be right back," Brown told Meade.

While Brown was tending to the horses, Sarah said to Meade, "why don't you let me go. You're in over your head and you know it. Tommy's not far behind."

"How do you know that?"

Sarah smiled. "I left him a trail that even a blind man could follow."

"I don't want any part of this, I'm going tonight."

"You're going where?" Brown asked Meade as he came back from tending the horses.

"I'm going to pack up and leave you two here. She told me she left a clear trail for her husband to follow."

"You're staying here tonight. You can leave tomorrow." Brown pointed his pistol at Meade.

Brown looked around the cave and could see that it was only partially covered, with two accesses. The other exit was one hundred and eighty degrees from the one he'd used. There were realistically only three sides to the cave, but the area inside the rocks was about ten by twenty feet. Sarah was sitting with her back against one of the boulder like walls, as Brown approached her and took off his vest. "Okay blondie, this is our time. Get your clothes off. Meade you watch the entrance while blondie and I get it on."

Sarah knew that when Brown made his move, she had to fight and now was the time. "Go to hell. I won't help you. In fact, you'll be sorry and wish you hadn't taken me. I'm not some frail female who's going to roll over for you."

Sarah lashed out with a foot and caught Brown in the stomach. Initially, he was doubled over from the kick, but immediately lashed out and slapped her across the face, drawing blood and knocking her down. Sarah got up and went at Brown with her nails clawing at his face. She drew two long scratches down his face, which cut the skin. He was enraged and hit Sarah with a glancing blown to the head with enough force to knock her against the wall. All this time Meade just watched in stunned silence.

As Brown took off his belt, three arrows flew one after another into the small enclosure. Meade jumped back as one of arrows nearly hit him. Brown stopped what he was doing and stared at Meade. "You think he found us?"

"I don't know but I'm getting the hell out of here. I didn't have anything to do with the woman. You're on your own."

Three more arrows entered the enclosure, but this time they came from the other entrance and both Meade and Brown pulled back against the wall. At that moment Sarah made her move and tried to escape, but again Brown was too quick. He grabbed her arm and tossed her against the rocks where she hit her head and crumbled to the dirt floor. But she was up quickly leaning back against the rock wall.

"I don't think you're going anywhere. This is where both of you die." Sarah was dazed but fighting to stay on her feet. Her face was swollen and blood was coming from lacerations on her forehead and cheek. Her lips were split.

"Well, if we die, so will you." Brown said.

"But I expect to die right here. You both didn't plan on him. He's going to be unmerciful when he catches you. You have nowhere to run and little chance to escape. Even if one of you gets out of here alive, he'll find you. He knows ever inch of these mountains. My husband's the greatest natural hunter and killer you'll ever see. He was a legend as a brave. He'd slip into the enemy's camp and neutralize all their guards. What chance do you have?" Sarah said.

Brown grabbed Sarah by the hair and pulled her in front of him, as he stood just inside the entrance.

"I have your wife Sanchez. If you don't let us leave, I'll cut her so much that she'll beg me to die."

Meade was standing near the other entrance one minute and the next he was lying on his face with an arrow in his throat. Brown turned quickly as Meade fell and a shiver went up his spine. He didn't know what to do but he still had Sarah Sanchez. She'd be his ticket out of this dilemma. He realized that his passion got the best of him when he abducted the woman. He'd have to deal with it. So he called out to Tommy. "You may be able to get to me Sanchez, but I'll definitely kill your wife, before you kill me. If you let's us go, I'll leave her on the trail to Santa Barbara."

Tommy was standing on the rock roof of the cave. He couldn't see either Brown or Sarah but the light from the fire cast their shadows, so he had a good idea where they were standing.

"The only thing keeping you alive is Sarah. If you kill her, I'll kill you, so it's in your inter- est to make sure she lives. The people in my village captured a white man who killed his Indian wife. They took him outside the village where the wolves, mountain lions and coyotes used to scavenge for scraps of food. They dug a hole five feet deep and put the man in the hole and covered him with dirt up to his neck. He couldn't move his arms and legs. He could only look as the wolves circled him. I was a boy of ten at the time, but I always remembered that experience."

It took an effort for Sarah to talk. Her mouth was swollen and still bleeding. "You don't have a chance and you know it. You can't stay awake and you can't kill me. Your only chance is to beg him to let you live."

"We'll see." Brown pulled Sarah down to the ground and forced her to lie in front of him. He had his left arm around her neck and his right hand held his pistol in front of her.

"If he comes in, I'll get him."

Brown waited throughout the night while fighting to stay awake; Sarah was asleep and snoring. He kept squeezing her and telling her to stay awake. His left arm was numb and he didn't know how long he could stay in this position. He wanted Sanchez to make a move but that dammed Indian just waited. Dawn came and he was tired, but the adrenalin kept him alert enough. The fire was out and still Sanchez didn't make a move. Brown's only hope now was to get Sanchez to make a move. With his left hand he started to strangle Sarah. She screamed out but still Sanchez didn't make a move. What's with that guy? "Don't do anything Tommy; he can't kill me," Sarah coughed and spit up blood.

Brown hit Sarah across the head with his pistol and she slumped, but she was breathing. He waited and still Sanchez didn't come. He smelled smoke. Several of the mesquite bushes at the east entrance were on fire. Brown took out a handkerchief and covered his nose and mouth. He did the same for Sarah. He knew that Sanchez was trying psychological ploys in the hope he'd panic and come out shooting. The smoke was just pouring into the entrance as though someone was directing the smoke. "Dam that Sanchez."

Brown crawled and pulled Sarah toward the other entrance while keeping her on the ground in front of him. As soon as the smoke coming into the entrance started to dissipate, Brown could see fire at the other entrance and soon smoke was pouring into the cave like area. He shifted Sarah's and his position back toward the other entrance and soon more smoke came in that way. There were small slits in the rocks above the cave and embers were being pushed into the slits and hot coal like clumps were falling into the cave chamber. Sarah was still un- conscious, so Brown got up and threw handfuls of dirt on the hot lumps and then went back to his position on the ground, behind Sarah.

Over the next hour there was virtual silence but Brown was too apprehensive to get up. Sarah had regained consciousness but she was groggy and did some moaning. Brown could hear someone moving on the rocks on top and he heard Sanchez say, "Sarah it won't be long now and I'll have you free."

Without Brown hearing it, someone had placed a lot of brush at the west entrance and lighted a fire. The smoke was over powering and Brown made a choice, they had to get out of the cave. He pulled Sarah off the ground by the hair and put his left arm around her neck and pushed her toward the east entrance while holding her in front of him. Just as they were outside the cave, Tommy leaped from above pushing Sarah to one side with his hands and landing on Brown's head with his body. Brown was initially stunned and his gun was thrown from his hand. But he got to his feet quickly and drew his knife and faced Tommy, "let's see how you do face to face Sanchez."

Tommy smiled and withdrew his knife and took off his poncho and threw it to the side. Brown could see a silver breastplate on Sanchez chest as the two men circled each other waiting to make the first strike and gain an advantage. Sarah was on her feet and had Brown's gun in her hand. "Let me shoot him Tommy."

"That would be too easy Sarah. Let me have him for a bit and then you can kill him." The two men were parrying when Brown made a thrust that Tommy dodged and leaped in the air and struck out with both feet hitting Brown in the chest. The blow was powerful enough to knock Brown backwards. He fell hard on his back. Tommy didn't press his advantage but waited until Brown got back on his feet.

Brown looked at Tommy as though trying to come up with a plan. The two men started circling each other again and when Brown parried again, Tommy pivoted around onto his left foot and struck out with his right foot again catching Brown in the chest and he went down again. Brown took his time getting back up this time. It was as though he was resigned to his fate. When Tommy moved forward, Brown backed up. Tommy cut Brown's right arm that held the knife and Brown dropped the knife. He quickly recovered it with his left hand and stood up. Tommy could see in the man's eyes that he knew he was going to die. Tommy turned and looked at Sarah. She shot Brown in the forehead and he fell over on his face. There was no need to check; Brown was dead.

Tommy picked up Sarah in his arms and kissed her on the cheek. Her lips were still bleeding. Tommy poured some water on a handkerchief and cleaned Sarah's face and dabbed her lips with the cool and wet cloth. "I'm so sorry Sarah for leaving you at the ranch alone. You never should have gone through this ordeal. I will never do that again. Can you possibly for- give me?"

"You are my husband and I love you. I knew you'd come. Now let's go home. Everyone must be worried."

# CHAPTER
# FORTY-FIVE

The beating Sarah took at the hands of Jason Brown showed on her face. Tommy had left his horse about three miles from Lizard's Mouth and he was worried that Sarah wouldn't be able to walk that far. Sarah was reading his mind. "Brown left a horse about fifty yards from here. You should be able to find them. I'll wait right here until you get back. Both men are dead and don't pose any problem now."

It took Tommy about twenty minutes to find the horse and return to the cave. Sarah was sitting down and leaning against the rock wall. She looked exhausted. Tommy helped her to her feet and lifted her into the saddle. "We'll take our time. I think the best thing for you is to go to Kinevans, as soon as possible. That woman is as close to a doctor as anyone I know. We should be there in a half hour."

With Tommy walking and guiding the horse, Sarah held on tightly, but she was weak. When they reached the stagecoach stop, Sarah fell into Tommy's arms and he carried her into the station. Mrs. Kinevan told Tommy to put her on the bed in her bedroom, which was next to the kitchen. "Let me take a look at her. She looks like she had a fight with a grizzly bear."

Mrs. Kinevan treated the lacerations on Sarah's face, head and mouth and applied some lotion. There was a great deal of swelling and Sarah had a slight fever. As soon as she was satisfied that the damage to Sarah was minimal, she called Tommy. "I think the best thing for your wife, is you. Why don't you sit with her, so she can get some sleep? She told me some of what happened, but I assume not all of it. You can stay here as long as you want."

Raul, Juan and three of Tommy's vaqueros were taking Singleton, Simmers, Jose and Hodges to the sheriff in Santa Barbara and decided to stop at the stagecoach stop on Kinevan Road. What a surprise they got when they saw Tommy sitting in the dining room having lunch.

Tommy told Juan what happened and said it was okay for him to go into the bedroom to see his mother. "Please don't wake her, she's had it pretty rough."

"Did you kill Brown?" Juan asked Tommy. "He's dead. That's all you need to know. I want you to tell the sheriff that he can find Meade and Brown's bodies at Lizard's Mouth. He knows where it is."

"We have Singleton and his three pals tied up outside. Yesterday, I received a letter from my friend who works for the bank. One of the guards at First National has a sister, who is married to Singleton's friend, Frank Hodges. I think we have enough evidence to at least hold Single- ton and the other two for the bank robbery."

After Juan visited his mother, he came back to the kitchen and sat with Tommy. I'll be back on the stage tomorrow. I hope my mother will be well enough to ride back with us."

The next day Sarah and Tommy boarded the stage at Cold Springs Tavern and made their way home. They were dropped off at the Central Hotel, rented a rig and drove to Altura Prado. When she saw the children, Sarah was her old self. Tommy smiled. It was good to be home.

# ABOUT THE AUTHOR

James S. (JIM) Kelly is a retired Air Force Colonel with over 100 combat missions in Vietnam. Prior to his retirement, Jim was program director for a communications program in IRAN. He and his wife Patricia currently own and operate High Meadow's horse ranch outside Solvang, California. All of his novels use Solvang and the Santa Ynez Valley as a setting. For the past ten years, husband and wife are active in a charity to Support Our Troops in forward operating locations, in hostile territory. To contact Jim, email him at, jkelly2020@outlook.com.

www.ingramcontent.com/pod-product-compliance
Lightning Source LLC
Chambersburg PA
CBHW031335010826
48972CB00012B/355